I0719103
FRANKENSTEIN

AN EDUCATION IN EVIL

ENDYMION COLLEGE
BOOK THREE

W.H. LOCKWOOD

I did not bow down to you, I bowed down to all the
suffering of humanity.

— FYODOR DOSTOYEVSKY

An Education in Evil

W. H. Lockwood

CONTENTS

CHAPTER I

DESOLATION

"Welcome to Russian Literature. You can call me Professor Worthing." He printed his name slowly on the blackboard in large, ugly letters. He turned to face the packed lecture theatre and fixed Anna James, alone at the back of the theatre, with his one cold, cruel eye. "Death, misery, regret, agony. This is what you have chosen."

Anna lowered her gaze to the page in front of her and watched as a few tears dropped into the ink, obliterating the tiny modicum of progress she had made.

"We'll begin, naturally, with Fyodor Dostoyevsky's masterpiece, Crime and Punishment. If you never wanted to drink a pint of vodka before, this may be the moment that pushes you over the edge, as you try to understand why our protagonist did what they did. As you try to put yourself in the place of a monster. As you wonder to yourself, are you even rooting for this person anymore? Or do you want them to suffer? Do you want to see them punished?"

Eve, or whatever he had become, looked around the crowded lecture theatre with his good eye. The other, still healing, was hidden behind a black eyepatch. He paused in his observation only once, to smile and look appreciatively over one of the attractive women towards the front, much to her delight, then he continued, "I wonder how many murderers we have in the audience today?" Anna looked up in shock, her heart pounding hard in her chest, a sick dizziness almost over-whelming her, while a cruel grin spread across his face. "Just one? Just one who smashed her best friend's head in with a wine bottle?"

She pushed her shaking hands hard together to keep them still and waited, breathless, for what might come next.

He only laughed and carried on with his harrowing lecture. "That's just an example, of course. But you never know who that really is sitting next to you, do you? Even your closest friend who you love, who you believe in, who you trust with your life—what would they do if they were pushed? Humans are ruthless when they need to be. Or perhaps, just when they want to be."

Anna turned to a fresh page of her notebook and pressed her ballpoint pen to the paper.

"This week, we'll take a deep-dive into a sick, depraved mind, and if you can stomach what you find there, I ask you: what shall the punishment be? What does she deserve?" Anna's terri-fied eyes found Demon-Eve's. He smiled a little wider. "'He'. I mean, does 'he' deserve it? Does *he* deserve *his* punishment? Choices were made and now he is going to pay the price as much as anyone else. What comes next might be absolutely appalling to a normal person, depressing, miserable, abhorrent! But, one thing's for sure…" Anna gripped the table as he suddenly stood tall and strong and let himself, just for one short moment, look exactly like Evelyn, a beautiful, handsome, sweet, boyish smile on the face she loved so much, before it returned to the malicious grimace she had become accustomed to. "I'm going to enjoy every second of it."

After the lecture, Anna went to the library and sat by the fire, forcing her eyes down to the page in front of her. She turned cold, and she focused completely, and she didn't exist, and Eve didn't exist, and the fireplace and the leather couch and the library didn't exist, and none of it had ever happened.

She no longer cared if she never felt anything again. The day had long since passed that she could tolerate her emotions at all, so she stayed there, in St. Petersburg, in the company of another murderer, until she could stay no longer.

Until she had to return home.

To his home.

To him.

Anna knew, if she didn't feed the demon, then Eve's body wouldn't be fed, so she walked home, over the moist green grass, past the bright yellow daffodils just blooming, past the lush viridescent tips of fresh shoots of leaves on lovely old trees all around her, and she saw nothing. She felt nothing. All romance, all poetry, every sensation of beauty and hope and new life was lost to her.

She made his food, and she made hers, and she forced it down, and she waited for him to come home.

Then she sat on the floor at his feet in silence while he ate, glaring at her all the while.

Finally, he placed his bowl down on the coffee table and he said, "I think... kidneys this time."

CHAPTER 2
AN APPOINTMENT WITH DEATH

"Oh, Anna…" The woman's big, sad eyes stared back at her from across the sombre desk. "I'm so sorry to have to tell you this. Mrs Sullivan passed away."

Anna stared back at the woman, her face full of devastated surprise. "When?"

"Not even an hour ago. I'm so sorry."

Anna's shoulders stooped, she pulled her hands into the sleeves of her sweater and wrung them as one bereft. She lowered her head and let her hair cover a good portion of her face, but for all that, the woman said, "Are you smiling?"

Anna fixed her with excited, dazzling eyes. "I am. I know that's not appropriate, but I'm just so happy for her. She's in a better place now."

The woman clacked her tongue and brought her hands to her hips. "You continue to amaze me. Your strong religious faith these last few months has been a comfort and an example to us all." Tears rose to her earnest eyes. "God bless you, Anna."

"God bless you, too, Macy." The words dropped like sugar from Anna's sweetest smile. "And God bless Mrs Sullivan. Is she… Is she in her room?"

"Did you want to say goodbye?"

"I just want to see her one last time."

Anna's stomach twisted with dread as the woman's face fell. "I'm so sorry. She has no family, and we weren't expecting you, so…"

A touch of gravel ground in her throat as she asked, "Is she in the morgue?"

"She is. They'll be here to get her soon." The woman cast a regretful glance down the hall. "I'm sorry, but it's not nice down there. It's best you wait for the funeral and try to remember her as she was."

"Thank you, Macy. I understand." Anna walked around the desk, as she had done many times before, and pulled Macy in for a long, close hug. Then she stood back and looked her kindly right in the eyes. "I'm going straight home, and I'm going to pray for Mrs Sullivan tonight."

Macy nodded proudly. "That's just like you, Anna. Always thinking of others. I wish there were more young women just like you."

Not even five minutes later, the fire alarm screamed through the hospice. Anna knew how to set it off. She had done it before. She had also left a basement window unlocked to come in and out as she pleased. She knew exactly how long it would take for the fire department to arrive, because she'd timed that. She had at least ten minutes.

From the basement to the morgue was a short, dark walk, surrounded by damp, mouldy concrete and lit only by flickering fluorescent lights. She waited a full minute down there, allowing time should any staff need to flee the morgue, then, when she was quite sure she was alone, she slipped down the corridor, rounded the bend, and there, not even shut away behind a steel door, was the corpse of Mrs Sullivan.

Mrs Sullivan had been stripped of all her worldly goods and now she lay on that cold, grim, metal table in that dank morgue, all alone with a tag on her toe. It would have been an affecting sight for almost anyone else, but Anna had no time for sympathy. She wrenched the white covering to the floor and appraised the old body.

Kidneys.

Kidneys would be at the back.

She pulled on her gloves, flipped the body over using all her strength, and accidentally sent the corpse crashing to the floor.

"Oh no. Sorry, Mrs Sullivan."

There was really a lot of blood from where her head hit the tiles and Mrs Sullivan became unfortunately disfigured in the instant.

Anna reached into her satchel and pulled out a short knife with a razor-keen blade. She had sharpened it religiously, never knowing when she would have to slice open a new human body, where it would be, or who it would belong to.

She dug the knife into the back quickly, and sliced lines down either side of the spine, just like she had seen chefs do on cooking shows on television.

This is how we skin a creature.

This is how we get at the meat.

The soul-crushing thought of Eve's vegetarianism jumped into her head, and she pushed it away with more revulsion than she had for the task at hand. It would have been morbidly funny once upon a time. Not now. Nothing was funny now.

She made four cuts along the flanks of Mrs Sullivan. She knew not to go too deep. She had pierced a liver once, when she was less experienced. The demon had made her pay for that. She was painstakingly careful now.

She took out her filleting knife and carefully ran it under the skin, edging it back and forth, back and forth, until Mrs Sullivan's back was spread open in all the blues, pinks, yellows, and reds of a grotesque butterfly.

The demon always wanted the organs fresh. He had told her to murder people to get them, but she had hedged her bets that if she could obtain the organs close enough to death, then perhaps he would know no difference. It had worked so far. Or so she thought.

Back to the short knife. She displaced and threw lumps of fat, muscle, and sinew to the floor. It was entirely too much for her to get through in the time she had, so she brought her scissors out instead. They easily cut through small bones, and the gristle of an old lady was no match for them.

In the last three months, Anna had successfully created a morbid network of contacts to get everything she needed. She had spent hours volunteering at the hospice, waiting patiently for someone to die. She had paid a nurse at a hospital to steal organs after transplant surgeries, but they had never been the right organs, or the right timing. It was still a contact worth keeping. She had found access to the funeral home and had obtained a very nice spleen from there. There were also the houses where drug-overdose victims were dumped so they couldn't be traced back to their dealers. She knew of at least three of those, and they were probably the most generous source of fresh body parts.

She had only had to murder two people so far. They were awful people and whether they deserved it or not, she felt she was no longer in a position to judge, but even if they did, she probably still would have felt terrible about it had she had the capacity to feel much of anything.

She sliced the kidneys free and placed them in a small plastic container. She put that container in her satchel, gathered her bloody belongings, and climbed back out the window.

What the demon wanted the organs for, she did not know. Perhaps he needed them for some hideous master plan—some sort of spell that would do untold evil to all humankind.

More likely, she thought, he did it only to torture her.

She returned home, and he was there, as usual, waiting for her. As usual, she sank to his feet and presented him with the stolen items. As usual, he cast an uncaring eye over the hard-earned spoils, and as usual, when he smiled his self-satisfied smile, she moved to stand.

Then something was different.

"Stay where you are."

Anna dropped back down, part of her terrified, part of her resigned to her fate.

Eve's gorgeous, beautiful, lovely face looked down at her, a malevolent smile swept across it, and he said, "Eat it."

CHAPTER 3
AN IMMOVABLE FEAST

Anna looked up hopefully at the demon. "Can I cook it?"

Eve's sweet, soft laugh and gentle voice. "No, Anna. You can't cook it."

She turned to the coffee table where the organs sat, soft, flabby, bloody, the stench of death upon them. She fought back a retch at the thought of it and did all she could to detach herself from the situation.

But this time, cruelly, her mind wouldn't let her detach.

She reached out tentative, shaking fingers and squeezed one of the cold, smooth, squashy innards. She picked it up, but it slipped from her fingers and plopped back down into its box. She picked it up, and it slipped again, making a hideous squelching sound.

By now, the horror and the foreboding were sinking in, and her quick resolve was fading fast.

She wondered what it would taste like raw.

She wondered how many hours of food poisoning she might get from this.

She wondered if she would have to eat both or just the one.

She should start with the biggest.

As she began to appraise the two kidneys to determine if one was slightly larger than the other, her mind unconsciously leaping to the smallest distraction from the task at hand, the demon asked, "Would you like to see him?"

Her heart leapt so violently that the kidney dropped from her grasp a third time. She pulled her bloody fingers into her sleeves and raised her eyes to him. She daren't ask. She didn't want him to see how hopeful she was because it gave him so much pleasure to tear her hopes away from her.

But she couldn't hide it.

Every day, over and over, she did what the demon told her to, and every day she wondered, was he really still in there?

Or was it all for nothing?

The demon smiled at her as he leaned back in the armchair, then, very suddenly, his eye cleared. One beautiful, grey eye cleared in an instant, and Eve's entire body began to shake. He looked first at Anna, then down at his hands. Anna leapt across to him, reaching her hands out for his. He grasped them tight and begged, "Don't!"

Then, half a second later, that same hand reached up and slapped her face, knocking her down. Eve's body laughed, loud and hearty, with that evil glint back in his eye.

He was gone.

Anna burst into tears. She remained on the floor, crying helplessly, until she felt a kidney thrown against her face.

"Eat it."

Eve was in there.

He was still in there somewhere.

She pushed herself up, picked up the kidney, sank her teeth into it, pressed down as hard as she could, and she took a bite.

Then she promptly threw up all over the rug.

She sat up, gasping for air, then screamed in pain and doubled over again as the demon delivered a sharp boot to her ribs.

The door slammed, and the demon walked Evelyn's body out into the night, she knew not where, or with whom, or what things Eve would have to see while he was trapped with that hideous being.

Anna lay on the floor and she cried for some time, then, when she was exhausted from crying, she stared at the wall in silence —not thinking, not feeling, just being miraculously empty.

A tentative knock on the door wrenched her back into the room.

She wiped her face on her sleeves, pulled her sweater straight, and opened the door a tiny crack.

"Aubrey?" Anna's eyes lit up for the first time in months. "I can't believe you came to see me. How's Candide? I went to the hospital and they wouldn't let me see her—"

"I told them not to," came the cold reply.

It felt exactly like a knife in her stomach, but Anna kept her tone light and casual. "Yeah, I kind of figured that. And they wouldn't tell me anything… and…" She looked up hopefully, sadly, at Aubrey. "Is she out of her coma?"

Aubrey's face was as hard as Anna had ever seen it. "Candide came out of her coma months ago."

"Oh. Really? I didn't know that…" Months. They hadn't told her, and it had been *months*. She wasn't surprised they hadn't told her. Or that Candide didn't want to see her. But it would have been so good to have at least known for all those months. "And is she okay?"

Aubrey's eyes bore into her. "Physically, she has made a full recovery."

"Oh, Aubrey, that's so good to hear," she whispered, some old knot inside her untangling itself with relief.

Aubrey soon tied it up again with her reply. "It's good to hear that you're not a murderer?"

"Yes…" Anna stared off into the nothingness of the dark hallway. "Yes… That I'm not a murderer."

"You came close."

She focused back on Aubrey. "How close?"

"Very close."

Anna nodded slowly. "Thank you for telling me. And thank you for taking care of her. I knew you'd understand. And you saved the day."

Aubrey's scowl deepened a little, from a frown of hatred to a frown of hatred mingled with a little interest. "What do you mean? Understand what?"

"When I told you to stay down that night." At that, Aubrey's face cleared to blank, but Anna barely noticed as she prattled on, anxious and overexcited to have any company that wasn't a demon. "I wasn't sure you were really awake, down there on the floor. But I thought you were. You were sort of… *too* still. Like you were scared to breathe. And I knew—I knew you would save Candide, because you're so smart, and you're so good, and that's what you do, isn't it? But I haven't seen you since then, so… So, I could never say thank you. But you probably don't want to hear that, anyway. Not from me. But I still wanted to say it…"

Aubrey's hard demeanour crumbled, just a little, and she softened her voice. "I always wondered. Until just now. When you said it that night… I wasn't sure—"

"No, I said it to you. I wanted him to think it was for Candide. I thought you knew. I hoped you knew. I thought if you stayed down and just waited, that maybe I could get him out of there, and we could save them both…" A few tears fell from Anna's eyes, so she blinked them away and tried to rally herself. "It's all over now anyway, isn't it? But can I see her? Is she coming back?"

"She's back already. But she doesn't want to see you." Aubrey's voice was hesitant now, her eyes regretful and sympathetic as she looked at Anna. "That's why I'm here."

Anna kept herself as strong as she could, though she felt her knees were about ready to buckle under her with the foreboding Aubrey's tone inspired. "What can I do?"

"She…" Aubrey let out a sigh. "We need you to move out of the apartment."

"Oh." She grasped the doorframe tight, her fingers turning white with how hard she pressed them to keep herself functioning. "Oh. Okay. I'll do it tonight." Anna smiled and fought back fresh tears.

"I thought… Haven't you been living here?" Aubrey looked past her shoulder and noticed for the first time the red mess, the vomit soaking into the rug. Her eyes met Anna's again, alarmed. "Anna, are you okay?"

"That?" Anna cast a careless eye over the evening's turmoil. "Oh, that's just… you know. Normal stuff. I dropped some things." She shrugged and plastered her smile back on. "I'll go over and get my things from the apartment tonight, and I'll be gone."

Another tear escaped Anna's eye, tickling her cheek on the way down. She reached up and wiped it away with her bloody fingers, her loose sleeve falling back to expose the bruises and the cuts, the shape of fingerprints purple on her forearm.

"Anna…" Aubrey reached for her hand to examine her injuries. "I don't think you should stay here, either. Have you got somewhere else to go?"

Anna yanked her sleeve back down and shrank a little deeper into her sweater. "No, it's better I stay here. I need to watch him."

Eyes wide, Aubrey asked, "Did he do that to you?"

Anna laughed, loud and unsound, at both her sudden concern and the stupid question. "Aubrey, I live with a demon. It's not all fun and games. But it is what it is. And you're right, yes, I pretty much do live here now. So it's no big change."

Aubrey observed Anna carefully, as Anna dropped her gaze to the floor, suddenly looking as though she was about to wilt with the effort of the interaction. She asked gently, "Is he almost healed?"

Anna's voice broke on her reply. "I think so. I hope so. I just hope…"

Aubrey reached out a hand for Anna's.

Anna instinctively pulled hers away.

"We'll get him back," Aubrey said.

Anna slammed the door in her face. She couldn't stand any more kindness or conversation or the thought of being hopeful about anything in the face of what she still had to endure.

She rolled up the rug and dumped it in the haunted bathroom to wash later. She picked up Mrs Sullivan's kidneys and put them in the fridge in case the demon still wanted her to eat them. She cleaned the blood from the coffee table and the carpet. She went to Candide's apartment and put her entire life into her suitcase, then she took her key, her beautiful skeleton key that Percy had given her so long ago, and left it on another new coffee table. Then walked out and closed the door. She went back to Eve's apartment, and she sat down on the floor and she disappeared into *Crime and Punishment*.

CHAPTER 4
ABSENT FRIENDS

"*I knew you wouldn't understand.*"

Strong hands wrapped around her arms. "Anna, I do understand—"

She threw them off, crossing to the other side of the fireplace. "Do you?"

"If I didn't understand, I wouldn't be talking to you right now."

"Then what do you want from me? Do you want to make me feel even more ashamed? Because that's not possible. You don't understand and you never will."

Percy had been careful with his tone. Careful not to push her any further than he and all the rest of the world already had. But still he said it, moving a little closer, leaning his shoulder into the mantelpiece, searching her eyes as if she had any sort of answer for him. "When you told that thing to take his body, it looked into your soul. And I was inside it and I saw into your soul. And I saw that it was black."

She refused. She wasn't going to apologise now or ever for what she had done. She raised her chin in defiance. "Only when it needs to be, Percy."

He narrowed his beautiful, sharp eyes. "And when is that, exactly?"

"How can you ask me that?"

"Because what I saw was terrifying. What you did was—"

"I did what none of you could do," she yelled, pulling away from him.

"What none of us would do!" he yelled after her. "Because it isn't right. It isn't what Eve would have wanted."

When she spun around to face Percy, she let him have every bit of her frustration, her anger, her terror, and her hopelessness all in one fast, desperate, incandescent tirade. "Don't talk about him like he's dead! What could you possibly know about what Eve wants? He wants me! There is no Eve without me. And there is no me without Eve. That's something you will never understand because you have never had half your soul torn away from you. And just after I found it! Just after I found him. And for the first time in my life, I felt complete and whole. And it killed him—"

"Anna, I know—"

"No, you don't! Even now you think it's because it killed him. Because I wanted him. Because of something so simple and base as grief. It's not. And that's why you saw what you saw. He is my soul, Percy. He's all the light and the loveliness and everything pure and meaningful and worthwhile in this world to me. And if my soul is black, if all you saw was darkness, that's why. He's all the light I have ever had. And Percy…" She swallowed down the lump in her throat, fixed him with her dark eyes, and made her voice just as hard and vicious as she knew how. "Understand, there isn't a person on this Earth I wouldn't sacrifice in a heartbeat for one more second with Eve."

Percy had let the comment sit there in the air between them for a time. A long time, during which he held her gaze, and she saw the hurt in his eyes as he tried to assess the truth in hers. "Are you threatening me?"

"I'm explaining to you."

"Eve would never forgive you."

"He would never know."

"Eve loves me. I'm his brother."

"And he deserves better from you," she finally whispered. "When I bring your brother back to you—when I'm burning in Hell for all the things I had to do to bring him back to you—you remember that."

Percy hadn't spoken a word to her since that day.

Mornings like these, when she didn't have class for a few hours, Anna would lay still in Eve's bed, staring at the ceiling, and go over that last conversation in her mind.

She missed Percy desperately. She never would have hurt him for all the world, but she said it anyway, and now he was gone.

Joe had been injured badly the last time she saw him. Worse than any of them realised. He had needed to stay in the hospital. Then she was told she wasn't allowed to have any more information about him, and that she wasn't allowed to see him, just like Candide. She assumed he'd heard what she'd done and that he, too, wanted nothing to do with her. He never returned her messages, and where he was now or what he did, she didn't know.

And every day she missed Candide. Every day she wondered what she would give for one word, one look—just one moment alone to try to explain. But what was there to explain? She did what she did, and she would do it again. She would do it again, over and over, because Eve was everything, and if she lost control of this situation, even once, everything would have been for nothing. There was no way Candide could understand that. No way she could understand that Anna loved her, adored her, would have given almost anything to be near her again.

Anything but Eve.

She rolled onto her side, and the memories replayed on the same sad loop.

"I don't care. Everything you've said, all the things I've seen, everything I know. Anna, let me stop it."

In two short steps, his arms were around her. She dropped her head against his chest and Percy sunk his fingertips into her hair, his other arm enclosing her completely. He had held her so close against him, and she had felt her strength ebbing away, like climbing into a soft bed at the end of the longest, most harrowing night of her entire life.

Percy was safe. He was warm. He was strong. And she knew would protect her from anything. She felt it in his arms. She felt it deep in her soul.

So she wrapped her heart up tight in a shield of barbed wire. "I can't see you again. Not until it's all over."

She felt the soft touch of his thumb running over her cheek, under the dark bruise she'd received only an hour earlier, turning her face up to his. "I can't stand to see you like this."

"He'll know. He'll know I've seen you, and if I don't do everything he tells me, we'll never get him back."

She tried to push herself away from him, but he only wrapped a gentle hand around her arm and begged, "Please, don't go back there."

"I have to. Don't let me see you again." How well she remembered looking up into his beautiful blue eyes for the last time, so full of fear and faith and intense adoration. How well she remembered saying, "It's too tempting."

Had Anna known then, two months earlier, what lay in store for her, she never would have had the strength to force Percy to make the promises he made that night. But she didn't know. She never could have imagined. And Percy, who had been her only friend and her only comfort in the world for a time, was somewhere, and he wasn't with her. And she still hadn't been defeated.

"Out," came the cold voice from the doorway.

Obediently, she climbed off the bed and followed the demon.

They had been summoned to Worthing House, a summons the demon only acquiesced to because playing the role of Evelyn Worthing until he recovered had been part of the deal. *Play the part until Eve is healed, then take Anna's soul to keep for all eternity.* Anna had never told Lady Worthing what happened. She had never told anyone the full extent of her morbid gambit. She just let everything happen around her and hoped it would all end.

After a long, silent drive, the demon opened the door to Worthing House with Eve's key, and they made their way through the dusty sitting room, then through the French doors and into the brilliant light of Lady Worthing's study.

Lady Worthing sat on the couch with her back turned to them and didn't even glance up from her book on their entrance. "Evelyn, be a dear and check the mail for me."

His nasty grimace fell on Anna and she shrank away from him, but he turned and he left the room as requested, the front door making a soft click as it closed behind him.

Lady Worthing rose, turned, and looked upon Anna with a full face of fury. "Why the hell is that thing in my son?"

Anna could barely force the words out with the shock of Lady Worthing's question. "How can you tell?"

"Of course I can tell!" she whisper-shouted. "Now quickly, before he comes back."

There was nothing for it but to tell the horrible truth in one frantic spurt. "Percy was possessed. He killed Eve. I made the demon get into Eve's body and bring him back to life. I traded my soul on the condition that it heal all Eve's wounds from the night it killed him, then give him back to us, whole. Like he was before. I made it promise to pretend to be him, so—so that Eve would be able to get back to his life when the demon gives him back his body."

Anna looked only at the floor as she spoke, trying to distance herself from the shame and sadness she felt, trying to prepare for the anger, bereavement, shock, whatever else Lady Worthing might feel now she had heard everything.

The silence hung heavily between them for a few moments as Lady Worthing made her appraisal of Anna. Then finally, in a low, calm, confident voice, Lady Worthing said, "Good girl."

Anna very nearly fell straight to the floor in disbelief. "What? Really?"

"Yes. You've done the right thing, Anna. I'm very proud of you."

The very rare sensation of reassurance made Anna brave enough to go on. "I'm... I've been living with it. Watching him. Waiting for it to heal him."

Lady Worthing glanced out the window for him. It was a long walk to the mailbox at the front of the property, but not long enough. "He's healed, Anna."

She gasped out, "What?"

"There isn't a thing wrong with him. Come on, you must realise by now how easily demons can heal people."

"But it said... It said because he was dead, it said it would take months."

"Demons lie."

"But how do you—"

"What does it want from you? Quickly, Anna!"

"I-I don't know," she stammered. "I already gave it my soul. It makes me do horrible things and I can't..." She broke off into tears, which she tried her best to shove back down.

Lady Worthing, only a touch paler than usual at Anna's words, nodded sympathetically, as though she understood. "Have you done them?" she asked, softly.

"No." Anna wiped her wet eyes. "Some things. But not like he asked."

"Did you tell him?"

"No. I lied."

"It knows you're lying."

Heart hammering in her chest at the idea, Anna's first reaction was denial. "Then it will know you're lying."

Lady Worthing gave a vague shake of her head. "No. I can… deal with demons. Some of them."

Something in the way she said that, some sort of avoidance, drew Anna's attention. "Why can you deal with demons?"

"I have a… slightly… possibly… *familial* relationship… with demons." It was said evasively enough, the way a child might own up to having taken something they shouldn't have.

Anna only stared, not in horror, because the revelation felt more like a piece of a puzzle sliding into place rather than having any sort of illusion of Lady Worthing's humanity shattered, but it still came with a modicum of shock. "What? So you *are* a demon!"

"Only partially." As though that made it any better.

"So it's true!" Anna cried. "Percy said it, and I didn't believe him."

"Well, Percy's a little shit."

"He is sometimes," Anna conceded sadly.

"And what about Candide?"

The brief moment of understanding and progress was snatched away. Anna would have to reveal what she had done. She took a deep breath. "It was me. I did that to her. I only did it because—"

"I can imagine," Adeline cut her off. "You did what you had to do."

Anna attempted a reply, but all that came out was, "Uh…"

Lady Worthing quickly jumped back in. "Is there anything else I need to know right now?"

Anna looked again at Lady Worthing and imagined it was only her partial-demon nature that could have let her respond in such a way. She swallowed hard and took the exit presented to her without another word on the subject. "No, I don't think so… But…"

"What?"

With the words unwilling on her lips, she asked, "If you're part demon, what does that make—"

"I don't know. That's a conversation for another time." The words were sharp and fast and Anna knew it wasn't a point to be pushed that day. To drive that very apparent realisation home, Lady Worthing continued her speech. "Now listen to me. That demon is just playing with you. There isn't a thing wrong with Eve's body, and there hasn't been for some time. It's going to know you know that now, so be ready for what it does next."

She walked swiftly across the room to Anna and put one gentle finger under her chin, lifting Anna's face up to hers. "You are strong. I've never met another woman as strong as you. Understand: no one else could have done this."

Anna attempted to lower her head as her eyes watered, but Lady Worthing pulled it back and held her there. "Head up. No tears. Stay strong. I'm going to be there for you both when you need me, and after this you will have Eve back and you will have my undying loyalty. I'm going to fix everything and we're going to save him. We'll do it together." She took her hand from Anna's chin, then just as Anna caught her breath, it was back, holding her head high again. Lady Worthing looked deep into her eyes. "And Anna, when you apply for the honours program, you will be accepted."

Anna, overcome by the revelations of the last five minutes, could do little more than nod an understanding of Lady Worthing's unexpected compliments and promises.

Lady Worthing's eyes shot to the left as she saw Eve approach the house again, then she turned them back on Anna. "Now get the hell out and don't fuck this up."

CHAPTER 5
AWAKENING

The drive back to Endymion College was interminable and just as silent. She fed the demon like she always did, and things carried on much the same way for the next three days. She hid in the library as usual; she went out on her grim errands as usual; she read her books and attended all her lectures as usual; she took his abuse, and she cried herself to sleep as usual.

On Friday, around midday, she went back to Eve's apartment to gather her study supplies, knowing he had a tutorial and would be absent from the apartment.

But this time, he wasn't absent.

Evelyn Worthing's beautiful body relaxed in his regular armchair, smiling sweetly at her, his lovely hands toying with her filleting knife.

Anna blanched white as her eyes caught the sharp blade, yet she bravely stepped into the room and closed the door behind her.

He wouldn't kill her. But how far would he go this time?

She began to shake all over as various scenarios played out in her mind, her heart beating fast, her blood pulsing loudly in her ears. In her panic, she spoke up in a way she hadn't for a long time, words slipping out before she could stop them. "You're not supposed to be here. That was part of the deal. You do the lectures, you do the tutorials, you don't fuck up his life any more than you already have. You need to go. You need to leave right now!"

The demon was calm and resolute. "The deal is done."

"What?" she rasped. "No. You can't do that. Demons stick to deals! Demons always stick to deals!"

"I remember our deal. Fix this man. Fix him and give him back to you whole and in one piece. Undamaged. And for that, you have traded your soul. For that, you have pledged yourself to a demon for all eternity." He threw the knife down on the table with a smile and a violent clatter. "It's time, Anna. He's better."

Her hands trembled, her lips quivered, her voice came as barely a whisper. "Do you mean…"

"Once I depart this body, my end of the deal is done. Whatever happens after that, well, I owe you nothing more. I will have delivered him to you as requested, as per our agreement."

The demon pulled the eye patch off, and Anna saw Eve's beloved face, complete, healed, exactly as he was before the demon murdered him.

She was wholly unprepared. She had never really let herself imagine it finally happening.

But he was better.

He was all fixed, and the demon had her soul and her allegiance anyway, so why not now?

Still, he had done it so many times before. So many times he had let Evelyn out, just for a few seconds, then ripped him away again.

But he had never told her before that Eve was better.

He had never taken the eye patch off and let her see his beautiful face in full.

She approached hesitantly and sat, as usual, at his feet. She looked up at him and watched and waited, barely daring to breathe in case she upset him and he changed his mind.

The demon regarded her for a few quiet moments, then said, "It was fun. I'll visit again soon. And again. And again. For as long as you live. Then, when you die, you will come to me, and you will stay by my side. Forever."

Anna gave a small, sad, resigned nod of her head as the demon smiled down upon her.

"Goodbye, Anna. For a short time."

The demon stared deep into her terrified eyes, and she looked deep into his, then suddenly they cleared. Eve's hands shook violently, his whole body trembled, his face changed in an instant to one of understanding, of horror, and she finally knew, for the first time in all those months, Eve was back.

It was truly Eve, and he was hers.

"Anna!"

"Eve, it's you!" He grasped her hands, and she squeezed his tight. She pulled herself onto her knees, reaching her fingers up to his cheek, touching him lovingly for the first time in so long as tears fell from both their eyes. Eve reached for Anna to pull her in tight, and she threw herself back against the coffee table in an automatic reflex at his sudden movement.

There they sat, frozen, staring at one another in shocked silence.

"I'm so sorry," Eve whispered.

"Don't be sorry," she said at once.

How she wanted to throw herself on him—to have him kiss her—to feel his gentle hand against her own cheek. But she couldn't bring herself to do any of it. She stayed exactly where she was, the wood hard in her back, staring up at the man she loved, trying to reconcile that love with the terror she began to realise she now felt for him. Not for the demon. For Eve.

When she didn't move at all, Eve understood. Silent tears fell from his eyes as he sank slowly to the floor by her side. His shaking hands reached out to touch hers, ever so softly. "Anna, everything you've been through… Everything." He shook his head, crying. "I'm so sorry. I couldn't stop him. I watched it all and I couldn't do a thing. I'm so, so sorry."

She forced herself to bring her hands to meet his, even if she couldn't make herself wipe his tears away, as desperately as she wished she could. "It doesn't matter now, Eve. It doesn't matter at all. Nothing does. I've got you back."

He wanted so much to grab hold of her and keep her safe, to feel his arms around her, and hers around him, but he forced himself to stay where he was. "It's over. We'll be okay. We will."

They sat there on the floor, with only the very tips of their fingers touching, and she cried, "Eve, I love you so much."

Eve stopped dead still.

The eyes were Eve's eyes, and they looked at her first in sad confusion, then in sheer horror.

His hand moved uncontrollably to the knife. She lunged for it, but his other hand formed a fist and punched her across the face with such force her back smashed against the wall, and her head hit the carpet.

His boot clamped down on her neck, and she shoved at him with all her strength, screaming to get him off. "No! No, don't do this!"

Tears were in both their terrified eyes as he lifted the knife, slowly, slowly, towards his throat. Eve's eyes, just the same—the desperation and the horror—but that smile, that malevolent smile, was no longer Eve's. He stood over her, the knife pressed to his skin.

She managed to shove him off. She pushed herself to her knees, and his boot met her chin, throwing her back again. Her head hit the wall hard, and she cried out in pain and despair.

Blood streaming from her temple, dizzy and gasping for air, she stared up at him. And she knew it was over. That she had lost at the last. He pushed the blade, and the blood came freely as he began to slice his own neck open.

She pressed her eyes tight shut.

But the body didn't fall.

Anna forced herself to look.

There he remained, the knife still pressed hard against the flesh of his throat. But it made no further progress. The sickening smile faded, the face turned quickly to confusion, then to rage, and suddenly Eve's eyes were no longer Eve's eyes. The demon fixed her with an incandescent glare of pure hatred.

Aubrey was in the room.

Anna watched on, stupefied, as she injected Eve's body with something and he fell to the floor. Alive. In one piece.

"Anna, get up and help me get him in that wheelchair. Quickly! Before he wakes up."

Anna, mechanically, did as she was told.

"I'm taking him to the apartment." Aubrey started down the hall while Anna ran after her.

"Why? What are you doing with him?"

"We're going to fix him. We can do that now."

"Really? Oh, this is wonderful! Okay, what do we do first?"

Aubrey didn't pause for a second in her procession. She spoke as calmly as if she had done this one thousand times before. "You stay here. You can't come."

"What?" Anna cried. "No!"

"I'm sorry, Anna. You brought his body back to life, but now you need to let us exorcise him. She can't do it with you there."

"No! Please, Aubrey, no. I need to be with him."

Aubrey pushed open the apartment door and shoved Eve through. Anna made a move to follow through the doorway, but her body slammed up against absolutely nothing, and she was knocked straight down to the floor.

"What the fuck?" she shouted.

She climbed to her feet, and she did the exact same thing again, only hitting the floor twice as hard in her desperation. She crawled to the door and held her hand to the divide, and sure enough, she met an invisible force, just as physical as if the door was still closed.

She searched around the door frame in confusion, then her eyes fell on Candide.

Candide stood tall and powerful and just as radiant as she had ever looked, but her face was furious and her eyes glowed green and she flicked one beautiful wrist and the door slammed shut in Anna's face.

"No!"

Anna pounded on the door, kicked the door, cried against the door, but eventually, she fell flat on the doormat, curled into a ball and variously cried and wailed and kicked the door again until, hours later, she had exhausted herself completely.

She lay there, staring absently into black nothingness, until she finally fell into a lonely, shivering sleep right there in the dark hall. Then, when she awoke a short time later, she repeated the whole process. This she continued to do, over and over, for at least three days.

CHAPTER 6
RESURRECTION

Anna heard a loud bang as the door slammed behind her. She felt the cool breeze of someone stepping over her, and she was aware of the sound of boots descending the stairs.

She sat up, slowly realising where she was, still sitting on the floor outside what used to be her own apartment door, having slept there countless hours.

The door opened again.

"Anna?"

Bewildered, she turned her face towards the familiar voice. "Joe?"

Joe was there. His arms were around her. It was the first time she'd had such a sensation—just a loving touch—in months. It was a feeling so wholly unexpected that she burst into tears, digging her fingers into his shoulders, and curling her whole body into him. Joe clung equally tight to her, knowing how much she must have needed him just then. She daren't move, not for a long time, believing that as soon as she pulled back, all the warmth would be gone with all the human kindness, and she would be alone in the cold, dark hallway again.

Eventually, she felt him loosen his grip on her, but he didn't tear himself away, and she wrenched him back in. "I thought you hated me."

"Hated you?" Now he did lean back, and he looked her in the face, a confused expression on his own. "No. No, I just got back last night."

"Back?"

"From Italy. I had no idea about any of this. Is that what you thought? If I'd known, I would have been here." He hugged her close. "Of course I would have been here." Then more quietly, "I can't believe they let this happen to you."

"No." She shook her head against his chest. "No, this is all my fault. I brought this on all of us. I messed everything up."

He tilted her chin up to look at her again, happy, exuberant even, and he said, "That's just not true. You did it, Anna. We got him back."

Her broken heart burst back into life. "Eve? You really did it?"

"We did. He's all better. And he's asking for you."

Joe pulled her to her feet, but she barely felt it. She ran into the apartment. The room was empty. Her eyes moved past the hanging door, to the hole in the stone wall, and she descended the dangerously creaking stairs in a matter of seconds. She ran around the edge of the half-built brick wall and she stopped in her tracks the moment she saw him.

Still seated in a chair, the last of his binds being cut from his battered body, Eve's eyes met hers. He was just as beautiful as he had ever been, yet she could see he had suffered greatly during the exorcism, just as he could see she hadn't eaten and had barely slept in three days. He was bruised and cut all over from whatever they had done to him, on his face, shoulders, arms. And there on his chest, bleeding profusely, was a new demon-warding symbol, in the exact same place she'd cut the last from him.

He staggered to his feet.

She took a step back.

The understanding, the overwhelming sadness in his expression, showed her it was absolutely, completely Evelyn Worthing.

And she was terrified of him.

"Eve?" she whispered.

"Anna."

She walked to him and very slowly, cautiously, he placed his hands gently on her forearms.

She flinched.

His tears fell fast and free as he knelt down at her feet. "I can never make it better, can I? Never. I can never fix this."

The truth of his words shattered them both completely on the inside, but they stayed there, close, neither willing to act on it.

Percy was there, and Joe and Aubrey, and even Lady Worthing, but Anna barely noticed them as they left the room. All she knew was that there, in that dark apartment alone with Eve, truly Eve, she was more frightened than ever, and she wanted to run.

She forced herself to reach out and touch his hair—his lovely hair that she adored so much—and the tendrils were hard and thick with blood and salt. She ran a hand over the edge of his delicate ear and down his cheek, and that was all she could bring herself to do.

Anna pulled back and burst into tears—tears she didn't think she had left after all the weeks of crying, but still she found more. "What have I done to you?"

He turned his beautiful eyes up to look at her. Then he turned them away again. "I don't know."

Always so honest, so sweetly honest, his words, spoken in a hollow, broken tenor, created a chasm between them.

The months of strength she had amassed to get through the ordeal came crashing down at once. All the awful things that had happened, all the awful memories that were too hideous for her to contemplate, all these horrors which she had believed to be her own challenges, now they were Eve's too. He had seen himself do things, indescribably awful things, and those memories weighed just as hard on him as they did on her.

Except he had had no say in the decision to let them happen.

She saw it in his eyes, in the way he held himself, in the way he knew better than to touch her.

Anna knew Eve inside out, and in that moment, she believed he was irrevocably changed. In that moment, she knew every awful thing she had done was for nothing.

She had destroyed him.

Whatever Eve had been, he would never be again, and he was just a shell now. She knew he would never recover, not ever, from the things he had seen himself do to her. The things she made him watch.

There was now only one sad, solitary thought that repeated itself, that overwhelmed every other idea, or reflection, or hope that may once have flashed through Anna's mind.

If only she had let him die.

CHAPTER 7
THE END OF EVERYTHING

Joe had offered to house either Anna or Eve, or stay with either of them should they need him. Percy had pressed Anna's hand in a quiet moment and fought with all his strength not to overstep whatever the thoroughly blurred boundaries were. Neither he nor Anna knew anymore. Candide had never returned, such was her abhorrence of Eve's all-consuming need for Anna after everything that had happened. Aubrey had bandaged Eve up, made sure they were all as well as could be, then returned to Candide. Lady Worthing had departed with barely a word to any of them once the job was done.

When Eve and Anna returned to his apartment that afternoon, the first thing he did was push the demon's armchair out into the hall. He pushed the other out for good measure. Then he turned to Anna, who stood silently, watching him, waiting to see what would happen next. "Tea?"

She made a move for the kitchen as though her life depended on it.

"No, I don't mean that," he said gently. "Let me make it for you."

"Oh. Sorry," she said, and stood awkwardly by the kitchen bench as he set the water to boil.

She trained her eyes on the kettle, and Eve saw her eyes, and he followed them. Then he remembered his own hands deliberately burning her with that kettle, and how she had screamed in pain, and he didn't know whether to turn it off or keep it going.

He turned it off.

He glanced around the room. "Do you want to sit down?"

"Okay." She walked to the couch and sank onto the floor.

"Anna, no."

"No?" She looked up at him, alarmed. "Oh. Sorry." She gave a small, scared laugh and crawled up onto the couch.

She hadn't sat on the couch in months. She hadn't been allowed to.

He took his place on the couch, but he kept as much distance as possible, saying softly, "Please don't feel like you have to say sorry to me."

"I'm sorry," she said. She let out another uncomfortable half-laugh at the comment, and when it drew only sadness from Eve, she turned her face away, then she turned her body away, and she stared at the wall.

Eve leaned forward, hiding his own face in his hands. Anna started to cry and so Eve started to cry. He turned towards her but she flinched, so he pulled back and turned away from her again, and they both sat in his living room and cried.

Eventually, so quietly she could barely hear him, Eve said, "I can't do this to you."

She made no answer.

He said, "I know you're trying to take care of me, and us, but I don't think it's good for us to be here."

Her eyes studied the wall. The carpet. The wall. "Do you want me to go?"

"No. No, I don't." She felt the couch move as he shifted a little, felt his eyes on her, but she still couldn't bring herself to make eye contact. "I don't, but I think… maybe one of us should. I need you and I love you so much and to see you frightened of me… Anna…" His voice broke again. "I'm so sorry."

"I don't want to leave you." Her own voice came out in a small, scared whisper as she clutched the edge of the chair tight with trembling fingers.

"Anna, I don't think we can do this."

The words had come so fast, before he could stop them, and then the silence was so, so heavy.

"What?" she whispered.

He wiped his tears away, and he cried, then he wiped his face again and said, "Do you really want to be here?"

"I love you, Eve," she protested, but she didn't touch him at all, and she stayed curled up on her corner of the lounge, her face averted and her shoulders hunched protectively as though he might, at any moment, raise his hand to her again.

"That's not what I asked."

She made no reply, then through his tears he said, "God, I love you so much, Anna. And I was the one person who was supposed to keep you safe. I love you so much and it was me. I did all those things to you. And I can see…" She forced herself to glance at him, then averted her eyes again, in fear, but also in shame that she couldn't do it. "You're so scared of me."

"I'm sorry!" she shouted.

"Please don't apologise to me!" he shouted back. "Anna doesn't apologise to me like that. It's not you! Please!"

When his words drew only racking sobs, Eve hated himself and all of it twice as much, and cried desperately, "I'm so sorry. I should never have said that."

But he was right. With every second that passed, Anna knew he was right. And the knowledge, the conviction, grew and grew inside her, until it was utterly undeniable, that Eve, her one true, perfect love, wasn't that at all.

Not anymore.

And she wasn't his anymore.

It was a fundamental shift, and for the first time, Anna grew to believe that love didn't matter a bit in the end. Because despite everything, she still loved him as much as she ever had, and she wasn't sure she wouldn't do it all over again, right now, if she was forced to make the same decision.

But she still couldn't look at him.

She whispered, "I don't want it to be over."

"Neither do I," he said. "You're my world. You're still my whole world. And you always will be."

"I know." She gave a small nod. "But we're not the same people." Anna let out a sharp, bitter laugh. "To think, all that time, you were so worried you were going to get me killed. And I did it. It was me."

"It wasn't your fault at all. I know why you did what you did—"

"I did it because I'm a horrible person."

"You're not, Anna."

"And I never deserved you," she sobbed. "And now I've ruined your life. I thought I was saving it, but I've killed you, haven't I?"

He moved closer, trying so hard not to touch her. "Anna—"

She cut him off. "I'm not Anna. And you're not Eve. And our beautiful romance… Everything we had… it's dead, and it's buried and it's all my fault." She wiped her tears away, took a deep breath, and steadied her voice. "I will never stop loving you, Eve, and I'm sorry I didn't let you die. You would have been happier, and look what I've done to you."

Anna's stark words cut off any reply he might have made at the throat. Because the simple fact was, Eve wished bitterly he had died that night. He would never breathe a word of that hideous truth to Anna, even if he knew she knew it, but every protest he wanted to make was caught in the knot in his chest and the grinding of his heart that pounded out its desperate plea for relief. For escape from this life. For escape from everything but Anna.

She didn't wait any longer for his response. "I'm going to go stay with Joe. And I'll drop your class. And we'll see what happens next."

The couch shifted with his body as he moved towards her. She heard the desperation in his voice. "No, I don't want to do this.

I don't want you to go. I'm sorry I said that. Any of it. I want you here. Please."

"I don't want to go. But I'm going, anyway." She sat forward on the lounge, looking around for her bag, trying to find the strength to stand. "Please, can you call Candide to come stay with you?"

His shoulder was so close by hers, but he didn't make contact, and she couldn't stand to. "Don't go. Please."

She said a little louder, "Please, will you call her?"

He sat silent for a moment, then, "Yes," he lied. "I will."

"Please do it. I can't stand the thought of leaving you alone. But if I don't go now…" She climbed to her feet, swiping her bag up from the desk. "I can't stay, because then I'll make things even worse for you."

"You wouldn't."

"I would."

He remained exactly where he was, watching her shove some books away. "Anna, I love you."

"I love you too, Eve." She pulled her bag onto her shoulder, and finally she turned around and made herself look at him. His heartbroken face. His beautiful, beloved face, and all the lines of it that she'd studied a thousand times over and never once imagined herself leaving. How desperately she wished she could look at him the way she used to. That he could look at her with the same love he'd always had for her. Every single time he looked at her, from the second she woke up, until that last kiss at night. Every night. "I'm so sorry I ruined this. I'll never love anyone else the way I love you."

"Please…" He wanted to ask her again to stay, or even ask if he could walk with her, but he knew he shouldn't and she understood anyway, so she only shook her head and wiped away her tears, trying to catch her breath to walk away from the man she loved.

"Can you call me when you get there?" he asked. "Just so I know you're okay?"

She wanted to laugh at the thought of ever being okay again. "Yes. Yes, I'll call you."

She put her hand on the door handle and turned to take one final look back at Eve. Beautiful, sweet, handsome Eve, with his tear-stained face and blood and cuts all over him. There was so much love in his eyes, but so much pain, and it was more than she could take, and in a second the door was closed behind her, and she was in the dark hallway of a building she no longer lived in.

She walked slowly down the hall as she tried to dry the never-ending tears with her sleeves.

She stopped outside Room 235.

There came a flash of herself opening that door for the first time and seeing her own new apartment. A memory of standing outside that door with Candide, or with Eve, or with both of them, and how confidently they had planned to face one supernatural challenge or another, always together. She thought of how she would never set foot in that apartment again.

She slowly descended the stairs and remembered the first time she had ever met Eve, just there, at the base of the stairs. The first time their hands ever touched. How much she adored him from the second she laid eyes on him.

As though he had been her one and only love.

Her soul mate.

As though such stupid things existed.

She proceeded down the hall and to the building's old, cold, stone entrance and stepped through.

What she had said to Eve was true. She had intended to go straight to Joe's cottage and stay with him as long as he would have her.

But then she walked out into the light of a gorgeous spring day and she saw Percy there, sitting at the base of the old tree in the centre of the courtyard, in his lovely blue coat, surrounded by daffodils, reading. And waiting for her.

He looked up at her as she stepped into the sunshine and there was so much love, so much care written in his expression, that she went to him. She collapsed onto the ground next to him and he wrapped his coat around her and he rested his head on hers until she stopped crying. Then he picked her up and took her home with him.

Meanwhile, Eve sat on his couch, alone, late into the night, and calculated as carefully as possible exactly how he could kill himself without Anna or Candide ever finding out what he had done.

CHAPTER 8

ENDYMION AGAIN

The next morning Anna woke, fresh and happy, with one thought on her mind: Eve.

She must see him. She must hold him. She must kiss him.

She sat upright in her own bed in her own apartment and stretched her arms high over her head. She flinched at the pain in her back and abdomen, but gave it little thought. The sun was soft and yellow as it streamed through her gigantic gothic window and bathed her in its gentle warmth. The huge ash tree outside was covered in a blanket of beautiful white flowers and she marvelled that only a few days earlier it had been completely bare. She pushed the window open and breathed deep of the sweet scent, the cool morning air of spring filling her with all the hope and romance and promise of a new day at Endymion College. She touched the tiny blossoms and felt the fragrant dew on her fingers, then suddenly, one of her fingers brushed something hard.

Tentatively, Anna parted the flowers, and there, tied to a small twig with a piece of red string, she discovered a small parcel, wrapped in plastic to protect it from the weather. She smiled as she disentangled it, imagining the look on Eve's face as he placed it there for her to find. His lovely delicate fingers winding the string around and around, the excitement he must have felt, wondering when she would finally see it.

How long had it been there? How many frosts and storms and winds had his romantic gesture weathered?

She pulled the tiny paper scroll from its wrapping and unfurled it. And there, in Eve's beautiful, elegant hand:

> O, for some sunny spell
> To dissipate the shadows of this hell.
> Say they are gone—with the new dawning light
> Steps forth my lady bright.
> O, let me once more rest
> My soul upon that dazzling breast.
> Let once again these aching arms be placed,
> The tender gaolers of thy waist.
> And let me feel that warm breath here and there
> To spread a rapture in my very hair—
> O, the sweetness of the pain!
> Give me those lips again!
>
> With double-distilled fire in his heart,
> Evelyn Worthing.

It was a full swoon. Not the middling swoon of a favourite book presented with a red rose on St George's day. Not the really quite considerable swoon of that first brush of fingertips or lips. Anna fell back into her bed and held the note close, reading it over and over, running her fingers over the words, then losing herself in her pillow again.

Evelyn Worthing.

That he thought it necessary to sign his name there, as though anyone else would have done such a thing.

Eventually, she calmed herself enough to climb out of her bed, and that was when she realised she was fully clothed. In clothes she had no memory of putting on. Her coat was slung across the foot of her bed. How did she end up here, alone, in her own bed and not with Eve? Did it matter?

She determined to run straight down the hall to him, pausing only to pick up her skeleton key from the bedside table where it sat sparkling serenely in the morning light. That was when she heard another key turning in the lock of the apartment door.

"Candide!" Anna cried.

Candide turned to face her, a look of shock, horror, anger, disgust written all over her.

Anna's face fell. "Are you okay?"

"What are you doing here?"

"Uh… I just woke up… So I'm here…" Anna looked around, still perfectly confused. "It's weird. I don't really know how I got here. But here I am."

Candide stared at her for a few angry moments, then she seemed to falter, to nod her head as though she understood something awful that Anna didn't understand at all. She ran her hands over her pockets, feeling for something, then she cast her eyes over the nearby surfaces, searching. Eventually, she pressed her trembling lips together hard, stared at Anna a little longer with hazy eyes, then said, barely louder than a whisper, "Did he give you a key?"

Anna pulled the skeleton key from her pocket and held it happily over her head. "Of course."

Candide slammed the door behind her and dropped down onto the coffee table in defeat.

"What is it?" asked Anna, walking to her. "Is Aubrey all right?" She reached for Candide's hand, but Candide pulled hers away, looking at Anna like she was an alien—a foul alien that Candide didn't want to be near.

Anna was surprised, confused, but she pushed on gently. "It was a pretty rough battle last night. Are you doing okay with everything?"

Candide narrowed her eyes. "Last night?"

Anna narrowed her eyes. "Candide, you're worrying me. Is everyone out of hospital? Is Eve okay?"

"Eve?"

"I was just going to surprise him with coffee. Come with me. We'll get it from the cafe then we'll go over. Oh, and he left me the loveliest note!" She jumped up and ran back into her bedroom to get the letter.

There came a knock at the door.

Candide stood and opened it mechanically.

"Candi!" Eve threw an arm around her and kissed her cheek. "Look, I brought you a flower!" He handed her a bright yellow daffodil. "And one for Anna too. Where is she?"

"I'm here, beautiful!" she called. "Look what I found!"

Eve advanced into the room, wrapped his arms around Anna and kissed her. "You finally found it!"

"How long has it been there?"

"Ages! I thought you'd never see it."

"I'm always with you! How did you think I was going to find that?"

"Do you like it?"

"I love it. I love you."

"I love you, too." He kissed her again. "And I brought you a flower."

"Eve! It's so beautiful." She snatched it out of his hand. "Where did you get this?"

He nodded towards the window, the vast expanse of sparkling greenery far below. "It's the weirdest thing. They're growing out in the courtyard. I could swear they weren't there yesterday. I've never seen daffodils in winter and I thought it was so special, so I stole them for you."

It was only now he glanced back at Candide and saw her pallid complexion, her shaking hands and the tears falling fast from her beautiful eyes. He was by her side in an instant. "What? What is it?"

"Daffodils in winter?" Candide whispered.

"What?" He looked at the flowers in confusion. "I don't understand. Should I not have stolen them?"

At that, Candide fell onto the couch and sobbed uncontrollably, unable to answer any of the well-intentioned questions Eve and Anna threw at her for the next twenty minutes. Even when she calmed down, she refused to say much of anything to either of them, but held Eve's hand and turned it over in hers, tracing the lines of it sadly but lovingly.

"Aubrey's fine," she said after some time. "Joe's fine. Percy's… Percy." She set her mouth hard, then said, "I have to go. Right now. Can you both do me a favour and be here when I get back?"

Eve was halfway to standing already. "Can't I come with you?"

She shook her head, stammering out, "N-no. It's… class… So you can't."

"Oh. Hey, do I have a class?" He furrowed his brow. "What day is it, by the way?"

"Uh." Candide licked her lips. "Saturday."

"You have class on a Saturday?"

"Not a class. A museum… thing. For class. Please, can you stay?" She tightened her hand on his and looked deeply into his eyes. "And I mean, really, not leave this apartment at all?"

Eve searched her eyes for a few moments, then said, "Candide, you look so sad."

Naturally, this brought a veritable waterfall of tears forth, and she flung herself against his chest and cried for several more minutes.

"What can I do?" he asked softly, stroking her hair.

"Nothing. There's not a thing you can do. Eve, I love you so much, and I can't…"

He watched her, his own eyes watering in sympathy with something he didn't understand at all.

"Please, just stay here." She stood and gathered her belongings, then left without even a look or a word for Anna.

Eve and Anna worried over her behaviour for about two more minutes, when the door swung wide open again.

"I thought she'd never leave," Percy said. "Whatever you do, don't let her find me."

CHAPTER 9
A STRANGE REUNION

"Percy!" Eve and his dazzling smile jumped up from the couch and he threw his arms around his brother. Percy held him very tight for some time until Eve said, "You saved my life, Percy."

"Of course I did." Percy pulled back to look at him. "I love you. There isn't a thing I wouldn't do for you." He kissed Eve's cheek, then let his eyes fall on Anna. "How are you?"

Anna, utterly delighted to see the love between Eve and Percy, said, "I'm really happy to see you again."

He coloured, only slightly, and replied, "I'm really happy to see you, too. Both of you." Then, with a slightly odd casualness to his tone, "That was some battle last night."

"Wasn't it?" Eve agreed. "How's Michael?"

"Amazing," said Percy. "You wouldn't think a boy who went through so much could make such a good recovery. There is some… telekinesis, you know, when he dreams at night, but nothing we can't handle."

Eve nodded his ready understanding. "And how's your mother doing?"

"So happy. So happy again. Very confused and still deeply traumatised, but… It's been a very good thing overall. I never could have done it without you both."

Eve smiled. "All's well that ends well."

Suddenly, there came a knock at the door.

"Shit," Percy whispered. "Did she forget her key?"

"Candide?" Anna whispered back. "Why are you hiding from her?"

"There's no time to explain. Quick! Let me out on the ledge."

Eve waited patiently by the front door as Anna secreted Percy behind the hanging door, then, "Eve!" Joe cried, when the apartment door finally opened. "I went to your place, but you weren't there."

"Joe!" Eve wrapped his arms around him warmly. "I'm so glad you're here."

"Joe!" Anna called. She ran over to him and hugged him tight. "Damn, you look so good!"

"Thanks, I guess," he laughed, blushing.

She threw her arm back around Eve's waist, also blushing, and mumbled, "I mean, you don't look beat up at all. Wow. I thought you'd be a mess."

He looked at her in some confusion, then running his eyes over their two happy faces, said, "I wasn't expecting this. You both look… like you're back to normal." Now Eve and Anna looked mildly confused. "Sorry," Joe said. "I was just so worried about you both, so I came first thing, and… you seem fine."

"Yeah, we're fine." Eve shrugged. "It was a pretty serious battle, but we all came out unscathed by the looks of it."

"Battle?" Joe said.

"Those weird dog things," said Anna. "I thought you were a goner, Joe."

Joe looked at them both very hard. "Why are we talking about—"

There were a series of angry kicks from the hanging door.

"Oh, I forgot!" Anna ran over to reveal Percy's furious, immaculately handsome face.

"You didn't need to lock it," he grumbled. Then, "Joe, I want you right now. In the kitchen."

Joe sighed and set his mouth, then followed Percy, silently and warily.

"Can I come?" asked Anna.

She received a firm 'no' from both Percy and Joe, so she shrugged and waited. Once they were safely secluded, she said to Eve, "Do you think Percy's about to pledge his undying love?"

"No." Eve laughed. "Joe's not the person Percy's taken with. I would love to know what's going on in there, though."

Anna blushed even more heavily, but before she could say anything else, there came another tap at the door. "Shit!" she said.

"Why is he even hiding from Candide?" Eve whispered.

"We don't have time to find out!" Anna whispered back. She opened the door a tiny crack, then flung it wide and cried,

"Aubrey!"

"Anna?"

"Aubrey!" Eve cried.

"Eve? Are you two…" Aubrey's eyes shot back and forth between them. "Are you *together*?"

Eve and Anna exchanged more confused glances. "Of course we're together." Anna said. "We're always together."

Aubrey threw her arms around both of them. "Oh! This is such a relief. I thought you two were finished for sure."

"What?" Anna half-laughed.

"Sorry, I probably shouldn't have said that. It's just…" She stood tall to look at them, hands on hips, shaking her head slowly. "You're honestly the strongest couple I've ever met. It's deeply inspiring."

"Thanks, Aubrey," Eve mumbled. "How's your back?"

"My back?"

"Yeah, those dog things. How are you feeling?"

She jutted out her lower lip, but kept smiling. "Fine. Totally better now."

"Already?"

"Yes, but…" Aubrey studied Eve suspiciously. "Where's Candide?"

"She went out," Anna supplied. "Some class thing."

Aubrey rolled her eyes. "That figures. Listen, Eve, I'm thinking you must have let Anna in here. You'd better not let Candide see her, or she's going to be pissed."

Both Eve's and Anna's mouths dropped open in another shared moment of befuddlement.

"Why would Candide be upset?" Eve asked.

"Seriously?" Aubrey practically yelled.

"Aubrey!" Percy shouted. "You're needed in the kitchen."

A frown hit Aubrey. She assessed Eve and Anna again, more curiously this time, then she sighed and muttered, "What now?" as she followed Percy's voice, resigned to whatever was to come next.

Anna watched her go, then said quietly to Eve, "Did you ever feel like everyone's talking about you?"

Eve cast his eyes around the room, then at the bright, sunny landscape outside the window. "Is it still winter?"

With his words increasing her own sneaking suspicion that something was very, very off that morning, Anna said, "I did notice the ash tree is flowering very suddenly."

"And the daffodils," he concurred. "Is it possible..." He paused. He went ahead. "Could it be spring?"

Their eyes met as they came to the same appalling conclusion.

Anna shouted, "Percy, get out here right now and explain what's going on!"

Percy strode quickly back into the living room and ordered everyone to sit. "All right. We have quite a lot of exposition to get through, so if you could all just—"

The door slammed shut.

"Percy!" Candide yelled. "You absolute bastard!"

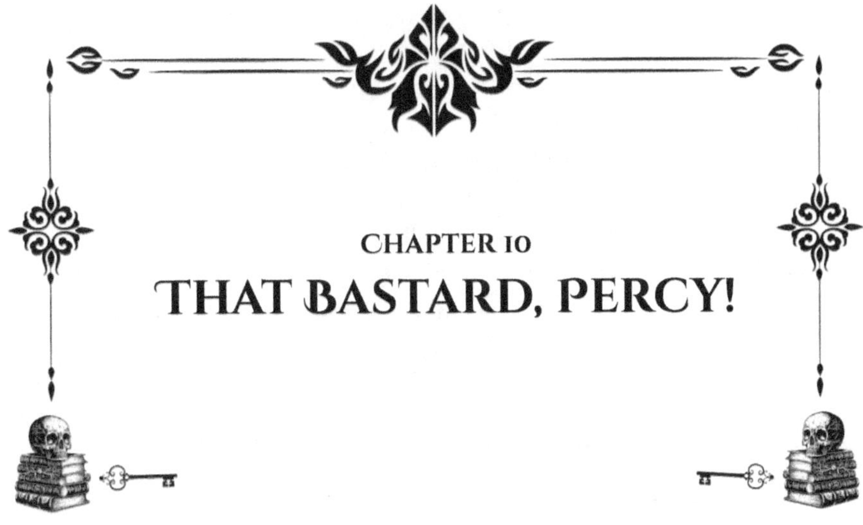

CHAPTER 10
THAT BASTARD, PERCY!

"Ooooh, what did he do this time?" came Anna's excited reply.

"Shut up, Anna!" Candide snapped. "I don't want to hear a thing from you!"

"What?" Anna and Eve gasped out.

"Don't speak to her like that," Percy said calmly. "She has no idea what you're talking about."

"Oh, really?" Candide turned furious eyes on Anna. "Let me be the one to fill her in."

"You shut your mouth this instant!" Percy yelled.

"Don't you dare talk to me like that!" Candide yelled back. "This is all your fault!"

"Well done you, figuring that out. Slow clap for Candide."

"Oh, you absolute—"

"Bastard, yes, I know," he finished for her, letting his voice drop back to mildly irritated. "I was just about to explain to Eve and Anna everything that's happened, and I'm sure you don't want things to be like they would have been, Candide, had I not fixed the situation, so tread carefully. Please, could you sit down and listen, and when we're done, you can do to me whatever you want to do. But for now, just look at them. They are very happy today."

Eve plastered an awkward smile on his face and Anna said, "I'm beginning to think we missed something important."

"When do you think it is?" asked Joe, looking at them exactly as if they were a fascinating science experiment.

"Spring!" Eve said proudly. "We figured that out already. Because of the flowers. Also, it's really hot."

Anna's eyes lit up. "You should take your sweater off."

Eve grinned at her. "I think I will."

"Amazing," Aubrey marvelled. "They're exactly the same."

Anna watched on approvingly as Eve pulled his sweater over his head, then she said, "Oh no, look, you're bleeding."

He looked down at the red patch on his crisp white shirt. "Oh yeah, that's really weird. My warding symbol opened up again somehow. I put a bandage on it but… yeah…"

Anna swiftly and expertly unbuttoned his shirt. "That's so odd. It was totally healed. Demon stuff?" She looked to the group.

"Yes," said Percy. "Demon stuff."

"But I *know* the battle was last night," Anna said. "I remember everything so clearly. But you're all fine…" She looked over the rest of the group, well-dressed and washed and perfectly healthy. "Why am I the only one who hasn't healed?"

"I haven't either," Eve said. "Check it out." He pulled his shirt the rest of the way open to reveal, besides the mouth-watering chest and abdomen, which just about sunk three members of the group that day, a series of cuts and bruises all over his chest, his stomach, his arms.

Anna pressed a gentle finger beneath a spatter of raised, reddish marks on his upper-left abdomen. "Is that burns?"

"I don't know. Looks like burns…" He examined the wounds with a wince. "Feels like burns… But I don't remember getting burned."

"That's nothing," said Anna. "Check *this* out." She ripped off her own sweater to reveal her slender arms, black and blue and covered in cut after cut after cut, all side by side in neat lines.

"Jesus, Anna," Eve cried, taking her forearm and turning it over gently. "What the hell happened?"

She shrugged. "I think Michael really hurt my wrist with that wrench. I don't know about the rest, though."

"When was the last time you ate?" Aubrey murmured, looking her up and down.

"I don't know," Anna replied. "I don't even know what day it is."

"I'm going to get you something." Aubrey disappeared into the kitchen.

"Put your sweater back on." Percy's shaky voice as he surveyed her wounds drew the quick attention of everyone else in the group. "Stay warm."

"I'm fine," she replied, extra brightly, not really sure why she wanted to reassure him, or what he was so bothered about, anyway. In a show of excess bravado, she went on, "But my stomach is really sore and I haven't even looked at that yet. Are you guys ready?" She stood up, grinned proudly, and everyone in the room turned pale as she pulled her shirt up to reveal pink, purple, yellow, brown and black welts all over. This accompanied by more cuts, more scrapes, the lot of it displayed on a sunken belly beneath protruding ribs. "Whoa, that's so much worse than I thought it was going to be." She laughed, a little nervously, trying hard to remember exactly when she could have received so many injuries during the battle.

"Holy shit." It took Eve a moment to form words more appropriate, but eventually he managed a whispered, "How are you still standing?"

Aubrey almost dropped the plate she was carrying when she saw Anna standing there. She carefully rebalanced, then placed it on the table in front of her. "I think you really need to eat something."

"Carrot sticks?!" Percy yelled.

"There's no nutritious food in there!" Aubrey protested in a shout just as loud. "I don't even know what Candide eats."

"She doesn't need carrot sticks, she needs calories!" With another glance at Anna, he adjusted his tone back to annoyed but controlled, shoved the plate forwards, and said, "Forget it. Eat, Anna, then we'll get lunch."

Eve placed a gentle hand on Anna's hip and said softly, "Turn. There's more."

"What?" She arched her neck, trying to see what he'd found. "What is it?"

"There's…" Eve faltered. "It's all cut up… but…" His fingers ghosted over her broken skin, eyes intent. "It's symbols… and it's… Some of this is fresh… Look at it all." Eve's brow contracted as his mind raced, then his eyes turned hard. He pulled Anna gently down against him and wrapped his arms around her, meeting the gaze of all the other sickened, horrified faces. "Who did this to her?"

No one said a word, but Eve and Anna's eyes both shot over to Percy, who refused to look at either of them as he wiped his eye with his wrist, then, with shaking hands, lit a cigarette.

"Open the window," Candide said quietly.

"You open the fucking window," Percy snapped.

"Don't yell at her," Eve said.

"I'll get it," said Anna. Then, to lighten the mood, "I'm sure it's just from the battle—"

"It's not." Eve's eyes remained on Percy. "Who did that to her?"

Percy leaned forward and tapped a tiny flake of ash off his cigarette. The others watched and waited for him, while he seemed to be making up his mind.

"Percy?" Eve pushed.

"It was a demon, and it's gone now," he said. "But what it did to you both, as you can see, is too awful for you to remember. So I took the liberty of…" He swished his hand in the air as if trying to think of the best words to explain it, but all he came up with was the plain, brutal truth. "Of deleting it from your memories."

Anna turned sharply back from the window. "I'm sorry. You did what?"

"I just…" He waved that same hand. "I got rid of it."

"What the hell did you do?" cried Eve. "How long? How much?"

"Three months."

Anna gasped. "Three months? Just gone?"

"Gone," Percy said simply.

Eve and Anna looked at one another. It was shocking, of course, but given the many clues of the morning, the idea that a few months had passed wasn't the greater part of the appalling revelation. Anna had been waiting—expecting—the demon that attacked them to return. The idea that it had been and gone and was over, but that she wasn't allowed to remember it, was its own kind of harrowing. Anna sank back down beside Eve. "What could have been that bad?"

Eve, whose intelligent mind was driven double-fast, relentlessly by his anxiety, saw all things flashing bright and clear before him, and with the bleeding wound on his chest smarting sharp, he fixed his eyes on Candide. "Who did that to her?"

Candide, who never could lie to Eve very effectively, said nothing, and stared back at him like a delinquent in the dock.

"I told you, it was a demon," said Percy, a tic flickering beneath his left eye as he watched Candide's mute response.

"Candide?" Eve pursued, never once breaking eye contact with her. "Did I do that to her?"

It might have been the small break in his voice, or the horror of the question stated so openly, but whatever it was, the panic left Candide's eyes as she reached her resolution to protect him. "No. No. Not you, Eve. It was a demon. It was a very difficult demon that we had a hard time getting rid of. It's gone now."

Anna squeezed Eve's hand as his thoughtful eyes dropped back to the coffee table. "So it wasn't a battle?" she asked.

"It was," Percy said. "And you were incredibly brave, Anna. In fact, you're the only reason we're all able to be here in this room together today. If not for what you did, I don't think any of us would have survived."

"Really?" She smiled wide, a happy blush colouring her pallid cheeks, and she leaned into the proud arm Eve passed around her.

Percy watched on, that same touch of melancholy about him. "Really."

"That's so nice to hear," she said. "I would hate to let any of you down."

Candide's glare at Anna was daggers, laced with poison, seeped in a good deal of bitter hate. Unable to unleash it properly where it wanted to go, she instead flung the lot at Percy. "You had no right to do that. That's their memories and their lives—that's who they are now. You have no right to just delete that!"

"It wasn't an easy decision to make," Percy said quietly. His devoted, devastated eyes rested on Anna a few moments too long before he wrenched them away again, and gazed at the blossoms of the ash tree pressed up against the window. He drew deep on his cigarette, and breathed out, "I believe I did the right thing."

Every person in the room caught the telling glance, and every person knew on some level what it meant and reacted differently.

Eve felt an almost overpowering love for his brother, strangely combined with a small spark of jealousy, which he promptly denied the existence of, and therefore, he doubled down on his belief that Percy was the best brother in existence.

Candide felt a vicious fury rise inside her, all the hotter for her complete inability to vent or process it, while every word seemed to add more fuel.

Aubrey felt a little surprise and a little guilt at how much she was enjoying all the drama.

Anna felt a combination of sadness, embarrassment, curiosity and irritation with Percy's look, as the last thing she remembered saying to him about their relationship was that revealing his feelings was disrespectful to both her and Eve and that he should keep them to himself.

But of all those thoughts and reactions, it was Joe's that was the strongest, and, to him, the most unexpected. It was Joe who finally saw a side of Percy that he had not, until that time, realised existed. Something inside him shifted suddenly, desperately, irrevocably, and although one heart appeared to be lost to Percy forever from that time, another became permanently, feverishly devoted to him.

"I also think you did the right thing," Joe announced. "It's very obvious to us all how much you love Eve."

"I agree," Aubrey whispered.

"He tried to murder him!" Candide yelled.

"And now I'm making amends for that the only way I know how," said Percy. "Candide, you brought him back to us—physically—you did that. But now I'm giving him everything else back. This doesn't need to touch him. Either of them. Why do you want him to suffer?"

"I don't! Of course, I don't!"

"Because it eases your misery." Percy cut straight to the quick, whether he realised he was doing it or not. "Because it's very lonely to have gone through what you went through and the only people in the world who would really understand, don't understand. And they never can. Not really. Even I can't understand what you've been through, but listen." He pointed his long, handsome finger towards Anna, eyes on Candide. "She isn't who she became. Anna is the same person she was before any of that happened. And even now that you know what she's capable of, even now you have those memories she no longer possesses, you must understand: it was all those things you don't like about her that gave Evelyn back to you. To all of us. I won't see her punished after everything she went through for that."

Candide snapped, "She didn't do it because she's a good person. She did it because she's selfish and careless and horrible."

"Maybe so." Percy shrugged, before tilting his head towards Eve. "But look at him. He's here with you now, living, breathing. And you can hate her as much as you want, but you can't deny she did something none of us could have done."

Percy's words had been hard to follow for Anna, her mind reeling, trying to figure out what she must have done, but his conclusion was like a knife through her heart. "Candide, do you hate me?"

Candide didn't hesitate. "Yes. Yes, Anna, I hate you."

Anna's mouth dropped open and a flood of tears rushed to her eyes. "But why? What can I have done to make you hate me? You're my best friend and I love you."

"Eve died," Candide revealed in cold, crisp words before Percy could stop her.

Anna took in a sharp breath and held Eve's hands even tighter.

Candide went on mercilessly, "Eve died, and to get him back, you did a deal with a demon. Part of that deal was apparently to murder me."

Anna's big eyes stared silently up at Candide.

"You tried to murder me, Anna. You sacrificed me for Eve."

"Oh," said Anna.

"Oh?" said Candide.

"Oh," said Anna. "Is that all?"

CHAPTER II
SHE MAKES A GOOD POINT

Eve's quick reflexes caught the book Candide launched at Anna.

"What do you mean, 'is that all'?" Candide yelled.

Anna blustered, "Well, I mean, I'm sorry, but that just sounds exactly like something I would do."

Candide stared at Anna, blank.

"I mean… I would die for him. And, I thought you would too? Wouldn't you have wanted me to do that?" Receiving only more incredulous silence from Candide, Anna continued, "I don't… I don't know what I did, obviously, but…" She let out an exasperated breath, and said, "I'm sorry, I'm just not really surprised I would do that."

Joe sent a disapproving look across at Percy's chuckle.

Eve, less amused than Percy, as usual, watched Candide and Anna anxiously, saying to Anna, "No, you might think you would do that, but you would never really do that."

"She did!" Candide yelled.

"Well, wait." Finally, Aubrey spoke up. "I talked to Anna a few days ago—"

"When did you talk to Anna?" Candide snapped.

"Just when you asked me to get her key—"

"You took my key back?" Anna cried.

"You bet I did," said Candide. "You shouldn't even be in my apartment."

"Oh." Anna frowned.

"Anyway," said Aubrey, "Anna seems to have had some idea that I was awake at the time, when the demon attacked, and she seems to have hugely overestimated my medical abilities. From what she told me, it appears that she may have made a snap decision that night, that if she did what the demon wanted, I could save you, and she could save Eve, and that everyone would be fine."

"That makes a lot more sense," Eve nodded confidently.

Candide narrowed her eyes at him. "Are you serious?"

"Anna could never do that!" he shouted.

Anna shrugged apologetically. "I don't even know what I did."

"She smashed my head in with a wine bottle!" Candide yelled.

Eve looked at Anna, aghast.

"But to be fair," Aubrey added, "Anna's not—no offence, Anna —Anna's not the kind of person to always... think things through."

"That's very true," said Joe.

"Yeah, that's true," Anna conceded. "Listen, Candide, I guess I really must have done that, because you're so angry with me… And I'm sorry. I really am sorry. I really wish I didn't try to kill you. Or almost kill you. Or whatever I did." She shuffled forward on the couch, trying to catch Candide's averted eyes. "All I know is that I love you. The Candide I remember from a few days ago knows I would die for her in a heartbeat… I still would. I can't imagine what happened to change any of that. I think I'm going to feel terrible when this all sinks in, but right now, all I can see is that you're here and you're fine, and Eve's here and he's fine, and… I guess whatever I did worked?"

Candide floundered and scrunched fists open and closed at her inability to argue with Anna's honest, artless answer.

"She makes a good point," Joe said.

"But you weren't even here to see what happened!" Candide cried. "Everything that happened after that night—"

Percy cut her off. "We don't talk about that now. Not ever again. As far as they're concerned, none of it ever happened."

Candide raised an exasperated hand to her temple. "She can't just get away with this like she did nothing wrong."

"Today, she can," Percy said simply. "I wasn't going to mention it, but she tried to kill me too, you know. I'm not complaining."

Anna's pale face snapped across. "I did?"

"Yes. Stabbed me right in the neck." He wafted his fingers upwards. "There's still some blood up there on the ceiling from whatever artery you severed."

For the first time that morning, Anna noticed the faded brown stains splattered in a long, thin line across the ceiling. "Sorry."

"Don't be. I'm fine now, too. You did what you had to do, and not to put too fine a point on it, but Evelyn would be dead and cold and mouldering in the ground if not for your quick thinking." He continued before anyone could voice their abhorrence at his choice of words. "I have two living brothers whom I adore and it's all thanks to you, Anna." He smiled at her proudly. "Now, just looking at you is making me ravenous." Anna's eyes widened and Percy hastened to add, "Because you look utterly emaciated. You need food. What do you want? Anything you like."

Anna thought for a moment, bit her lip in excitement, then said, "Steak and kidney pie!"

"Kidneys!" Eve cried. "Anna, that's disgusting."

"I like them." She grinned. "They're chewy."

"Ugh, I have to kiss that mouth," he replied. Then he went ahead and kissed her, anyway.

CHAPTER 12

LUNCH DATE

"Oh my god, this is so good," Anna moaned between mouthfuls of offal.

"Take my chips," said Aubrey, piling them high onto Anna's plate, then shoving a hot chocolate at her, all of which Anna accepted delightedly.

"All right," said Percy. "That's done. Now, lean in everybody."

A few worried glances were exchanged around the table, then Eve, Candide, Joe, Aubrey and Anna hunched forward expectantly over their cups and plates.

Percy looked around the cafe to make sure they wouldn't be overheard, bent his head close, fixed them with an inappropriately dashing and conspiratorial smile, and said, "I'm sorry to have to tell you this, but there's more."

CHAPTER 13
MORE

Percy continued, "When Anna made that deal with the demon, I was there. In exchange for resurrecting Evelyn, she had to pledge her mortal soul for all eternity."

"What!" Eve shouted, slamming his cup down and turning his full body towards Anna, as much as the booth would allow.

"It's what demons do," Joe shrugged.

Anna kept her shocked eyes on Percy. "I'm damned?"

"Damned," Percy confirmed.

"Really damned?" asked Anna.

"Damned! I'm telling you!" said Percy.

"Well, you know, I think I would have liked to finish my lunch without knowing that. What did you tell me that for?" Anna shoved three more chips into her mouth.

"Anna," Eve said, drawing her attention back with his firm remonstrance, "don't you ever pledge your soul for me again."

"I wouldn't," she lied.

Eve wrinkled his beautiful lips, then to Percy, "There must be something we can do."

"There is," Percy replied.

Aubrey leaned a little closer. "Is it incredibly dangerous?"

Anna looked at her and smiled. "I could swear you're beginning to enjoy this."

"Just a little." Aubrey smiled back, then looked very slightly sorry to Candide, who narrowed her eyes at both of them.

"Well, what do we do?" came Eve's impatient voice.

"We need to kill the demon she made the deal with," Percy said. "Then the deal is null and void."

"Perfect," said Anna. "Let's summon this asshole."

"It's a little more complicated than that." Percy took another breath to continue the explanation, but was surprised into silence by Joe's hand, which squeezed his biceps firmly, allowing Joe to take over.

"A demon can't be summoned unless he wants to, so he probably won't come. But then, to be honest, he might want to. He didn't go willingly. And I think he'll come back if we do nothing at all. He's… very attached to Anna."

Candide's worried eyes flitted over to Eve, whose eyes were still fast on Anna, him fighting hard against creating an intense public display of affection, despite the kidneys. "Why would it want to come back? It already thinks it's got her soul, right?"

"It said some things during the exorcism—" Joe started.

"What exorcism?" said Eve, his hand moving unconsciously to the warding symbol on his chest.

"Uh—when you exorcised me," Joe lied quickly, with a panicked look into Percy's stern eyes.

"Wait," said Eve, "that's the same demon? It came back?"

Joe nodded, pouring a little more milk into his tea to avoid making eye contact with Eve. "It came back. And I don't think it's going to stop coming back unless we stop it. It—it enjoys upsetting Anna, for whatever reason. All of us, but especially Anna."

"That's at least two reasons to kill it," Eve muttered, reaching for Anna's hand. "So, if we can't summon it, what do we do?"

"There's only one thing we can do." Percy dropped the words dramatically and cast his gaze expectantly onto Candide.

Candide rolled her eyes, sighed heavily, looked disparagingly at Anna, apologetically at Eve, then said, "We have to go to Hell."

CHAPTER 14
GOOD INTENTIONS

Eve gave a confident nod and an even more confident smile. "When can I leave?"

Before Anna could speak a word of protest, Candide cried out, "What? No! You're not going to Hell. I just got you back!"

He fixed accusing eyes on hers. "Back from where, Candide?" She looked away guiltily, so he continued, tapping his finger on the table for emphasis, "I'm going straight to Hell. I'm going to kill that demon. Then all supernatural things are done. Forever. And then me and Anna are moving to the village and…" He caught himself with a sheepish glance at his beloved. "That is, if… if you want to, Anna…"

"I do," she breathed, her delighted eyes shining adoringly at him.

He smiled, emboldened, "And then we're going to get one of those stone cottages you like, write our books and live out our days drinking sangria in the sun!"

"Yes!" Anna clapped her hands. "Yes! And we'll get a cat?"

"I'm getting you that cat for your birthday!"

"Oh, Eve! You're the best thing ever!"

"You're the best thing ever! How did I even find you?"

Percy coughed vaguely in the background.

"But, Eve," Anna continued, staring lovingly into his faithful eyes, "I really want to kill that demon myself."

"Then that settles it." He brought her fingers to his lips with a hearty kiss. "Let's go to Hell together and kill a demon."

"It's a goddamn date, Eve. I love you so much."

"I love you so much, too." It was all either of them could do to not climb over the table to each other.

But then Percy interrupted in his flat way. "You're both adorable. Truly. But you're not going to Hell. Not together anyway."

"What!" they cried in unison.

"I didn't actually *delete* your memories. That's just shorthand. I've used a very good cloaking spell—very good magic—and it's strong and it will hold, here, but my concern is, if we went to Hell and that magic was challenged, I'm not sure I'm powerful enough to hold it." Eve opened his mouth and Percy shut it with, "And under no circumstances are you two allowed to remember what happened, because then the whole thing is ruined and out the window because neither of you will be capable of doing what you need to do."

"What are you trying to say?" Anna asked.

"I'm saying," he cast his eyes around the table, "I need to know who else, other than Eve and Anna, would be willing to come to Hell with me."

"I would follow you to Hell, Percy," Joe sighed.

In the quick glance Percy gave Joe, he realised for the first time in months how remarkably long Joe's eyelashes actually were. "Thank you, Joe. I would love to take you."

"I'm in," said Aubrey.

"Sorry, no," said Percy. "I need you here for reasons yet to be disclosed."

"Oh… Okay, then…"

Percy paid no attention to her fallen face, explaining, "Aubrey will need protection, which leaves Eve, Candide and Anna to stay here and take care of her, while Joe and I go to Hell."

"I'm going to Hell," Anna protested. "Of course I'm going to Hell!"

There broke a small, circuitous argument between Percy and Anna in which she insisted that this was her demon and it was her right to kill it, and in which he argued that she'd be useless to him down there if he lost his grip on the magic for any reason.

"Will…" Candide sighed and tsked loudly. "Percy, will your protection on Eve hold if you're in Hell and he's here? Or if you die in Hell?"

Percy shook his head at his ignorance of the answer, and said only, "If it doesn't, I hope you'll do what you need to do."

Candide probed, "And what if the demon comes back while you're gone, and I don't have your help to fight it here? It's so much harder to send a demon back to Hell than it would be to just kill it there in the first place. In theory. Especially without you here to deal with Eve and Anna…" She looked across at Eve, who by that time was staring down at his barely touched plate, forehead wrinkled with worry.

Percy followed her gaze, saying regretfully, "It's the only way. You take care of them here, and Joe and I will do our best."

"It's not good enough," Candide decided.

Percy glanced up at her, and some kind of silent understanding passed between the two of them, as Candide said, "Someone with stronger powers could take Anna to Hell and keep her safe. And they would have a better chance of preventing the demon from coming back to Earth. And all that trouble would be avoided… But they would need a guarantee things would be looked after here in case anything goes wrong."

Eve came back to the conversation with the shift in the atmosphere. "I'm sorry, what's happening?"

"I swear it," Percy said to Candide.

"Swear what?" said Eve. "I don't think I like where this is going."

Candide glared at Anna, grimacing as she did so, then she sighed out, "I'll do it. I'll take Anna to Hell."

"Huh—" Anna began inarticulately enough, but she was drowned out by the screech of Candide's chair pushing back, and the clatter of Eve's crockery as he jumped up to chase after her.

"Meet at my place!" Percy called after them.

"Ah, it's such a nice day, and we're all going to hang out in Percy's weird demon sex dungeon," Aubrey said.

Joe, with a tremble to his beautiful lips that no one had ever seen on him before, asked, a little breathlessly, "Percy has a weird demon sex dungeon?"

"No," Percy muttered. "It's my living room. Aubrey here has painfully pedestrian taste."

Anna pulled her gaze back from the window, where Candide and Eve were swiftly making their way across the courtyard in furious argument. She smiled over at Percy. "Finally, I get to see your place."

"Yes. Finally," he said, adding his own sad, resigned smile before ushering them all out of the cafe.

CHAPTER 15
WEIRD DEMON SEX DUNGEON

"I don't believe it," Joe exhaled, long and enamoured.

Percy's home was nothing like Anna had imagined, which she had done more times than she would have liked to admit. It was apparent Joe felt the same as they found themselves standing side by side at the edge of a very neat green lawn, leading up a slight incline to an adorable old church. The church sat quietly overlooking a small, ancient graveyard, respectfully kept clear of vines and long grass, weathered headstones leaning here and there, soft green moss clinging to them all over.

"It's incredible," Anna gasped out.

Percy looked down at her with a fond smile, obviously buoyed by her enthusiasm. "I'm glad you like it."

The grey granite, sparkling serenely in the delicate sunshine, was frigidly cold to Anna's appreciative touch as they wound their way around the building. The church doors were thick and solid and opened with a delightful creak directly onto a breathtaking scene.

Inside, the stone was exposed as much as it was on the outside, decorated with glorious artworks that looked to Anna to be the genuine thing. Various odd artefacts and curios were displayed all around. From the floor to the very high arched ceiling were stained-glass windows, throwing a rainbow of colour onto everything below. There were two enormous brown leather sofas facing one another in the centre of the room, and on the floor beyond that, the softest-looking, fluffiest, thickest white rug Anna ever saw. The whole thing must have looked marvellous on a winter's night when Percy lit a fire in the gigantic fireplace at the far end of the room, particularly, Anna considered, if Percy himself were seated by the fire on that soft rug, though she kept that last thought quite to herself.

"Look, he's got the chains and everything," Aubrey laughed, pointing at the ceiling.

"They're attached to the lights," Percy bristled. "And they cost a small fortune."

"I like them," Anna said. She did. They emanated from huge hooks high up in the stone wall, then threaded through more huge hooks hung from the ceiling, lowering a beautiful, black metal chandelier over the room. She turned to Aubrey. "Have you been here many times?"

A slight frown crossed Aubrey's face as she remembered Anna's memory loss. "Just a few times."

"Oh," came the somewhat-melancholy reply. "It's funny how much I don't know now."

Anna walked over to a wooden chess set and started fiddling with the pieces in exactly the same way she had the first time she visited.

Percy watched her fingers for only a few seconds before throwing himself down on the couch and lighting a cigarette.

Anna came over and sat down on the rug, and Percy couldn't help but think of how he had sat right there next to her, and how he had looked deep into her eyes in the firelight…

"Anna, wouldn't you rather sit on the couch?" Percy asked.

And he thought of her lips, and his hand lost in the tangle of her hair…

"No, I'm good here," she said.

And how cold and delicate her hands were when he held them in his own, and how much he adored them…

"How long do you think Eve and Candide will be?" he asked.

And how he had pulled off her wet overcoat and wrapped his arms around her…

"You know those two." She laughed. "They could argue all day."

And how she had snuggled in close against his chest, and how he had wanted nothing more in the world than to stay there with her forever.

Percy walked over to the side-table and poured four glasses of scotch with an unsteady hand.

"What are we even doing here?" asked Joe, finishing his tour of the room and sliding into the seat next to where Percy had just been.

Percy placed the drinks on the table, wondering slightly if Joe had always moved his hips quite like that. He pushed his golden cigarette case towards Anna. "I have a lot of weapons and a lot of relics that I think can be very useful to us."

"About time." Anna flipped the case open—a new movement to her, but an achingly familiar one to Percy. "Eve and Candide have no weapons. Like, none!"

"I thought that was so odd," Aubrey replied. "I mean, if this kind of thing keeps coming up…"

"Right?" Anna puffed out some smoke from her freshly lit cigarette and pushed the case away. "It's all kitchen knives and skewers with them."

"He's in denial." Percy flicked his lighter open and held the fire to Joe's cigarette. "If he buys real weapons, he accepts that this is his life."

"It's not," said Anna. "When I'm done with this demon, nothing bad is going to touch him ever again."

Joe breathed out his own meditative plume of smoke. "He's not just going to let you go to Hell, you know?"

"Eve trusts me," Anna replied, wondering exactly how much denial she was in as she made the statement.

But Percy said, faintly, "He shows good judgement."

"He does," Joe agreed, a little more forcefully. His hand, resting on his own leg until just then, flipped over, and he pressed a finger against Percy's outer thigh. A small gesture, but one that drew Percy's full attention. "Now, let's see these weapons."

With clear consternation etched across his handsome brow, Percy traversed the room to a set of six of Goya's Disasters of War etchings and pulled one from the wall. Behind was a small cavity in the stone. From there, he took a little silver key.

Anna loved Francisco Goya, one of the many painters she had studied in Gothic in Art. She made a quick assessment based on everything she knew of Percy. "Those aren't real, are they?"

He didn't look up. In fact, he lowered his head a little, but what she could catch of his smile was as mischievous as ever. "I'm just holding them for a friend."

"A friend?"

He sent her a wink. "Not a word to Candide."

Aubrey groaned and threw her head back. "Please don't make me keep secrets from my girlfriend."

Anna cast her eyes over the other artworks in the room and wondered how many of those were being held for 'friends' too. But before she could wonder about anything else, Percy flung open a huge set of doors belonging to a gigantic cabinet that towered high above him, and Anna's jaw just about hit the coffee table.

The entirety of the cabinet's interior was covered in tightly packed, shiny weaponry and dozens of even more bizarre relics than those on display throughout the odd and increasingly bewitching room.

Aubrey, who must have had prior knowledge of the bounty, only raised an eyebrow and said, "See what I mean? Demon sex dungeon."

"Yes!" Anna bounded over to the cupboard in an instant. "He's got even more chains in here." She reached out to feel the cold steel of a golden set, shining in the dappled light of Percy's church.

"These are warded too," he said proudly, watching Anna's fingers trace over the tiny inscriptions that ran along the edge of each loop.

Anna suddenly felt an all-too familiar warmth while looking over Percy's chains. She glanced up at him, and he snuck a peek down at her, and all the spark of their intimacy was back in full force.

She blushed and made herself walk away, hating that the feeling was still there, always simmering so close to the surface, and confounded as to what she should do to get rid of it.

Joe, having watched the brief, telling interaction, sauntered over to Percy's side, and said quietly, "I wonder what's good for killing demons."

"I have no idea," Percy muttered, still fondling his chains. "I was just going to put a few things on display so Anna can decide what she likes best."

Joe, thrown by the unguarded statement, said, "Percy, you can't be serious."

"What?" He threw half a glance over his shoulder at Anna. "She needs to decide what she really wants. I can't decide for her."

Joe arrested his arm as he reached for a large knife. "Don't do this."

"Don't do what?" Percy leaned in close. "Why are we whispering now?"

Percy looked so genuinely perplexed by Joe's sudden concern that Joe wondered if there had been any double-speak in the conversation at all. He searched Percy's eyes a moment longer, then said cautiously, "Just remember, Anna has terrible aim."

"I can still hear you," Anna called.

"And you know that's true," Joe retorted.

Percy and Joe proceeded to lay down a series of weapons on the coffee table, and Percy set about regaling them with endless, fascinating tales of where each highly illegal item had been obtained. The more time passed, the heartier the conversation became, all of them having missed such easy company over the last few months, except Anna, who was just happy to be with them, even if it felt like only one night since they last met.

Aubrey took free rein in Percy's kitchen, and the pair of them took turns to ply Anna with fattening foods until she had to refuse any more. They all sipped their drinks, topping them up again and again, and Anna, Percy, and Joe smoked endless cigarettes while Aubrey tolerated it.

As it got dark, and as it was only early in spring, Percy lit a fire. They settled on the white rug, where Percy took his place as far away from Anna as possible, which was not very far. They were all comfortably relaxing on the floor in such a way, with a just-opened second bottle of scotch, when Eve and Candide finally arrived.

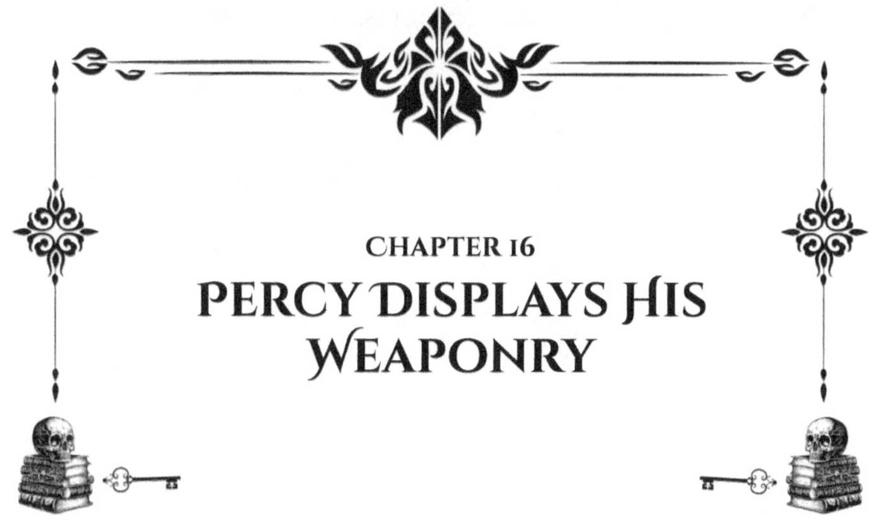

CHAPTER 16
PERCY DISPLAYS HIS WEAPONRY

"Did you just get more beautiful?" Eve called across the church the moment he was let in.

Anna's heart thumped proudly in her chest as he took his place by her side and kissed her. Percy flung himself back down unobtrusively yet dramatically, and Joe leaned back on his elbows and stretched his legs out quite deliberately, at which time it was noted by Percy (and Eve and Anna) that yes, he did indeed have very nice legs. Meanwhile, Aubrey skipped across the room to Candide, who had, as yet, disdained to join the group on the rug. A quiet chat was had, culminating in Aubrey leaning in for rather a sweet kiss and leading a reluctant Candide to the fireside.

In seconds, it became clear that Eve and Candide had also been drinking, as Eve, though still insistent he would be accompanying them, was far less upset about the idea of Candide and Anna's trip to Hell than anyone expected.

Anna would have sent a sly and approving smile to Candide had she felt Candide was ready to receive that look from her, but Candide kept her face turned away and her lips ready to make a cutting remark should they be provoked.

Percy drew her attention to the weapons on offer. Candide studied them for a time, lifting a knife here, turning over a shuriken there, then she turned to Percy and asked accusingly, "Are there more weapons?"

"Everything in the cupboard," Percy replied, a little too immediately.

Candide tilted her head to the side. "And?"

"And…" He assessed her. He shrugged. "Well, a few other things, but I'm not sure they'd be any good."

Something in the reluctant, vague way Percy worded the answer made Anna's eyes snap over. "What other things?"

"Uh…" He hid his mouth with his scotch. "Very old things."

"Antiques?" Anna pushed.

"Yes."

"Like your nice dagger?"

"Yes." He coloured a little and mumbled, "Like my nice dagger."

Eve leaned in, grinning handsomely and irresistibly. "Where do you keep the good stuff, Percy?"

"It's not even good." Percy shoved him off. "It's very nice, but it would probably fall apart if you tried to kill a demon, but…" He sighed and ran his eyes around the expectant group. "Do you want to see them, anyway?"

All were in loud and enthusiastic agreement, so Percy had them all stand, undid yet another button on his shirt because he was really very hot after all, what with sitting so close to the fire, and once they were all a good distance back, he flung the rug aside to reveal a trapdoor.

"You have a real demon sex dungeon!" Aubrey cried.

"Yes, more or less," he drawled. "More demon, less sex, but you get the idea."

Percy slid a latch and pulled the trapdoor open on a square of pitch black in the floor. Joe picked up the bottle of scotch and they descended what little they could see of a wooden ladder. All but Percy could barely contain their excitement as they made their way down, setting foot moments later on dark, dusty, bare earth. Percy hit a switch and illuminated a long tunnel, lit from above with a series of flickering electric lanterns. At the end of the tunnel was a dim metal door, some disconcerting way off. There wouldn't have been much to intimidate a group like this in a secret underground tunnel beneath a church graveyard, had it not been for the endless rows of coffins sitting upright, on both sides of the passage, as far as the eye could see.

"Are they…" Aubrey started. She lowered her voice to a whisper. "Are they occupied?"

"Of course," Percy replied.

Aubrey took a step closer to Candide and Joe said, "What are they doing here? You shouldn't move bodies from consecrated ground."

"Oh yes, I know that," said Percy. "I think it's still consecrated ground down here. Unless the estate agents unconsecrated it. But I had to dig out the old graveyard to make my dungeon, you see, and I didn't want to just dump the bodies, so here they all are. Still buried. Sort of."

"This is some Poltergeist shit right here," Candide said.

Anna could hardly believe her ears. She knew the comment must have been for her benefit, but Candide only took a sip from the bottle Eve passed to her, then gave it to Aubrey, then started down the dark passage. Anna desperately wanted to step forward and take her arm and lead the way with her, but instead she stood back and said quietly, "You son of a bitch, you left the bodies," and Candide laughed a little, and it was more than enough for Anna.

"So, this is the way to my exorcism room," Percy said. "That's not a protected space. I think we're all warded now, except maybe you, Aubrey?"

"No. I'm totally warded now," Aubrey replied, a touch of reproach on her lips.

"You are?" asked Anna.

"Yeah. I think it would be a bit remiss of me to not be, given the kind of stuff that keeps happening to us."

"Yes, point taken, Aubrey," said Percy. "Repeatedly."

"I'm just saying—"

"Stop saying!"

Anna glanced up at Percy's magnificent, but increasingly annoyed, face. "You've always been warded, haven't you?"

Along with her innocently spoken words, Percy was hit by the sudden and gut-wrenching memory of Anna's beautiful fingers covered in his own blood. This was followed in quick succession by a vision of his own hand, ready to snap her neck, then another of his hand forcing her fountain pen deep into his brother's skull. He visibly shuddered, but he quickly straightened his shoulders, set his jaw, smiled, and forced himself to speak softly, jovially, as though there wasn't a thing wrong. "It may have taken a little longer than it should have, but it's done now and that's what's important."

Aubrey stopped. She turned to look back. "What was that?"

Candide paused by her side and surveyed the long tunnel behind them. "I didn't hear anything."

"There are rats in the walls," Percy suggested grimly.

"So just ignore those scratching sounds?" Aubrey asked.

"It would probably be for the best," Percy replied.

They were about halfway through the tunnel when there came a very distinct scraping sound. Much louder than the scratching sounds Aubrey had referred to. The sound, most likely, they each reflected, of bare bones scratching at ancient, rotting wood.

Percy stopped, turned, pulled his dagger free and passed a key to Eve. "Perhaps a little faster into the exorcism room."

Eve didn't need to be told twice. He took hold of Anna's hand, unnecessarily insisted Candide keep up, and they ran down the hall. Percy kept a fast backward pace behind them, blade outstretched, while Joe kept a close eye on him and whatever the hell the situation was.

The lock opened easily, Eve thrust the door wide, and they all tumbled into a new, pitch-black space, just as the lights to the tunnel were cut.

"Fuck!" Percy slammed the door shut behind them then flicked his lighter open. Then, with a little light to think more rationally about the situation, he offered, "It's probably just… a generator thing."

Joe, back to the door, shoulder to shoulder with Percy, asked, "You use a generator?"

Percy shrugged bashfully. "I thought it would be rustic."

"No, it is." Joe smiled. "It's a nice touch. Under normal circumstances. I bet the sound's comforting."

"You know, in an odd way—"

"Shhh!" Candide pressed an ear against the door. There was some more scratching, followed by a decidedly loud crack. "Is this door locked?"

"Oh shit." Eve flung himself around and turned the key in the lock. "Sorry."

Candide scowled at him. "Is your brain back to normal yet?"

"It was your idea to get the second bottle!"

Percy crossed the room and set alight a huge stone fireplace, which threw its radiance onto the surrounding expanse. They saw at once the space was enormous. The walls were hard-packed, exposed dirt, roots breaking through here and there, metal clasps and hooks thrust deep to hold chains and more chains, bizarre instruments of torture, fascinating weaponry. There were wooden tables and shelves scattered about the place, covered in herbs and spell books, bowls and jugs, knives and the ancient stains of spilled potions. Two huge candelabras with wax dripped all down the sides in fascinating patterns sat on either side of a gigantic, indestructible-looking metal chair in the centre of the room. As a final, impressive flourish, the entire dungeon was presided over by a gigantic marble altar that Percy must have had transported down from the original church.

Anna gasped, and managed, "Oh my god…"

Percy had been watching, waiting for her response. "Do you like it?" He couldn't help himself, hiding none of his pleasure as he lit his oversized candelabras.

"I love it!" she cried.

Percy gave a warm laugh. "I had a feeling you would."

"Yet it's a gas fireplace?" Joe asked, loudly cutting through the increasingly thick atmosphere.

"It gets incredibly cold down here in winter," Percy explained, successfully distracted. "And I thought, what's wrong with a bit of luxury?"

Joe gave a wide, handsome smile. "Nothing wrong with that."

"Plus, it's helpful to heat the implements."

"Implements?" asked Aubrey. "You mean like all these metal things? For torture?"

Joe cast his eyes appreciatively over the walls. "Sometimes you have to be cruel to be kind."

"Bless your Catholic heart," Percy said, before giving considerable pause over the wink he received from Joe.

"In the nicest way," Aubrey said, "I think it's a little weird you do your exorcisms by candlelight."

"Only when the lights go out," Percy replied, "which, if you're going to claim to be such an expert, you should know, happens a lot when you're dealing with the paranormal."

"I never claimed to be an expert."

"Know-It-Aulbrey," he said.

"Shut up, Percy!"

"Will do." And he threw himself back languorously into the huge exorcism chair.

"No, don't," said Candide. "Where are the weapons?"

"Oh, yes. I forgot." He jumped up and walked across the room to another locked cabinet, as the noise of cracks and scrapes sounded loudly outside the door.

Candide looked around anxiously. "And how much air do we have in here?"

"Um. Some."

"So maybe we should cut the fire."

"It does get quite cold."

"Cut the fire."

"We may need it."

All six heads turned in alarm as there came three distinct, bony taps on the metal door.

"That's not good," Joe said.

"How many corpses would you guess are out there?" Eve asked.

"I never counted. But let's just calmly look at what old, rusted, antique weapons we have down here. Not like the nice, new, sharp ones upstairs." Percy threw the cabinet open.

The scrapes and taps increased, and with it the urgency in Joe's voice. "Is that door attached to the bedrock? Or just in the dirt?"

"Do I look like a door salesman?" Percy snapped. "Now everyone come and choose a weapon. Quickly!"

Eve grabbed a large, sturdy-looking knife. Aubrey, quite ambitiously, grabbed a nice-looking scythe, and Joe went for a flail, with rather a heavy spiked ball at the end.

Anna sighed a little.

Had it been anyone else, Percy would have been furious. But it was not anyone else. "What is it?"

"I just want to know why none of you demon hunters ever have guns."

A shocked silence fell around her.

"Anna, guns are awful!" cried Aubrey.

"They kill so many people!" Joe agreed.

"I've gotta say, I'm a little surprised you would say that, Anna," said Eve.

"I'm not," huffed Candide.

Percy also sighed, but he said, "Listen, I do have one gun."

"Don't give her a gun!" Eve all but yelled. "Guns are very dangerous."

"No, I mean, I'm not even sure if it works, but it's pretty nice." He swiftly pulled open a drawer lined with red silk, and there lay the most beautiful, and only gun Anna had ever seen. Its hilt was a smooth and rich mahogany. The steel that decorated the handle curled in intricate patterns inlaid with swirling gold, until it disappeared into an exquisitely long, cold, grey barrel. "This is the gun"—Percy paused for dramatic effect—"that killed Alexander Pushkin."

"Oh, well, I'm taking that then." Eve grabbed the thing before Anna could utter a word of protest. "Gunpowder? Shots?"

"Here." Percy passed them over.

Anna watched in wrapt admiration as Eve ripped open a packet of gunpowder with his lovely teeth, poured a tiny amount into his palm and the rest into the barrel of the gun. He threw a metal ball down there along with the paper package, and then used a metal rod, attached to the base of the barrel, to pack it all down. Next, he put the remaining speck of gunpowder into a little metal tray at the top of the pistol, extended his arm, then paused only to say, "Cover your ears." They did as told and he pulled the trigger, firing a bullet straight into the wall across the room.

"It leans left," he said. "I'll have to correct for that."

"Well, it is very old," Percy muttered. "And I'll want it back."

Anna stood on her tiptoes and kissed Eve's cheek, her heart all aflutter at yet another side of him she was just discovering. Then she reluctantly selected a shiny axe for herself.

Candide, all the while, had been assessing the weapons, until finally, her eyes lit on a glint of metal peeking over the edge of the top shelf. "What's that?"

Percy followed her eyes, and gave a gruff, "Not that."

"What is it?" She reached up regardless of his tense glare and wrapped her hand around cold steel.

"It's…" He swallowed. "It's just a sword."

"I like swords." She pulled, and it seemed to go on and on forever as she freed it from its dusty hiding place to reveal a well-loved, well-oiled, shiny, intensely sharp blade. A blade she recognised on sight. "You shouldn't have this!"

"You weren't supposed to find it!"

"No one even knows this exists anymore!"

"That's the idea!"

"I'm taking it!"

"Don't you dare!"

"What is it?" Anna asked quietly.

"It's the sword of Joan of Arc," they said at the same time.

"Holy shit!" Anna cried. "You've got to take it."

Candide nodded in agreement. "I'm taking it."

Anna watched her turn it over, the muscles flexing in her arm as she tried it out. "You look so good with it."

"Thanks." Candide smiled, so Anna smiled, too.

Percy, watching the pair of them, let out a resigned groan. "You can take it to Hell only. And that's a personal favour. You bring that and Pushkin's killer's gun straight back here, or I'll enchant them, and everyone who visits whatever museums they end up in will regret it."

"It's so nice," Eve said, ignoring the threat because he was too busy looking his gun over.

Anna glanced up at Percy hopefully. "Is my axe special, too?"

He looked back at her apologetically. "It's just a nice axe."

"Oh."

The taps and scrapes and bangs on the door had been increasing for some time and were now reaching a worrying crescendo.

"Okay," said Joe, advancing towards the enemy, whatever it was. "They're in a tunnel, so we've got the advantage. Is everyone ready?"

All agreed except Aubrey, who looked slightly more worried still at the large swig of scotch Candide downed.

The scotch, however, gave Candide an idea. "Oh, hey. Molotov cocktail?"

"Perfect!" Anna shouted. "Let's use Eve's shirt."

"Yes!" Joe said. "Let's do that."

"Rip it, Anna!" Percy said. Eve reluctantly let an unnecessarily large portion of his shirt be cut away with some kind of medieval torture shears that Anna had to hand, then Percy smiled approvingly and continued, "But you're not using a Molotov cocktail in my tunnel. You'll cave the whole thing in."

"What?" they all cried, especially Eve.

"We have two options available. We stand and fight an army of the undead—"

"Hardly an army," Eve scoffed.

"Or we go straight to Hell right now through a portal and kill that demon together!"

"Couldn't we make a portal to somewhere other than Hell?" Aubrey suggested.

"There's no time for that!" Percy snapped.

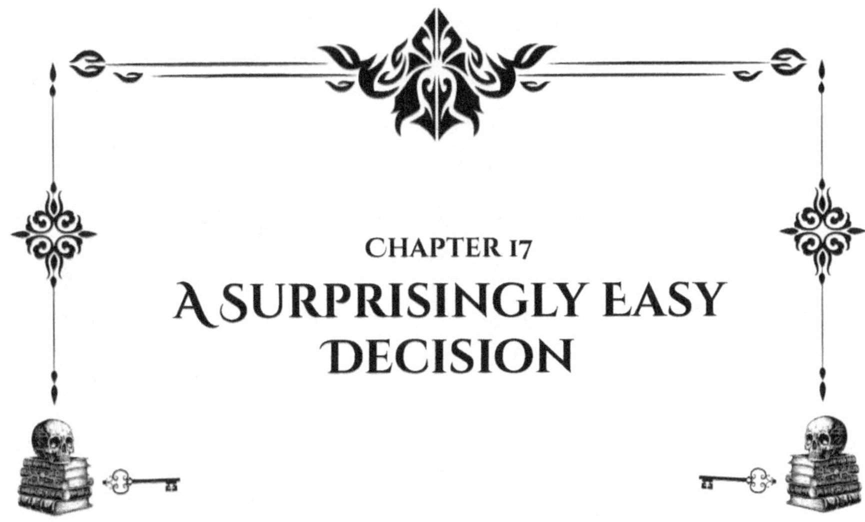

CHAPTER 17
A SURPRISINGLY EASY DECISION

"I vote Hell!" Eve yelled, like a man drunk on scotch and wine and misplaced bravado.

"Me too!" yelled Anna, also drunk, but especially on Eve's enthusiasm. "Hell!"

"I also vote Hell," said Percy.

"Yeah, I vote not Hell," Aubrey replied.

"I really don't mind either way," Joe put in.

Candide gave a vague shrug. "I'm good with Hell."

Aubrey sent a grimace her way, and asked, "Wasn't there a reason we weren't all supposed to go at once?"

"Not now, Know-It-Aulbrey," Percy replied.

"Stop calling me that!"

"It's pretty good," Candide chuckled.

"Bowl!" Percy pointed at a large silver bowl, which Anna grabbed and dumped on a table. "Eve, in that drawer there, some herbs." Eve seized them as directed. "And my nice dagger," said Percy, dramatically unsheathing his blade. "I'll need blood from each of you, so arms out."

"No!" Aubrey pulled her arms tight around herself in anticipation of his next move. "How old is that blade?"

"Four-hundred years," he announced. "Now arm out or I'm leaving you with the skeletons."

"Fuck!"

Everyone having thrust their arms forward, Percy made one large cut in each arm, not pausing to wash the blade in between, much to Aubrey's shock and disgust, and they all stood around the table letting their blood drop-drip into the bowl as the sounds at the door became near deafening.

Joe sent an anxious glance towards the noise. "They're using the wood from the coffins now. It won't be long."

"Have we got bandages?" Aubrey asked.

"Eve's shirt!" Anna cried.

"Yes!" shouted Percy.

"Do that!" said Joe.

"Fine," said Eve, pulling it over his head. "I guess it's hot down there, anyway."

"It soon will be," Anna joked, and Eve grinned a bashful smile, and Percy and Joe watched on happily as Eve's back arched and his abs flexed, and the indecently beautiful body was revealed.

Aubrey, unmoved, said, "Can we maybe use the scotch to sanitise the bandages?"

Candide spilled a little on her shirt as she pulled the bottle away from her lips. "Yes, but only a bit. It's very good scotch."

"Isn't it?" said Percy. "It was a gift from—"

"Please, could you just get us to Hell?" Aubrey snapped, watching the door with frightened eyes while dousing strips of Eve's shirt.

Percy sighed and threw the herbs into the bowl, then turned to face the fire. He held the hideous concoction over his head, his own blood spilling down his still-unbandaged arm as he began speaking in Latin. "Di nobis propitii Acherontis. Vale trinum numen Domini. Grati spiritus ignei, aerii, aquosi. Beelzebub, Orientis rector, inferni monarcha, et Demogorgon, regnum inferni impium intrare rogamus. Accipe hoc donum sanguinis peccatorum et da nobis iter liberum!"

With that, he threw the bloody mixture into the fire and dropped the bowl to the ground. "Grab your weapons. Time to go."

"Through the fire?" Aubrey shouted, holding a hand tight over her alcohol-soaked bandage.

The metal door finally gave and perhaps fifty skeletons, or at least the reanimated remains of them, poured onto the floor of the exorcism chamber, clambering over one another in a sickening, stinking, dusty wave of death.

"Hurry!" Anna yelled and shoved Aubrey through after Percy, tugging at Eve's belt as she stepped in, Joe and Candide coming last.

Seconds later they tripped and tumbled over Aubrey, who had tumbled over Percy, who had tripped on a very nice, late eighteenth-century fireplace grill, and landed in a heap on an excessively plush and expensive rug in one of the most beautiful rooms several members of the group had ever seen.

But unfortunately for Eve, he had seen it before. "Oh no," he whispered, looking around the room, horrified. "This is my mother's drawing room."

The group looked to him for explanation.

"Oh no!" Eve said again. "Have we arrived in my own personal Hell? Is this like one of those things where we have to delve into the darkest realms of our subconscious and battle through each person's own nightmarish vision of Hell, one after another, to survive?"

"Not quite, dear," came the familiar voice and cigarette smoke from the doorway. "But I won't keep you long."

CHAPTER 18
CELEBRATION

"Sorry, Mum," Eve mumbled, his cheeks aglow with a fierce blush of anxious embarrassment. "I didn't mean it like that."

"Of course you did," Lady Worthing replied coldly, but with a wry smile.

"Addie! I should have known!" Percy jumped up, threw his arms around her, and kissed her cheek.

"What!" Eve and Anna shouted in unison.

Adeline paid no attention to their aghast faces, leaning a shoulder into Percy. "What were you thinking? Trying to drag everyone to Hell!"

"I just…" He waved his hand vaguely. "A lot of scotch."

"I can smell that. We're just lucky I was able to redirect your exit point in time. The last thing I need this week is a trip to Hell. Take this." She handed Percy a bucket of water, which he promptly threw onto the fireplace, dousing the fire completely and closing the portal in the process.

Adeline walked over and pulled Candide to her feet. "Look what he did to your arm." She sent a reprimanding frown over her shoulder. "There are better ways, Percy."

"It's not entirely his fault, for a change," Candide said. "There were skeleton things."

"I saw," Adeline replied, pressing her lips together. "Still, let's get it bandaged up properly. Aubrey was right. As usual."

"Thanks, Lady Worthing," Aubrey squeaked.

"Will you stop calling me that?"

Eve, still on the floor, sank back against Anna with a defeated sigh.

"I feel like a lot must have happened in the last three months," she whispered to him.

"I can't," he replied. "It's entirely too much. I just want to sit here with you." He put his arm around her and kissed her hair, then rested his head against hers, closing his eyes against a sudden, overwhelming exhaustion.

Adeline regarded the pair for a time, then looked to Percy with a smile. "Seems to have worked."

Candide followed her gaze each way before her own eyes flared. "You were in on that?"

"You never would have let us do it," Adeline said calmly.

"He's your son!" Candide yelled.

Adeline only smiled placidly, saying pointedly, "He is now. Thanks to Percy." She turned her back on them, dropping the instruction, "Everyone into the dining room to celebrate."

Candide watched on furiously as Adeline linked her arm through Percy's and led the way. She followed only when Aubrey gave her arm a solid tug. Joe climbed to his feet next, and he and Anna pulled a reluctant Eve up.

Once they were all assembled around the austere dining-room table under the opulent crystal chandelier, Eve having made a small diversion to obtain a new shirt, a magnum of champagne was opened by the servants Anna never knew the family had, and Lady Worthing stood and raised her glass.

"A toast. The last few months have been difficult for all of you. You all showed courage, bravery and skill beyond anything I could have dreamed of. What you did brought my son back from the dead. I cannot thank you all enough for that. So, let's toast first to the two people whose dark magic is dark enough to bring down the very forces of Hell. My darling, Candide, and my darling, Percy. Cheers!"

They all drank, even Anna and Eve, who exchanged looks of utter perplexity over the top of their drinks.

"And next," Lady Worthing continued, "to you, Aubrey. You beautiful, bright, sweet girl. I've been proud of you since you set foot in Endymion College, and I couldn't have imagined such a fruitful alliance as you and Candide have made. The care you showed my goddaughter and my son these last few months will not be forgotten. To Aubrey!"

"To Aubrey!" They all drank.

"Joe, you are one hell of a priest, and I believe you would give any demon a run for his money. I'll never forget what you did for Evelyn. To Joe!"

"To Joe!" They all drank.

"And finally, to the two people responsible for us all being here in this room together. To the woman who showed the strength, courage and fortitude to literally bring a man back from the dead. A woman who, in only her second semester at university, has been approved to enter the Endymion College honours program. To Anna!"

"To Anna!" Candide surprised them all by dutifully drinking with the rest, while Anna watched on in shock as if the whole thing was a bizarre play.

"And to the man of the hour," said Lady Worthing. "That lovely, sweet, smart, brave boy who I'm so very proud of…"

Anna readied her glass, glancing over at Eve lovingly.

"To Percy!" Adeline announced.

"What!" Anna slammed her glass down so hard it almost broke.

Eve let out a short laugh and drank.

"Aunt Addie, why do you have to be like this?" Candide sighed.

"He knows I'm joking." She smiled airily in Eve's general direction, then continued, "Before Anna throws her champagne at me, let's drink to my beautiful son. I know I've been a wily old bitch, but I hope you know how much I love you."

He smiled a bashful smile, looking down at the table, inasmuch to say he had no idea how much she did or did not love him, but would happily accept the affectionate claim.

Adeline's tone changed, taking on that tenor that had, several times in the past, touched a sympathetic nerve with Anna. She sounded perfectly earnest when he finally met her gaze and she said softly, "I can't begin to describe the hole that would have been left behind without you, my darling. You are everything to me, and to so many people sitting around this table. Don't ever get yourself killed again." She raised her glass high. "To Eve."

"To Eve!" And they all drank.

"Now, kids, no one is to go to Hell tonight, or ever again without my say-so. You may all have the run of the house this evening, sleep it off tomorrow, then Tuesday, after your work, a select few will go to Hell. I'll be in my study for the rest of the night. No one disturb me." She smiled at the group one last time and swept out of the room.

Anna saw the change in Percy's face the second Lady Worthing turned to leave. The sparkle fading from his eyes, the slightest grimace of disgust at the corner of his lips as the smile fell away. His eyes shot across to her when he felt her studying him, then an entirely different, far more genuine smile appeared—the mischievous one she loved so much—and he winked at her. Anna flushed pink, and he immediately shifted his gaze, as though the interaction had never happened.

Anna spent a brief time unnecessarily assessing her fingernails, then cast her eyes back over Percy, then the entire group. Percy was already leaning over to whisper something in Eve's ear, and Eve's head was tilted down, listening intently, a smile widening across his beautiful face. Candide was carefully tipping the giant champagne bottle to fill their glasses, while Aubrey, with Percy's golden lighter, was roundly encouraging Joe in his attempt to light five cigarettes at once.

Anna found their apparent lack of concern more disconcerting, perhaps, than the events of the day. She wondered if Eve was feeling half as alienated as she suddenly was, but then Eve laughed at whatever Percy had said, Aubrey shoved an over-full champagne glass at her, and Joe passed over a successfully lit cigarette with such a triumphant air that she had no choice but to take it.

"That's a good point, though," Eve said, referring both to Adeline's parting speech and whatever Percy was talking about now. "What is my work Monday? I don't even know. Have I quit Endymion yet?"

"No." Candide grinned. "You're very much still the best professor of literature in town."

Anna sent a satisfied smile over to Eve, who, despite his very pure intentions in planning to quit Endymion College, always enjoyed having Anna's approval.

"So, what am I teaching this week?" he asked.

"Russian Literature, nine a.m., Chekhov," Percy replied.

"Chekhov? I love Chekhov!" He must have, because Eve would have appeared the wrong side of thrilled in any other group. "Do you know which one I picked?"

Percy, taking in Eve's charming exuberance, revealed softly, "Uncle Vanya."

"Ah, I love Uncle Vanya. I'm looking forward to that."

Anna leaned forward anxiously, eyes darting between the two. "Am I enrolled in that class?"

"Of course you are," Percy said. "But you may need a little refresher on Crime and Punishment from last week."

"We already did Crime and Punishment?" she asked, aghast. "And I missed it?"

Percy gave a slight shake of his head. "It's a grim story."

Anna gave a little shrug. "Yes, probably, but that doesn't mean I want to just skip over it like it never happened."

He pushed her champagne glass a little closer to her. "You can reread the miserable bits any time you like."

She took the drink in hand, pausing. "Yes, but I completely missed my lesson. Isn't that the whole point of all this? Shouldn't I have some sort of lesson?"

"No, I don't think so. Why should the experience of reading a book be any less just because there's no lesson?" He held out his glass for her to tink with her own.

Anna narrowed her eyes at him. "Lessons are important. It's how people learn."

And that dazzling smile of his was back on full display. "You don't need to learn anything. You're perfect the way you are."

He moved his own glass a little closer, so she made the small cheers. "Uh, that's not really what I meant." He took a drink, so she did too. "Also, some people might disagree."

"Hang them," he replied on a derisive puff of smoke. "You'll enjoy Uncle Vanya much more, anyway."

"It's not grim? I thought Chekhov would be grim."

"Chekhov's lovely," Eve sighed.

Candide laughed from across the table. "Still nursing that crush?"

Percy's head turned sharply towards his brother. "You too?"

"He's just an incredible writer," said Eve, blushing a little.

"He's a hot writer," Candide corrected.

Anna, dramatically warming to the idea of studying Chekhov, asked, "Was he very good looking?"

"Oh yes," said Eve.

"Number one literary conquest," said Percy.

"I don't think he was into men," said Aubrey.

"He never met me," came Percy's appropriately lascivious response.

As Anna had never seen Anton Chekhov, her mind was, unfortunately, unable to go the places Eve and Candide and Percy's minds went. As though that wasn't bad enough, she was then hit with an even more miserable revelation. "Hang on. And there's all of last term. Oh no. Did I miss Gothic Literature? Did I miss the whole term?" With fingers gripping the table tight, "I missed Gothic Lit!"

"You can take it again," Percy drawled.

"All those nice books I bought…"

"I don't remember teaching any of those classes at all," Eve said. "Except for The Picture of Dorian Gray. Did the rest go off okay?"

A silence fell over the room.

"I dropped that class…" Aubrey mumbled, eventually.

Eve looked to Candide.

"I dropped it, too." She shrugged, keeping a suspiciously blank face.

Eve frowned, so Aubrey offered a painfully enthusiastic, "I heard it was surprisingly good, though."

The indent in Eve's forehead deepened. "Surprisingly?"

"I mean—no—they weren't surprised. The person who said that wasn't…" Eve raised a suspicious eyebrow and Aubrey shut her mouth and let her eyes wander around the room.

Eve, for whatever reason, evidently wasn't willing to pursue the mystery, so Anna said, "I wonder what else I'm studying."

At that, Percy pulled a small notebook from his trouser pocket, flipped it open, ripped out a page, and pushed it across to her. "I'll get your timetable and notes from the first class to you tomorrow. You've bought all the books for the term already, so they're…" He gave pause. "Probably in Evelyn's apartment somewhere."

She looked over the note, the first time she'd ever seen Percy's handwriting, and she took especial notice of how beautiful it was. This she did in an attempt to hide how touched she felt that he seemed to have kept things in order for her so well, arranged everything for her return, from whatever had happened. With pink cheeks and a touch of panic about her bank account, she said, "I wonder how I managed to afford all those books."

There was a beat of silence, in which Percy, for the first time, apparently had no answer ready. Then he said, in a way that sounded exactly like deflecting, "You'll be pleased to know that despite everything, you never missed a class and your work is incredible."

She dragged her eyes up to his, a smile about them, asking softly, "You've been reading my work again?"

Percy blushed. Actually blushed. A vanishingly rare occurrence. "I won't anymore. I just wanted to—to make sure everything was entered into the system fairly and correctly. So things would be as they should when you came out the other side."

Even if her comment had caught him off guard, he was only mildly flustered for a matter of seconds. Whatever had happened in the last few months, Anna could see he was exactly the same Percy, except that it was a recurrent sadness in his eyes that replaced the anger she had become so accustomed to, before he and Evelyn had cemented their apparently now-impenetrable bond. With only the snap of his cigarette case and the flicker of flame, Anna watched him reassert his calm, happy, organised manner.

Perhaps Eve, also watching Percy a little curiously, was thinking similar thoughts. He said, "Thanks, everyone, for taking such good care of us. This has to be one of the weirdest things that can happen to a person, but you've made it so much easier than… I don't know what. And Percy, you've really thought of everything. Whatever happened, the last few months… We must have grown close, I think. You've been so good to us."

Percy's dark eyes had remained trained and hazy on Anna's dark eyes as Eve spoke, then they moved over to Eve and regarded him with such loving, sweet warmth, no one would ever have believed they spent so many years hating one another. "I sincerely love you both."

Eve took Percy's hand and leaned in close, and they spoke quietly again, secretly, but as they did, Anna's eyes were drawn to the doorway by a movement.

It was Eve.

It was Eve with an identical fresh shirt, his sleeves rolled in exactly the same way, his hair tossed to the side just the way Eve's was.

He walked past the doorway, pausing only to look over at her, his face nerve-shatteringly expressionless, before he continued on his way.

She heard his footsteps on the stairs, fading into the distance.

Anna wrapped frantic fingers around Eve's arm and turned back to him in alarm.

He placed his warm and very present hand on hers, asking, "What? What is it?"

"I just saw…" She looked again at the doorway in bewilderment.

Eve took in her pale change and now-shaking hands, and a look of recognition crossed his lovely face. "Was it me?"

Her head snapped back so fast it's a wonder she didn't snap her neck. "Yes, it was you! How did that happen? Why do you know that just happened?"

He exchanged a knowing glance with Candide, then focused back on Anna, leaning close, saying in a disconcertingly serious tone, "He's… probably okay. Just don't ever follow him."

She looked wonderingly between Candide and Eve. "What happens if I follow him?"

"We never found out." He held her hand a little tighter and added, "But I think it's probably very bad."

CHAPTER 19
THE LEAST HAUNTED ROOM IN THE HOUSE

Eve picked 'the least haunted room in the house' for him and Anna to sleep in. He moved the bedside table and lamp out of the way, and pushed the iron-framed bed right up against the swirling, twirling, somewhat-unsettling yellow wallpaper. He chose the outer edge of the bed for himself in an attempt to help Anna feel as safe and protected as he could make her feel in the strange and occasionally dangerous mansion.

Everything about him had changed as the bedroom door closed, and whatever act he had been putting on up until then, being the best version of himself that he sensed everyone else wanted to see after all the work they must have put in to fix whatever had happened, fell away. He suddenly looked very tired, considerably aged, and she wondered how he had kept it up for so long.

He didn't seem to notice her watching him as he took off his shirt and sat down on the edge of the bed, watching her as she undressed. His face was lined with worry—a troubled expression, behind which she could see his mind working overtime, going through all the possible scenarios that had resulted in her skin being left bruised and broken.

Finally, she caught his eye with hers. "That's not how I like you to look at me when I'm getting undressed."

His face softened and his eyes sparkled, just a little. "Come here."

He stood as she walked to him and he wrapped his warm, gentle arms around her waist and kissed her. He swept her hair back from her face, pushing it around behind her ear like he always did, and it fell stubbornly forward like it always did, and he kept his hand there, soft and strong on her cheek, and he still looked so sad as he said, "I hate that this happened to you."

She stood on her tip-toes to kiss him again. "It's just bruises."

"And your soul," he said.

It wasn't something she wanted to think about. She couldn't. If she let it in, then it was all horror. And it wasn't something she wanted Eve thinking about for that same reason and more. All day she'd watched his mind take little shortcuts that left him thinking this was somehow his fault. And here he was now, the misplaced guilt putting a screen between them. His mind somewhere else, far away from her and them and the shield they were for each other.

And she needed him.

She promised, "It will all get better. We just need to keep going."

The soft huff of a melancholy laugh grazed her cheek. "You always say that." His eyes searched hers, a dark shade of despair all about the grey-violet irises, but somewhere deep, in the way only Eve ever looked at Anna, there was a touch of hope.

"Because it's true." She wrapped her fingers around his hand and kissed his open palm, then held his hand against her cheek. "We keep going and we don't ever stop and nothing can catch up with us. That's how it goes."

There was a breath of silence, in which Eve was caught between wanting to believe her, and believing the proof of their downfall written on her skin. "What if something already caught up with us?"

"It didn't." She shook her head. "Or we wouldn't be here." She slid a hand down his abs and pulled his belt open. She kissed him again. He got undressed, then she pulled his hand and sank down onto the unsurprisingly soft bed, leading him under the bedspread beside her. The small chill of the sheets sent a shiver across her shoulders and she moved up against his arm for warmth, laying with the fingers of one hand running over his chest, playing with the hairs there, tracing around the curves of his muscles. Eve stared up at the ceiling, lost in thought. Lost in his own mind, no doubt running those circles it always did. She cut through, saying, "Did you see how surprised they all were that we're together?"

He rolled over towards her, leaning on one perfectly sculpted arm, his lovely face resting on his lovely hand. "Yeah. I did notice that."

She shifted a little closer so her legs were stretched out all the way down against his. "I think whatever happened—well, there must be a reason they thought we might not be together anymore." She kissed his arm, along his biceps, closer and closer to his shoulder. "And I don't want to be without you. Not ever."

A hand on her hip pulled her in a little closer again until her belly was flush with his. "I don't believe there's anything that could do that to us. But if there's any chance it could ruin this —what we have." He paused, unsure of the best way to ask what he wanted to ask. His eyes met hers tentatively, and on a melancholy whisper, he said, "Anna, I don't think I want to know what happened. But I need to know how you feel about that. About not asking, and just moving on. Like it never happened."

The words were music to her ears.

She only smiled and raised an eyebrow, then suggestively looked down at his hand still resting on her hip. So he let his own eyes drift down to that hand.

The first hint of a smile since they entered the bedroom played at the corner of his lips. He ran his fingertips softly and slowly over her hip, along the curve of her waist, and all the way up the side of her body, until she leaned back as alluringly as she could manage and stretched an arm overhead so his fingers were forced to change their path. He shifted their trail, featherlight, in a teasing circle of her nipple, then along her arm and right to the tip of her elbow, studying her body every inch of the way. The body he loved—worshipped—coated in marks he was terrified he had put there. His fingers swept back down to her waist, but she slapped her hand down on his, closing his hand tight on her hip. "Kiss me."

Christ, he was beautiful, the shock of the sound of her hand and her confidence bringing a shyness into his smile. He leaned over and kissed her again, and she draped an arm around his neck, keeping him there until one kiss turned into another, and another, and the atmosphere began to shift.

When he pulled back, she looked into his eyes and he looked into hers and she smiled, because finally, that was exactly how Eve was supposed to look at her.

Her fingers slipped under his arm and closed on his back, savouring the feeling of the curve of every muscle as she went. She pulled herself up, pressing her breasts deliciously against his warm chest. "I suggest we say nothing." She kissed his neck, his lips, his jaw, his cheek, while he closed his eyes, disappearing into the unrelenting, inviting, exquisite oblivion of Anna, who said all the things he wanted so desperately to hear. "We don't ask questions and we keep going and we don't ever look back. And no matter what we have to do, we always protect this." Then she sank her teeth into his shoulder and felt him melt.

"I love you, Anna."

"I love you."

He reached a hand around behind her neck, the tips of his fingers twisting in her hair, making her shiver delightedly. He pulled her in and kissed her again, more forcefully this time, then with his lips brushing her ear and his warm breath on her neck, "Do you want to do this?"

"Yes, sir."

The tension broke with his laugh. "Don't call me that."

"Yes, Professor."

He shook his head to kiss her cheek. "You'll pay for that one." She wanted to goad him some more, but her left nipple was already between his lips, and her ability to form words disappeared into the clamour of pleasure somewhere at the top of her skull.

Eve's teeth pulled at her until she gasped, and before his lips switched sides he said, "Are you sure?"

Her entire body tense with anticipation, she rasped out, "Please."

He let go on another delicious nip, then placed his hand under her chin, bringing her lips millimetres from his. "Then listen to me: tonight, you're not to make a sound."

Her lips trembled with excitement as she whispered, "I don't think I can—"

"You'll do everything exactly as I say."

Eve's other hand slipped between Anna's legs, and her brain short-circuited with pleasure around that time. He held her there, kissing her cheek, expert fingers on her clit, and her shoulders curled forward in an attempt to control herself. It was all she could do to nod her approval. His lips moved to her neck, his fingers straightened, then curled with such perfection that she moaned, "Eve, fuck!"

He pulled his fingers away, and she snapped back to the brutal reality of not being finger-banged by Evelyn Worthing. Her mouth wide open in shock, eyes large in lust and fury, she felt his kiss by her ear and heard his provoking, "What did I say?"

"But…" Her lower lip wobbled, and she complained, "You're very good at that."

"And you're very sexy when you try not to scream." A blush took her over, and Eve's mouth took hers before she could reply. "Want to try again?"

She gave a small, desperate nod. "Mmhmm."

"Will you be good?"

"I promise. But…" Her teeth sank into her lip. It was very, very nice having Eve in control, but if he wanted her to keep quiet, the least he could do was offer her some help. She threw back the sheets and dove for Eve's gorgeous dick. He let go his own expletive, twice as loud as hers, and she let out a small chuckle, as best she could as she took him into her mouth, before forgetting her small victory over him with the first taste of pre-cum. Knowing Eve wanted her, tasting it, set Anna's entire being on fire. She wasn't about to have it taken away, so she controlled her volume, letting her deepening breath carry the pent up energy away as best she could as she went to work on his cock.

But Eve wasn't playing fair. His fingers were on her clit within seconds and she grasped the base of his dick twice as hard in her frustrated pleasure. He wasn't giving her a second to catch her breath. He worked her clit like a man who loved fucking her, and he took a hand in her hair, teasing her with its soft intrusion. He knew what she wanted. She loved him to fuck her mouth every bit as violently as he wanted, but today it was only a soft tease, which relieved none of her exasperation. That hand on top of her mounting orgasm and her forced silence, the lot of it layering one intensity onto another until she thought she might explode. Her lips moved faster and firmer over his cock, his fingers tightened in her hair just a little as he tried to keep control of himself and her, then all at once she collapsed onto his leg, whimpering a helpless "Please" on a fracturing breath.

She bit into his thigh, but he only increased his pressure as his gravelly voice rasped, "Look at you. You were just made for fucking, weren't you?"

The thought of Eve's gaze on her sent a new thrill through Anna's body and she took his cock again, twice as desperately,

Eve's dick being her only release from the building ecstasy, while also being a tool to, hopefully, drive him crazy enough to fuck her. Loudly. She let her hair fall to the side and snuck a look up at him. His eyes were locked on, glazed with lust. She formed her fingers into a tight ring over the crown of his dick, and soaking the lot with her craving tongue, slid them down firmly, following closely with her hot mouth until his dick hit the back of her throat and he let out a long, harsh breath. She moved back up, his dick slick and the sound deliciously filthy, and she did it again, a little faster.

His hand was a fist now. He was losing control—losing himself. And she was loving every second of it.

But Eve had the exact same plan in mind as Anna, and determined that she should be the one to forget their life and their room and their reality, he slid his thumb inside and squeezed her clit with his fingers, and he was lucky Anna loved dick as much as she did, or he would have had a life altering injury on his hands.

Anna's back curled and she attempted to push herself up, but only fell down in a pathetic heap on Eve's leg. He, with the advantage now, fucked her with his hand, drinking in her utterly helpless form as she bit into the sheet, fingernails in his thigh, and he said, "I want you to come. Right here on my knee."

It wasn't as though she had much say in the matter. She couldn't find her way back to his dick even if she tried. She couldn't do a thing but give into his demand. She came hard on a tiny cry that belied the explosion of ecstasy in her body and her brain, because as lost as she was, she knew, if she behaved, that Eve was just getting started.

As her body relaxed a little she became twice as desperate for him, but before she could beg him for mercy, he pulled her up to straddle his thighs and kissed her, and she thought, finally, she would get some dick. But then he said, "You'd better hold on tight." Eve took strong hands around her waist, lay back, and took her with him, settling her on his face.

Anna, since the first time they had slept together, was Eve's own personal heaven, and there was nothing to annihilate the horrors of the world like her thigh's wrapped around his face—the smell of her, the taste of her, and fuck if he wasn't cursing himself for telling her to be quiet. But how gorgeous she was in every hopeless attempt to do it.

Eve's tongue was on Anna before she could even grasp the iron bars of the bed, a growl of approval in his throat as he lapped at her cum-laden pussy, and then it was straight back to her clit, so warm, and just the right amount of wet.

His hands on her ass supported her, pulled her wide, and she gripped the bars of the bed tight and threw her head back, slipping into euphoric abandon. The moans came softly at first, just as quietly as she could, but Eve didn't seem to hear. They moved up her throat into a choked wail, and her hips bucked forward. Eve protested with a grunt and a flick of his head that made her shout, "Fuck!" He must have heard that, but he kept going, and she thought she might pass out if she didn't scream as the intensity built and built. He gripped her so hard she knew there would be new bruises—beautiful purple bruises of Eve's fingerprints in her skin—that would replace the old, wipe away every speck of everything they didn't want, and make it all her own again. She gave in completely, the sound of her indulgence bouncing off the walls, and she let the waves of rapture eclipse every rational thought.

A rumble of approval crept from Eve's throat so that she felt it rip through her. Her fingers turned white gripping the rails, and she tried her best, she really did, but before she could come again, her fist slammed down on the wall and she snapped, "No! No. You fuck me right now!"

Her word was as good as done. Eve's strong hands wrapped around her ribcage and brought her down, settling her, thighs wide, just above his cock. He drove his hips up, impaling her with perfect, delicious aim, eliciting a full scream of contentment from Anna.

He lifted her, he slammed into her again. "You're so beautiful. Fuck!"

Anna dropped her head back, breasts rising, the length of her body stretching before him. He shifted her hips and fucked her, because Anna, despite her best efforts, was no longer in any state to be in control of anything, which is exactly where Eve wanted her. He shifted her faster, his perfect dick the whole core of her existence. "Eve," she panted. "Eve," she shouted. Then on a whimper, "Sorry."

"No, beautiful. You make all the noise you like." Keeping the one hand working her hip, he slid two fingers into her slick cunt, and she slammed a hand down onto his chest for stability. Her fingernails dug into him so deep they broke the skin, and the pain, the visceral link to life and to Anna, was like a drug to him.

He sat up, wrenching her body against his chest, placing a molten kiss on her hot, red lips. She broke the kiss with a cry as he pinched her nipple and she rose a little higher on his dick, taking control of them both.

Anna's breasts against his face, Anna's scolding hot body soaking his dick, Anna's soft hair drifting across his cheek, and those moans, those sweet, hot gasps of ecstasy, drove Eve crazy. He put every shred of self control into Anna's building orgasm. He kept her steady, kept his hand where it needed to be, and when her hazy brown eyes looked down at him like pure sex, it was all he could do to tighten his grip and hold on.

She rode his cock and his hand, slower, deeper, and with an intoxicating, feminine sexuality that he wanted to drown in. She owned him so completely—she was so spectacular in every shift and every breath, and he wanted to kiss her, desperately, but he didn't dare move and upset the perfect, tense, airless moment that she held him with her gaze.

Anna drank in his beauty, his adoration, that little line in his brow that she didn't want to smooth this time. The little line that said he had forgotten everything else. He didn't see the bruises now. He didn't see the cuts and the scars. There was no secret past where anything could have threatened the fortress they had built around themselves. He saw Anna. He saw only Anna, happy, in control, satisfied, confident, and his. So completely *his*. Safe, alive and vibrant in his arms and so perfectly, wonderfully, completely Anna. She filled him with love, with belief in the two of them, with belief that he could still protect her, and be there for her, because she was so vital and so real beneath his hands.

She knew on some level that she was—had always been—his link to this world. His final shot at life. He'd never said it, not in so many words, but that bond between them that was forged in the fire of their brutal pasts and shared trauma held her invincible against the world in just the same way it did for him. She understood him in her soul, in her blood, and in her heart. In that moment, they both knew this was it. This love was their last stand against the world, and whatever happened next, they would do it together, and it would be magnificent, and it would be eternal.

Anna's arms tightened around Eve's shoulders. Her head slipped to the side as his teeth found the skin of her neck, and she let herself drop safely into the madness of extreme bliss. She fucked him, she willed him to let himself go and sink just as profoundly into her as she had into him. She felt the next wave come for her, higher and higher, her muscles tensing, the complete helplessness as the orgasm took her, but this time she reached around, grasped Eve's balls, and pressed a finger right on his perineum. With that simple, confident move, timed to perfection, he let go a moan every bit as loud as hers, clamped his hand down on her ass and let go. He came hard, and Anna came again, and the two of them disappeared into ecstatic obliteration, bodies taut, pressed together.

He held her there for a long time, kissing her, never wanting to let go, but eventually she pushed him back, kissed him again, then slid down into the nook of his arm, both utterly exhausted, panting, spent, but so, so content.

His face nuzzled into her hair and her neck, dropping kisses, whispering that he loved her, and everything was perfect in Anna's world. So perfect she insisted on a few minutes of basking, even if they were both dangerously close to drifting off to sleep when she knew she would have to go back out into the cold, terrifying mansion to use the bathroom soon.

She rolled towards him and leaned her head on his chest. His arms wrapped firmly around her and he pulled the blanket up to her cheekbones, letting his sleepy hand stroke her hair as she listened to the calming of his beating heart. Then he said, with a voice thick with sleep, "You should know, if you go to Hell, I will follow you." Anna would have snuggled in even closer had it been possible. She made no reply, because she would go, and he would not, but they were happy now, so she let him keep the illusion.

Then he said, "Oh, and if it looks like the walls are weeping, they aren't really. Just wake me if anything happens."

Seconds later, Eve was sound asleep.

And Anna was wide awake, watching the yellow wallpaper.

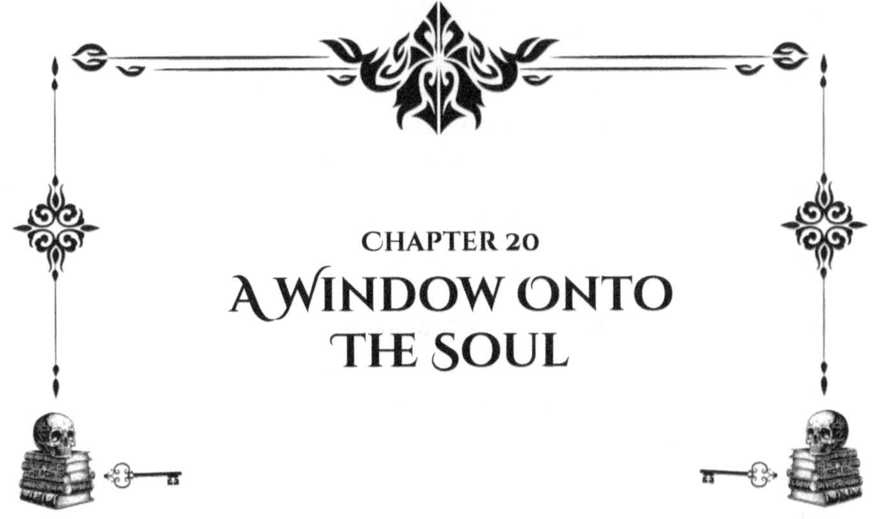

CHAPTER 20
A WINDOW ONTO THE SOUL

It was probably a stupid idea to slip out to the bathroom by herself, but Eve was so tired, and he looked so peaceful wth his head resting on the pillow. And when Anna stepped out into the hall and heard Percy and Joe still awake, still talking and laughing downstairs, she felt quite safe. It was only when she attempted to return to her room that she got the small fright of finding Evelyn stationed outside the door, waiting for her.

"Jesus, Eve!" she sputtered. "This is a very scary house for you to just stand around unexpectedly in."

His face cracked into a beautiful smile. "Sorry," he said. "It is a scary house. That's why I came. I'll take you back."

It was strange behaviour for Eve, who was generally only clingy at times when she almost died right in front of him, but given all they had been through recently, she considered it under-standable. And when he held out his hand and gave hers a little squeeze, and he was warm and tempting as always, she thought no more of it.

He led her back to the bedroom, but then paused at the door and leaned in close, his cheek against hers and his breath hot on her ear. "Can I show you something special?"

Her big eyes lit up. "Again?"

He laughed. "Come with me."

He continued up the dark hall, pulling her hand excitedly, so despite the cosy bed waiting inside for them, she followed him. They took a turn up and around another flight of stairs, past the big stained-glass window at the front of the house, then down along another, narrower hall, to a door at the end. He opened it to reveal an almost pitch black space inside, the scant light of a partially obscured full moon being the only illumination on offer.

She stepped onto the wooden floorboards of a room obviously rarely opened. She felt the thick dust between her toes and shivered a little as she felt the surrounding temperature drop substantially.

"Eve, is this very important to do right now? Can't it wait for morning?"

"It's better at night," he said, and gave her hand another tug, so she followed him again, as he led her to a tiny door in a wall at the end of the room. She virtually had to crawl through to follow him, but once she did, she realised they were inside the walls of the house.

In here, there was no illumination from the moon or from anything else. It was perfectly black. The space was only wide enough to walk through single file, and barely that. The floorboards creaked with age and she took her steps tentatively, wondering what, besides the thick dust, her bare feet might encounter.

Eve let go of her hand, moving swiftly ahead, disappearing completely from sight or touch.

A strong and frantic panic began rising within her.

It wasn't right. None of it.

It wasn't like Eve at all to do this, and she had no idea how she got here. She turned and looked back, but she couldn't see a thing and Eve wasn't there. "Eve? Eve, this is really scary. I want to go back. Eve!"

She felt him, sensed him by her side again. "It's just a few more steps. I promise it's worth it."

She looked around and realised that in her confusion, she didn't even know which way was back or forward now. She felt his hand take hers, and as she had no other choice, she followed.

Another doorway, this one the proper height, creaked open, and to her great relief, light cascaded through.

It was, after all, a magical sight. There were a few stairs, bathed in moonlight, leading up to an odd, circular window right at the top of the house. The window was almost as tall as Anna, and as she approached, she saw the full moon in all its glory, wide and yellow, lighting up the trees, the gardens, the statues, the walkways of all Lady Worthing's land. All Eve's land too, she supposed.

"It's so beautiful," she breathed, sitting on the top step to share the peaceful, intimate moment with him.

But Eve did not sit. Instead, he pushed a handle down, and the round window swung wide open. "There's more."

"Seriously?" Now they had found their beautiful, well-lit, secret place, Anna decided she was beginning to enjoy the adventure, and she leapt up quite happily. He stepped out first, onto the ash-grey tiles of the rooftop, incalculably high, incalculably dangerous. She paused for only a second until he offered his hand once more, and she took hold and stepped a foot gingerly through. It came down on a tile that shifted just a little with the pressure, but she glanced up at Eve, he gave her an encouraging nod, and she pressed forward.

"Anna!"

Eve wrenched his hand free from Anna's. The movement put her into a spin, her foot slipped on the loose tile, her whole body came plummeting down on the steep ledge, and she felt the lot give way beneath her.

The sound of a dozen tiles smashing into a million pieces on the stone ground far below reached her ears before she realised that another hand was holding hers tight. Candide pulled her sharply back inside, with a frantic, "What are you doing!"

Barely able to answer the question, as bewildered as she was, Anna blustered, "Eve's out there! He's out on the roof!" She poked her head back through the window to find him.

Naturally, he was gone.

"For goodness' sake, Anna," came the agitated, irritated reply. "We told you not to follow him. That was Bad Eve."

"Bad Eve?"

"How could you not know that was Bad Eve?"

"You call him Bad Eve?"

"Yeah, that's Bad Eve!"

Anna was quiet for a few seconds, thinking things over. Then, "You should have called him Evil Eve."

Candide smiled and let out an anxious laugh as she dropped down onto the stairs. "That would have been better."

Anna sat down next to her, searching out the window for him. "Was he trying to kill me?"

"Probably." Candide reached across and pulled the latch closed. "I don't know. We just think he's bad. We've never really found out what he wants. Maybe he just wanted to show you the incredibly unsafe rooftop for some reason."

Anna looked back out the window, aware of a stronger sense of longing to explore than was probably right or healthy. "It's very pretty."

Candide watched her warily. "I think it's more likely he would have tried to kill you, though."

"Oh."

"It's a good thing I heard you."

"Thank you for coming in here to get me."

Anna braced herself to hear Candide say she only did it for Eve, or that Anna was an idiot, but she didn't say either of those things. She wrapped her arms around her legs and rested her chin on her knees. "Do you want me to take you back to your bedroom?"

With her heart pounding like she'd just run a marathon, a slick of cold sweat all over, there was no chance she could sleep in that scary room. But more than that, Candide was talking to her again. She gave a hesitant, "I don't know. What time is it?"

Candide slid her sweater up to check her thin silver watch. "Around five."

"I could try. If you want to get to bed. Which I guess you do. I don't think I could sleep, though. Did I hear Percy and Joe downstairs?"

"Yeah," said Candide. "With Aubrey. They all refused to sleep here until the sun comes up."

"That's smart."

"It probably is."

"Maybe I should go sit with them…"

Candide made no move to leave, so neither did Anna, and she wondered if she should say something about everything that had passed, or if she should just shut up and hope Candide would love her again one day.

"Anna…" Candide reached out and took Anna's hand in hers, which Anna gave happily, until Candide said, "Can I show you something special?"

With a slightly shaky voice, Anna joked, "You're not Bad Candide, are you?"

"No," Candide replied, her eyes steady on Anna's. "I'm Evil Candide."

CHAPTER 21
SUNRISE

Anna's face dropped and she must have turned a disturbing shade of grey, for Candide quickly made profuse and sincere apologies for having terrified her, and with a great deal of anxious laughter from both of them, assured her that she was the one and only Candide, good and bad and everything in between, and that if they hurried, they could obtain enough coffee and blankets in good time to watch the sunrise together.

Much like Bad Eve, Candide dragged Anna though dark and dusty tunnels, tiny doors, large doors, ramshackle secret walkways, until finally she pushed open a hatch at the end of an ancient attic, and up a black, steel staircase, they stepped out onto the widow's walk at the very precipice of the mansion.

It was a clear, 360 degree view all around, and just as the moon disappeared on one side of Worthing House, the sun began to rise on the other. Wrapped in their blankets, they huddled together for warmth, their hands wrapped around hot coffee, and they both knew the silence between them was finally a comfortable one, neither of them needing to say anything. But Anna did anyway. "I love you and I'm sorry I tried to kill you."

Candide must have known it was coming. She smiled softly. "That's okay."

Anna studied the lines of her face intently. "Do you still hate me very passionately?"

"Not very passionately," Candide replied. "You were right. It's exactly the sort of thing you would do. I don't know why I was so shocked. There's no way you could have foreseen how things would go."

"With your recovery, do you mean?"

"No. With Eve's. With yours." Candide made brief eye contact, then trained her eyes on the horizon. "I can't tell you what really happened because Percy will kill me, and I don't think it's right to anyway, because you're different now, to how you were, but I still think you did the wrong thing that night."

"Oh." That was only natural, from what little Anna knew, but still, her heart sank inside her.

Only to be buoyed a second later when Candide continued, "But I'm glad you did it. You really did bring a person back from the dead. The person I love most in the whole world. The person you love most in the whole world. But you'll never know what you both went through to make it happen. And, if not for Percy, I don't know if either of you would have made it at all. I would never have made you forget everything like he did. It feels very wrong. But I guess it was the right thing after all."

Anna sipped her coffee and took in the pinks and purples of the fresh new day, watching the last few bright stars slip away. "If it was all as bad as you say, I think Eve and I are happy with Percy's decision."

Candide looked her over briefly, then went back to studying the sky. "You went through a lot. And… and I think that's why I haven't been managing well with you being back to how you used to be. I've been thinking about how this must all appear from your perspective, because you don't have three months of… of—"

"Candide?"

"Yes?"

"Did you have to see it happen?"

Candide wilted with the direct question. She turned her fallen face away, closed her eyes, and covered her trembling lips with her fingertips. "Yes." Her voice came out on a sob, she wiped away her tears and caught her breath before she tried to go on, as calmly as she knew how. "I saw the whole thing. It was horrible. And I fell apart completely. And you did too, I think, but in a different way. I keep wondering, maybe if I kept fighting that night, or did something else, maybe you wouldn't have done what you did. But I just… I wanted to be dead, like Eve was. I didn't care about anything. I didn't notice what you were doing, and I didn't feel a thing." She pulled the blanket up to her chin, before leaning her head back against the cold iron bars. "I woke up a few days afterwards, and Aubrey told me Eve wasn't dead at all, and I was so happy. So, so happy. But then she told me the rest. And I couldn't see him and I couldn't see you because…" Candide shook her head, her lips taut with the effort to hold back her speech. "I still can't tell you why. But the way it was, I was still grieving for him because… because I watched him die. Right in front of me. But then I also couldn't grieve for him because he wasn't gone at all. Not really. But… he was… And you can't understand, I know, but… I was just stuck and it was all so horrible and I was just stuck. And then all I had to think about, for months, was what you had done, and I just put all my—*everything*—I put it all on you." Candide shook her hair back and wiped away the tears. "I was so angry with you. And now I'm so sorry I didn't come to you, and I'm so sorry for what happened to you. Because everything that happened to you is my fault, too. I let that happen to both of you."

Anna, trying hard to wind her mind around the oblique clues dropped before her, said, "No. No, you didn't. Percy said you were the one who fixed Eve. None of that could be your fault."

"No, I did. I did that. That's true. I fixed one part of him and I know he wouldn't be here now without me. But what Percy did also fixed him. And you. Especially you." She sighed and ran her eyes over the dark wilderness, searching for the words. "Things happened, and I wasn't able to face them. Like I wish I could have." She let out a small, slightly bitter laugh. "I mean, in my defence, I was in the hospital for some time."

Anna's eyes grew wide with horror. "I'm so sorry."

"No, it's fine, it's just that, when I got home, I couldn't walk and all that—"

"You couldn't walk? Fuck, I'm so sorry."

"Seriously, I'm just trying to make a point, not make you feel bad—"

"I feel so bad."

Candide twisted her mouth to the side, shrugged lightly, then went on, "Anyway, there was some rehabilitation, so I couldn't have been there even if I wanted to. At the start. Percy did some things for me too, magic things, and what should have been much worse, physically, wasn't as bad as it could have been, and I made a full recovery faster than I should have."

"Well, that's something." Anna attempted a conciliatory smile, the weight on her stomach lifting ever so slightly.

"It still took months, though."

"Yeah." Anna swallowed, staring hard at her knees. "I am sorry. In case I hadn't mentioned—"

"The point is, I couldn't be there at first, but then, when I could… I wasn't. I chose not to be. Maybe I didn't know how bad it was for you until today… until I saw what happened to you with my own eyes. But I think…. No, maybe I knew. I think I must have known deep down that you were suffering…" Candide let out a long sigh. "Of course you were. I knew that. I knew that and I was in denial because I didn't want to see you and so… I left you. I abandoned you when you really needed me and maybe I could have helped. And I didn't." Candide made her eyes drift across to meet Anna's. "And I'm so ashamed. And I'm so sorry."

Anna hated the thought of it—of Candide's guilt and suffering because of, and on top of, the awful things Anna had done that she had no memory of. "Please don't apologise to me. I don't remember, anyway. And you know, I tried to kill you, so that's definitely worse."

Candide smiled sadly at Anna's attempted reassurance. "I'm not sure it is. And you shouldn't make excuses for me. I fucked up. I was supposed to be stronger than this. I should have been able to help or fix things, because you're my best friend and Eve…" She trailed off, her voice breaking again. "I couldn't do a thing… I just fell apart."

"Then we both fucked up." Anna shuffled across, leaning against Candide. "I don't think many people ever go through the things we have, so maybe could we just give each other a free pass this time?" Candide didn't look convinced, so Anna added, "You know, to me, it's only been a day since we were best friends. I miss you so much already."

"Only a day." Candide laughed sadly. "I've been stewing over this for so long."

"I don't..." Anna hesitated. Maybe it was too soon? She pushed forward, regardless. "I mean, I don't want to suggest that you and Eve have an unhealthy codependency—"

"Oh, we totally do."

"Then maybe—"

"But I'm not ready to change that."

"Uh, no. I would never suggest changing that. It's just, maybe don't be so hard on yourself about how you reacted to everything. He's a part of you. And you had to see something... something that no one should ever have to see that." Anna watched Candide's eyes water at the memory, so she changed direction. "You know what I think the problem is?"

Candide blinked. "Besides all those things I just said?"

"Yes, besides that." Anna smiled. "It's that you're a better person than me. And you're a better person than Percy, too. And sometimes it's shit to be a good person because you have less control. When the world is set against you, sometimes you have to fight dirty. Some of us learn that at a very young age, and maybe we don't turn out as nice, but we survive."

"I really don't believe you're a bad person, Anna. Despite everything."

The words very nearly made Anna burst into tears, so she looked away and pressed on as though Candide had said nothing. "Good people tend to either lose their battles or end up feeling terrible for what they did to win. And that's a kind of weakness. Which isn't to say it isn't endearing, but it makes you vulnerable. That's why you feel so bad right now, when you really shouldn't."

Now it was Candide who watched Anna carefully. "Are you saying it's better to embrace the darkness?"

"I think, sometimes, we have to be just as dark as the other side if we want to balance things out. Eve always says you should never feel bad about doing what you had to do to survive, and I believe that. Or I try to. You take care of yourself and the people you love as best you can, but if something comes and messes with that… I won't feel bad for doing what I had to do to protect that. Don't think for a second I wouldn't smash just about anyone else's head in to protect you."

"Anyone except Eve."

"Yes. But I think I was always very clear about my feelings for Eve."

"I always found it a little unsettling. And now I know why." Candide chuckled. "He loves you so much. And it's very obvious how much you love him. And that's what I always wanted for him. I am glad you did what you did. I haven't said thank you, to you, but…" Their eyes met, their expressions reflecting one another, two melancholy smiles. "Thanks, Anna. Thanks for bringing Eve back to us."

"I would do it again in a heartbeat."

"Please don't," she laughed. "But I appreciate the sentiment."

The sunrise had begun to take on a pale yellow hue by that time, beneath the purple of dawn, and above the trees, pitch black in contrast. It was increasingly, tentatively, beautiful. Anna said, "It must be so strange for you, having us wake up suddenly with no memory of any of this. I can see why you're mad at Percy for doing that."

Candide let out a sharp laugh. "I think that's the most galling part of all. Who the fuck even is Percy? I still don't understand. He terrorised Eve all through his childhood, tried to kill him at least twice, and then he just turns up and you all love him so much and now everything—everything—depends on him."

"You still don't trust him?"

"I do. Even I love stupid Percy. Not as much as Aubrey. Not as much as Eve. Not as much as Aunt Addie, of all people. Not as much as you." She glanced over at Anna, a line of concern at her lips. "But then you two have that weird thing."

Anna furrowed her brow and gave a quick, bright blush. "We don't have a weird thing."

Candide rolled her eyes. "You do."

Anna pushed her shoulder a little harder into Candide. "You and I have a weird thing."

"We do. But not like you and Percy."

Unable to get away with it, Anna said nothing, wondering what her weird thing with Percy was exactly, or had become.

"You should know," Candide pursued, somewhat hesitantly, "you and Percy got close in the last few months."

Anna kept her eyes trained on the tree line, a new twist of apprehension squeezing her gut. "Close? What do you mean?"

"I don't know. One of the many annoying things to come from all of this is that Aubrey and Percy are pretty much besties now, and it turns out she's an awful gossip, so never tell her anything you don't want me to know... But it's my understanding that you two spent some time together. You and Percy. And what happened, I don't know—"

"I love Eve!" Anna protested, entirely too fast and too loud at the suggestion in Candide's words.

Candide spat out a guffaw. "We're all very well aware of how much you love Eve. Don't worry about that. I'm just letting you know because, Percy… I don't know if he would say anything to you or if he's just going to pretend there's nothing going on."

"But there isn't anything going on," Anna insisted.

"I mean…" Whatever tension was in Candide's mind won, and she concluded the worrying report with, "All I'm saying is, I don't think it would be fair for you to not know what we all know. Which is really only that you and Percy were close. Very close. In some way. So there's that."

Anna's mind reeled. She didn't believe herself capable of hurting Eve. How close? "Is there anything else I should know about the last few months?"

"I don't think so. Eve died, you saved him. I feel like a walking pile of shit. You and Percy and your thing… Oh, and I'm a very powerful witch now."

"What!" Anna shouted, realised, then whispered harshly, "What?"

"Yep." Candide nodded with a distinct air of pride. "Way stronger than Percy. Stronger than Aunt Addie even."

"Because of the Necronomicon?"

"Yes. I still sleep with the book, and as far as I can tell, I haven't been driven insane. I absorbed a lot of power, but I also practised a lot over the last few months. I got more books, too. And I have actually been busy fighting things that came for the book this whole time."

"That never stopped?"

"No. When I was hurt, and while I was recovering, Percy helped Aubrey take care of things, and they both took care of me, and then Aubrey, wow, she's an incredible fighter now. Percy trained her. She's hardly scared of anything. Then, when I was feeling better, while you were dealing with other things, I was practising magic. I thought we might need it to help Eve, so I worked really hard, and turns out, it did help."

As though the Percy situation, her guilt about whatever the hell she'd done to everyone, and her loss of memory wasn't enough, a new trouble settled right at the forefront. "Have you told Eve any of this?"

"Not really. Only a little. I think he has enough going on. I don't want to give him an extra thing to worry about."

Slightly relieved that Candide was taking care of that side of things, Anna said, "That's fair. He'll probably have a small breakdown when he finds out."

"Yes, probably." Candide laughed, the smile lingering, then slowly fading, until her face fell to serious again. "What you were just saying, about embracing the darkness…"

Anna waited, but Candide became silent. "What is it?"

"It's only that…" She gave Anna a nervous glance. "How do you know when to stop?"

Anna meditated on her words for a time. "I wish I knew. I guess that's what separates us from those other things… Those darker things. But I truly don't know how far I would go if I was pushed. I would like to think I would know when to stop.

But maybe I already didn't. When I should have. Or maybe I did. I just don't know."

A thick silence, broken only by morning birdsong and the rustle of leaves in the soft breeze, settled for a long while, until Candide said, "Do you know what I do when I can't sleep?"

Anna shrank from the thought of the images in Candide's mind that, for months now, must have come to her whenever she closed her eyes. "What do you do?"

"I go for a run. I go for a run, outside, by myself at night. I run around the campus at two a.m. on a Saturday night if I want to."

Anna gasped. "Candide, no. That's so dangerous."

Candide smiled a bitter smile. "Do you hear yourself? You're not even talking about supernatural things now, are you?"

Anna didn't need to answer. It was Endymion College, prestigious, elite, but it was still a place full of young women, and places full of young women will always attract human predators.

"That's the thing," Candide continued. "I'm powerful now. Not as powerful as I can be. I can feel it." As she spoke, Anna's skin raised in a million tiny goosebumps. Candide didn't seem to notice the way Anna's eyes became fearful, or the way she pulled her blanket a little tighter around herself. But it was at the next words that Anna's stomach dropped. "All the true power in this world is in that book."

"Candide—"

"I could snap a man's neck without even touching him. I've never tried, of course." She laughed, so Anna tried a little laugh and failed. "But I can feel it. I know I could. I'm strong

now and people can't hurt me. And if I was stronger still…
None of that would have happened that night." After a few
seconds of Anna's stunned silence, she looked her in the eye
and said firmly, "Or any other night."

Anna was almost whispering as she spoke. "Is that why you
want to know how far you should go?"

Candide nodded.

Anna understood completely. Too completely. She knew what
it was to live a life in fear. She knew what it was to feel some
small modicum of power. She could barely comprehend how
Candide must feel with real, life-changing power in her hands,
and she understood. She reached across and took Candide's
hand. "I won't let you go too far."

Anna was perfectly serious when she said it, but within about
five seconds, neither of them could fail to see the humour in
the statement, especially Candide. "Twenty-four hours ago, I
never would have thought I'd be taking morality advice from
you. But I do think you're the only person who can understand
this."

"I do. And I promise, I'll never let you down again. And I
won't tell Eve." They searched one another's eyes until Anna
said, "You will. Tell him however you see fit, and I promise, I'll
back you up on this."

"Thank you." Candide squeezed her hand tight, and they
leaned their heads together, back against the black bars of the
widow's walk.

By now the sun's light was bright and warm, and all was aglow
around Worthing House. The birds' morning chorus was loud
and cheerful, and the forests and fields were endless and green
and glorious.

"Oh, and there's one more thing you missed." Candide's eyebrows drew hard together, and she seemed unsure how to go on. "Percy and Aubrey… They have this…"

Anna leaned in sympathetically as Candide trailed off. "What do they have?"

"They have this…" Candide sighed out reluctantly, "Soup thing."

"They have a soup thing?"

"They started making soup, you know, because I wasn't well and it was winter, and then there was some weird soup competition thing and, Anna…"

She looked so genuinely distressed that Anna's heart went out to her. "What is it?"

"Anna, now it's spring, and they're talking about doing cold soups. A whole series of them."

"A whole series?"

"And I just can't. I can't take any more soup at all, but not cold. I can't—I *won't* live like that and, Anna… I need my best friend back."

Anna's face lit just as bright as the morning sunshine. "Can we be best friends again?"

"Yes. We can. But I need you to do something else for me."

"Is our being best friends dependent on me doing that thing?"

"Not at all. That's a done deal."

"Okay. What do you need me to do?"

"You have to help me convince Eve to stay here. He can't come to Hell."

"That's another done deal. There's no way I'm risking him. I would never do that anyway, but apparently, we really lost him. Never again. Eve is staying here and we'll go together. I think we'll have a better time anyway, just the two of us. We'll sneak out if we have to."

"Sneak out to Hell?"

"I'm sure Percy would help us."

"I bet he would, too."

Anna laughed. "No. I'll talk to Eve. He's not dealing with things as well as he looks like he is. I think he could use… I mean, I guess we could all use a break from supernatural things trying to kill us. But I don't know what it's like knowing you died. Then knowing something awful happened, but no one will tell you what it is. I think he's blaming himself somehow for what's happened to me."

Candide said softly, "Don't let him do that."

"I'll do my best. It's hard though, when even I don't know what happened."

"It's only a few more days. We'll get your soul back and then it's done, and we don't ever need to talk about it again."

It sounded reasonable. No doubt it's much easier to recover from trauma you don't even know you have. Or had. And just seeing the damage it had done to her friends… "Candide, Can I ask you something?"

"You can."

"Why are you doing this? I can see how hard you're trying and I really appreciate that, but it's not possible to just flick a switch and stop being angry overnight. Going to Hell with me isn't a small thing. You could stay here and protect Eve, and Percy could come—"

"No. For lots of reasons, no. I still remember everything. I remember how much we loved each other. I know how much Eve loves you. More than you could know. I know what would happen to him if something were to happen to you. So I am doing it for Eve, but I'm doing it for you, too. And for me. I need to…" Anna watched Candide's face go through a range of emotions, her eyes searching the distant gardens, as though looking for the right answer, which Anna thought for a second she must have found. But then the resolve disappeared and Candide smiled and said simply, "It's just something I want to do."

CHAPTER 22
AFTER SUNRISE

Candide's bedroom was directly above the yellow room, where Anna said she intended to go back to sleep with Eve now the sun was up. Candide offered to escort her down the staircase, but Anna said she was more than capable of going such a short distance by herself, and despite the coffee, Candide looked exhausted, so Anna insisted, and Candide relented.

As soon as Candide's door shut safely behind her, Anna turned to descend the staircase.

Then she heard the noise below.

Perhaps two flights down.

She thought, for a moment, of running straight back to Candide.

She did a quick calculation to figure whether she could reach the door of the yellow room before whatever was making the sound could cover the same distance.

It was a step on the stairs, a creak, then a dragging sound, as though something were sliding along the wall.

Without a second to waste, as per her ill-calculations, Anna ran swiftly down her set of stairs, then paused.

The sound had reached the top of its set of stairs, and whatever was making the sound would soon be at the other end of the hall she needed to walk down.

She decided she could just peek around the corner to see what it was, then bolt to Candide if necessary.

Slowly, tentatively, Anna moved her head around her corner, and that was when Percy turned his corner, and there he was at the end of the hall.

He stopped for a few beats when he saw her. She did the same.

Then they walked towards each other.

They had been quite close.

Anna's mind raced as she wondered exactly how close. Had they been friends? Good friends? Had they ever kissed? Had they slept together? Did he know her that way?

No.

It wasn't possible.

Percy must have been showing off his scars again because his shirt hung open in the way it did when he showed off his scars, and she could see everything beneath, including his new demon-warding symbol. She wondered if he did it himself. Or who gave it to him.

Anna tore her eyes away from his glorious body to look up at his face again. God, it was a beautiful face. How could his eyes be so blue and so dark at the same time?

Percy stumbled a little, and Anna realised he must not have stopped drinking all night. He was filthy drunk, and she wondered exactly how that played on his inhibitions, which were barely existent to begin with.

She would need to walk straight by him and he was Percy, and they had some kind of history.

Would he tell her he loved her again? Would he take her hand? Would he stand in front of her and block her path with his hair swept to the side and his chest hard against her and not move until she admitted her shameful attraction? Would he pick her up with his strong, manly hands and thrust her against the wall and kiss her lips and her neck so that she had to fight against herself with every ounce of her integrity and self-respect to not give in and make love to him right there in the hallway?

His smile was as rakish as it ever was, his eyes as knowing, his whole presence as utterly captivating.

He was close by now. Almost within reach. His smile deepened a little. She knew he knew what she was thinking.

"Goodnight, Anna," he said, and he walked straight past without even brushing her hand.

"Good morning," she said.

He laughed softly and continued on his way, and she did look back at him, and he didn't look back at her.

Perhaps there was no history after all. Perhaps her imagination had entirely run away with her, as it so often did.

Perhaps.

It wasn't disappointment she felt at his behaviour in the hallway just now. She would have been appalled had he actually done any of the things she liked to imagine him doing. Yet there was some unspoken something deep inside. Approval, yes. Respect, yes. Unrequited something…

Perhaps.

She walked straight past the room where Evelyn slept and descended the stairs quickly, walking around to the left, through the sitting room, and straight to Lady Worthing's study. She peeked through the glass door and saw her there, still awake, sitting at her desk. She knocked lightly and entered.

"Anna. Finally."

Anna's bare feet scrunched to a halt on the lush carpet. "I thought you didn't want to be disturbed."

"Not you, Anna," came the tired voice.

"Oh. Okay." Anna stepped into the room, shutting the door quietly behind her.

"We need to talk."

"I suppose we do, yes."

"I'll have tea brought in." Lady Worthing hit a very old-fashioned button that presumably rang a very old-fashioned bell somewhere deep inside the mansion. Still, Lady Worthing continued to write whatever she was writing, so Anna slid onto the couch and waited in silence. She stared out the window at some small, colourful birds in the garden. The first time she visited, Worthing House had been deep in winter and all the branches were bare and it was grim and gothic. Now flowers and fresh shoots were abundant, the sun was shining, and after her very long night, Anna's eyes closed slowly on the pleasant scene.

"Anna. Tea."

She snapped her eyes open. She must have drifted off, but for how long she had no idea. Lady Worthing sat opposite, and someone had brought in an impressive array of cups and pots and nice things to eat. "Thank you, Lady Worthing."

"You're going to call me Adeline when we're not at Endymion."

"Okay. Thank you." She pushed herself upright.

Anna watched Lady Worthing's long, thin fingers as she served the tea, and she wondered what had shifted in their relationship. The last time they were together in that room, Adeline had tried to trick her into breaking up with Eve. Clearly, she knew what had happened to Eve and Anna since then, and things felt very different.

"How far back did Percy take your memory?" Straight to the point, as always.

"Three months. The night we exorcised Michael."

"All right. So you won't remember seeing me after that. Sugar?"

"One please. And no. I don't remember any of it. That was you that night, though, wasn't it? You helped us?"

"Yes, that was me. Had I known Candide was so powerful then... But we needed Percy too, and he would never have worked with me. But that's all beside the point." She picked up a small, elegant silver jug. "Milk?"

"Please."

"Why did you come in here just now?"

"I need to ask you something. About... It seems so strange to say it now..."

Lady Worthing placed the cup of tea down in front of Anna. "You want to ask me to choose you to go to Hell and to stop Evelyn from going."

"That's exactly right. And thank you," Anna said, picking up her cup.

"Good. I wanted to tell you that you will be going with Candide only. She will keep you safe. Evelyn will not be attending."

"Perfect," said Anna, setting her cup back down, ready to crawl back into bed.

"No. There's more."

"Of course there is." Anna picked up her cup.

"You won't remember something I told you, and…" She paused. She sucked a breath over her pert lips. She said, "Anna, if you go to Hell, and you meet a demon, and they tell you that they are Evelyn's true father, I'm going to need you to cover for me."

Anna put the cup down. "I'm sorry… What now?"

"There is some small doubt as to Evelyn's parentage." How very casual she was, leaning back on her couch, drinking her tea, only the twist of her slender ankle to indicate there might be any small disturbance within. "Now, I know you're not a stupid girl and, well, look around. This estate is entailed on the future Lord Worthing, which, as you know, is Evelyn. But if some creature from the abyss should make a claim like that, and Evelyn or Candide were to believe it… That might throw the whole inheritance into disarray."

Anna stared at Lady Worthing, quite blank, for about ten seconds. "Did you sleep with a demon?"

She shrugged. "Paranormal club wasn't all séances and spin-the-bottle, let's put it that way."

The tea was spilled as Anna sat forward in disbelief. "Oh my god! Are you saying you don't know if Eve's dad is human or a demon?"

"Quiet."

"Sorry," Anna whispered.

Lady Worthing set her own tea down and also leaned forward. "This is not something Evelyn wants to know. More importantly, it's not something anyone else needs to know."

"But what does that mean? Is Eve—"

"I honestly don't know. And more importantly still, you should wonder what that makes you." Adeline raised knowing eyebrows.

Anna's mouth could have caught flies. "Me?"

"Anna…" Lady Worthing let out a long breath and looked to the ceiling, out the window, to the floor, and finally back to Anna. "I'll put it plainly. When you lay with the demon… you *become* the demon."

Anna flushed a shocking red. "You… I'm sorry… No, that wasn't plain enough for me."

More sighing and evasive eye movements. "If Evelyn is part demon, then there's a good chance you are too by now."

"I'm sorry…" Anna leaned to one side, trying to catch the great lady's eye. "Lay with the demon… as in…" Lady Worthing nodded. Anna stared back in horror as her pulse began to race. "I don't know how to react to this."

"It could only happen if Evelyn *is* part demon, so it may be nothing at all. Then there's no need to get worked up about it. But if he is, then he inherited that through a demon father."

Anna nodded her swirling head, trying her best to understand what she had never imagined was possible. What she had never imagined at all, because it was too, too ludicrous. "Right…"

"Meanwhile, I became part demon the other way," Adeline helpfully explained.

"The other way as in…"

"Yes. By sleeping with demons."

"You're part demon?"

"Yes."

What else could she say? "Percy told me that, but I didn't believe him."

"Well," Adeline shrugged, "Percy's a little shit sometimes."

Anna narrowed her eyes. "You seemed to be getting along just fine before."

"Enemies close, dear," said Lady Worthing, dropping another lump of sugar into her tea. "He's still a little shit."

"He's very lovely, and—Oh my god! Are you telling me that Eve and Percy might not share a father?"

"That's exactly what I'm telling you," was the calm reply. "And that's something you're not going to breathe a word about."

"No. I can't keep that from them. I won't!"

"Where does your loyalty lie exactly? One wrong word and all this," she motioned around the room dramatically, "disappears from Evelyn's future. Now, do you want to inherit this house or don't you?"

"But Percy! His whole life, all those things that happened to him—"

"That's all over now. And the fact is, they may be brothers. They may share the same father. I don't know, I couldn't keep track of things. The way I see it, I did the hard work dealing with that bastard Lord Worthing, and therefore, my son inherits. Inheritance laws be damned! This whole world is stacked against women and unless you want to support that, then support me now."

Anna's world was spinning, and she began to wonder if she had woken up at all, or if she was still dozing in Lady Worthing's study, hoping to escape from whatever bizarre nightmare she was having this time. "I don't understand why you're telling me any of this. What is it you want me to do?"

"Simply this, Anna: Evelyn can't go to Hell. If the worst is true, then the beings down there will see that in him. His demon father will come to him and then the jig is up. Now, I'll do my best to keep Evelyn here, but I want you to double down on your part of this."

"How did I end up with this part?" Anna hissed.

Adeline ignored the question. "Talk him out of it. You have to keep him out, and more than that, when you get to Hell, you need to stop Candide from finding any of this out."

"And how am I supposed to do that?"

"How should I know?"

"Well, shit!"

"Shit, indeed."

"Wait." Anna searched Lady Worthing's annoyingly expectant eyes. "Candide's mum was in paranormal club too…"

"I suggest you try not to think too much about it."

"But… Is it possible…"

Another shrug. "Anything is possible."

"Why is your family like this?"

"I wish I knew."

"So maybe Candide and Eve are brother and sister, and maybe Percy isn't Eve's brother after all, and maybe Eve and maybe Candide and maybe me and certainly you have some kind of demon something in them, and maybe this whole estate rightly belongs to Percy?"

"In a nutshell. Though technically the estate would go to Michael, though technically he's dead, and they would never be able to convince anyone he's the older brother anyway, so in essence… Yes. This would all go to Percy."

And just like that, the last bit of Anna's energy slipped away. "I haven't even had breakfast yet."

Lady Worthing looked over the plentiful selection between them. "There are muffins and rolls here…"

"That's not really my point. I think maybe… I think I need to sleep."

Her attempt to rise was stayed by Lady Worthing's voice, unusually questioning, unusually worried. "You will work with me on this, won't you?"

"I don't know," Anna replied honestly. "I don't want to keep anything from Eve. Not from anyone, but especially not from Eve."

Lady Worthing continued to watch her, assess her, but she gave a slow nod. "You play it how you see fit, Anna. Whatever you say to Evelyn won't be worse than anything Percy has already told him, so if you tell him his father isn't his father, and you drive a wedge between those boys, well, that's up to you. But don't mention the demon. Evelyn can't ever find that out. You know as well as I do how hard he would take that. And you also know, if Candide knew about her parents, she would be heartbroken. She loved her father and her mother. We don't want to destroy her memory of them, do we?"

She was right. She was right about all of it, which only made Anna angrier, or at least it would have had she not been so exhausted, so she only said, "I'm not happy you've put this all on me."

"Well, I did try to warn you off Evelyn, dear."

"I thought you were just being possessive."

"No." Adeline smiled, one of those rare, genuine smiles. "I wouldn't ever want another person mixed up in this mess, but it had to happen sooner or later, and you're the person Evelyn has chosen. You won't understand, but it has become quite clear to me recently that he has made a very good choice in you. And as you may well be at least part demon by now, there's really no going back, so we may as well push on."

"I don't think that last bit is as comforting as you may have meant it to sound," Anna muttered.

Lady Worthing rose. "Get some sleep. You'll feel better about it."

Anna stood to leave as directed, made it halfway to the door, then turned back. "Um... What effect would that be likely to have on me? The being part demon thing."

Adeline, sitting again, topped up her tea in a long, steaming, amber stream. "That remains to be seen."

"Any advice or guidance about that would be really nice…"

She placed the teapot down carefully. "It's not a bad thing, Anna. Not at all."

"Because…" Anna hated to let herself be vulnerable with Adeline, after everything, but she really was the only person she could talk to about it. "I don't want to be a bad person."

Lady Worthing looked up, her face strangely kind for the first time that morning. Almost sympathetic, but not quite. "Bad is subjective, Anna. You like Evelyn, don't you?"

"I love Eve."

"So if he's part demon, then what have you got to worry about?"

"Well, I have no idea. I don't understand any of it."

Lady Worthing stood and walked over to her, but the only physical contact she made was to turn her around and push her gently towards the door. "Off to bed now. I'll come and see you on Tuesday to discuss the trip. Until then, you do everything you can to steer Evelyn away from the idea of going with you."

Lady Worthing returned to her desk and began scribbling again, so Anna placed one tired foot in front of the other and walked to the doorway.

"Oh and Anna."

Anna turned, spent, to look at Lady Worthing, who still didn't glance up.

"Do look around the estate a little when you wake up. If you play your cards right, all of this will belong to you and Evelyn one day."

Anna left without another word and started up the stairs.

What kind of strange bribery was this?

It wasn't much of a stretch to imagine Lady Worthing was part demon, but Eve? Lovely, sweet Eve.

Footsteps sounded ahead, and she lifted her heavy eyes to see Joe descending the stairs.

"Why aren't you asleep?" she asked.

He jogged down a few more steps. "I have church. I have to get a taxi all the way back. Do I look very drunk?"

"No, you look fine. You look good."

"Do you want to come back with me?"

"No, I really need to sleep right now. Will I see you later?"

"Of course. I think we're all meeting tonight." He paused, hesitant, and added, with what she could have sworn was a blush, "I wanted to talk to you about something, actually. Can we do that tonight?"

She nodded. "Of course."

While he stood there, his eyes focused a little more on her, and his face took on a note of concern. "Are you okay?"

She wasn't at all. How nice it would have been to sit on the stairs and cry on Joe's shoulder for a little while. How nice to have someone to tell her what to do. Instead she said, "I'm fine. I think I really need to sleep."

He remained reluctant, but said, "Okay. I'll see you tonight."

"Bye, Joe."

Joe left and finally Anna made it back to her bedroom. She crawled into her bed, back between Eve's arms, and he shifted a little and kissed her cheek. Then, somehow, all the worry went out of her. She loved the sleepy smell of Eve, the feeling of his arms around her, of his stubble on her skin. And she considered fleetingly, as she drifted off to sleep, that perhaps she did have a weird thing for demons after all.

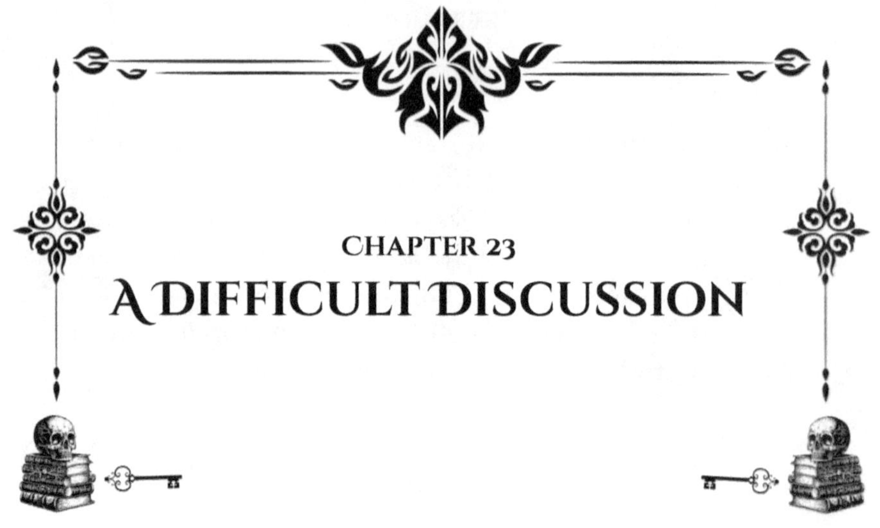

CHAPTER 23
A DIFFICULT DISCUSSION

Anna woke several hours later to find Evelyn sitting by her side, reading silently, as though he wasn't slowly starving to death. She wound her arms around his waist, lay her head on his abs, then remembered the billion or so horrible things that had come to her attention the day before.

She closed her eyes and went to sleep for another hour.

Everyone else having made their way back to where they needed to be, Eve and Anna eventually ate lunch together on the wide and elegant back verandah, bathed in early afternoon sunshine. The grounds were just as gorgeous to walk through as they had been to look at from high up on the widow's walk, and from their current vantage point, well away from the house, the old mansion looked magical.

It was, really, Anna supposed. To live in a haunted mansion took a certain kind of person. Lady Worthing was a match for any spirit, but Anna… Her shoes came to a silent stop on the springy, well-trimmed grass. "Eve?"

"Mmm?"

"Doesn't it bother you how haunted your home is?"

He glanced back, as though she could have been talking about anywhere else. "The mansion?"

"Yes."

He let out a small chuckle. "It bothers me very much. But it's not my home."

She recommenced the slow walk, arm linked through his, which was shoved into his pocket. "You never seem like it bothers you."

"You haven't seen me here when something new turns up."

With another nervous look over her shoulder, "And whatever's in there now, like Bad Eve, that doesn't scare you?"

Eve looked down at her, that same cloud of worry forming behind his eyes. "How do you know he's called Bad Eve? He didn't come to you, did he?"

Eve would probably never sleep soundly again if he knew just how close she came to death the night before, so she said, "No. Candide told me."

He nodded, furrowed his brow, and kept walking. She wondered if the conversation was over, until he said, "He tried to take her once. Did she tell you that?"

"No." Again, Anna pulled to a stop.

"He took her right down the back of the garden there." He pointed off into the distance. "I saw her just in time. I don't know what would have happened, but she was disappearing into the trees, holding his hand. I've never run so fast in my life."

Anna shuddered as she gazed down at the dark, lonely-looking copse. "She didn't tell me."

"She doesn't like to talk about it. It was pretty scary for her. She acts brave, but she's still terrified of him."

"She is brave. Incredibly brave," Anna said, realising only now how much it must have taken for Candide to come and find her in the walls of the house. "What is Bad Eve?"

"I don't know. I don't think he's a doppelgänger because he's never directly tried to hurt me. He's not me from the past or future, like a time-slip thing, because he always looks exactly the same. He's not a ghost, because as far as I know, I'm not dead. Not anymore. He ages with me and he's always dressed the same as me. He never talks to me or interacts with me, though. And he's always been there since I was a kid. He's just Bad Eve."

"Fuck your house, Eve."

"Yes. Fuck this house." He laughed. "I don't like the ghosts and things here, but there's nothing I can do about it. It's a package. So long as I have to come back here, I have to deal with them."

Anna didn't want to ask if he would ever like to live in the house permanently, or what he would do with it otherwise. She felt there was something untoward about discussing his inheritance with him, as though she had any say in his money or his future. That and the fact that Lady Worthing wasn't going anywhere any time soon, she imagined. Instead, she quietly thought very hard to herself, while Eve waited patiently for her to make up her mind about whatever it was she didn't want to say to him, until finally she managed, "Eve, would you really be happy living in a cottage in the village with me? If we could afford it."

"Yes," he said, without the slightest hesitation. Still, she stayed silent and pensive, so Eve attempted to save her the trouble of an awkward conversation. "Are you trying to tell me you don't ever want to live in a weird, haunted mansion? Because if that's what you're trying to say, you should know I don't want to live here either."

Anna's face and heart lightened with the news. "Really? You wouldn't miss it if you couldn't come here whenever you wanted?"

Plucking a few leaves off a nearby tree, he said, "I never want to come here. I don't even know what I'd do with the place if it was mine. It's beautiful, and it's a piece of history, but I don't want to be here. But then I couldn't imagine selling it either. It's too dangerous to let anyone else live here. I wouldn't want to let it fall into disrepair. I don't know. I wish someone else could just take care of the whole thing. But that's all a long way off and it doesn't matter, anyway. If I'm with you, I don't care where we are. Worthing House be damned."

That was it. She had to tell him. He didn't even want the house. Percy did. She would have to tell him what she knew. She took a deep breath, but then Eve went on, "It's weird to be talking about this. I was always so convinced I was going to die young that I never really considered the estate. And then I did die." He glanced over, eyebrow raised, eyes sparkling and set with adoration. "And then you fixed that. And now… Now the future seems really precious because I never really thought I was going to have one. I'm alive, I've got you and Candide, and now I have two brothers. It all seems too good to be true."

Anna slammed her mouth shut.

"I never imagined Percy and I could be close like this. And it turns out he's probably the best brother I could ever have.

Everything he's done for us… It's so touching. I feel awful for all the things I said about him."

"To be fair, he said a few things about you, too."

A light laugh rose in his throat. "He did. But I don't want to think about all those wasted years. You brought us together and now nothing can take that away. I feel like, if I can hold on to Percy and Michael, to you and Candide, I don't care about anything else."

Then *that* was it. She couldn't say a word. She wouldn't. She shouldn't.

But didn't he have a right to know?

Walking together along the tree line, Eve continued to throw furtive glances towards Anna as she continued to say very little, and as the lines on her face deepened, so did his. "Anna, if I'm moving too fast for you, just say the word."

"It's not that—"

"Because I know we haven't been together long. I don't want you to feel like you have to commit to anything right now." He turned her, pulling her arms around him. "I just want to make sure you're happy with whatever direction things are taking because… whatever future it ends up being, I don't see one without you in it." He bit his sexy lip. "Oh god, that sounded awful. That sounded like… What I mean is—"

She laughed. "I know what you mean, Eve."

"I know. I know you do." His thumb traced down her cheek, and he looked into her eyes with all the love that made everything, whatever had or hadn't happened, worth it. "That's a really long-winded way of saying we'll do whatever you want.

If you don't mind me tagging along. Maybe somewhere sunny. With you."

She looked up at him appreciatively. "And we'll read books and not die?"

"Exactly that."

"I think we have compatible life goals. Is Endymion sunny enough?"

"Yes! Of course Endymion. I hear you've already made the honours program, so I guess your PhD comes next."

She dropped her head to his chest. "It's a slightly shallow victory. All I had to do was resurrect the son of the boss-lady."

She felt the laugh in his chest as his arms tightened around her. "You make it sound so easy." His fingertips found her chin and tilted her face up. "But don't let her take that away from you. Not that or all the things Percy did in the past. You're brilliant. You don't need anyone's help to be brilliant. You were always going to do this."

She squeezed his hand and leaned her head against his shoulder as they recommenced their walk. "Do you know you're the first person who ever believed in me like this?"

"Maybe the first, but not the last. We're going to Hell, we're going to get your soul back, and then everyone is going to see how brilliant you are. And you're going to be rich and famous—"

"I don't think that many people care about my thoughts on Keats."

"Is that what you'll do your PhD on?"

"No, I'm going to do it on…" She stopped and took both his hands, looking deep into his eyes. "Why Wordsworth is the most boring poet who ever lived."

His face didn't change at all as he held her gaze. "I can see into your soul, Anna. And it's black."

She laughed. "The people need to know."

"Every word is like a dagger in my heart."

"Then there's only one thing to do, Werther."

"Pushkin's killer's gun?"

"Chekhov's Pushkin's killer's gun?"

He shook his head softly. "I can't believe I fell for a woman who hates Wordsworth."

"But you did. There's no going back now." Anna pulled him in for another hug.

"No. Not ever. It's you and me." And he kissed her.

When they finally returned to Eve's apartment that afternoon, they marvelled over some odd stains here and there, and Eve told her how he had only just saved his lovely armchairs from being taken away the previous morning. They showered in their haunted bathroom and ate again, and they discovered some hideously overdue library books that Eve insisted on returning that afternoon. All the while, Anna sighed only occasionally and carried on more or less as usual. Eve noticed but kept quiet about the issue until Anna finally looked at him long and hard and blurted out, "I have something awful to tell you and I don't want to tell you because it might break your heart but I can't not tell you."

Anna proceeded to give Evelyn a very watered-down version of what she had heard from Lady Worthing, never mentioning demons, and communicating only the pertinent information that his father might not be his father, that Percy and Michael might not be his brothers, and that Worthing House might not be his house.

At that, she was met with the rather pleasing information that Eve and Candide had long suspected what happened in paranormal club was more than simply séances and spin-the-bottle. In fact, they had come to the conclusion that it was entirely possible Candide's father was his own father too. To lose two brothers would be sad indeed, but to gain such a sister, such a father, was sufficient compensation, even if Candide's dad was gone now.

The only sticking point in the conversation was that Eve never believed his mother truly suspected his supposed-father wasn't his father. And he told himself, as much as Anna, that this must have been a very new revelation to Lady Worthing, as it was to him, and that, for all her very questionable behaviour, Lady Worthing would never have deliberately cheated Percy and Michael out of their inheritance. Indeed, it *must* be all very new and abstract information that Lady Worthing was mulling over, because the man she claimed was Eve's father was a monster, and to put Eve through that childhood with that man just for money which wasn't rightly theirs… Well, of course it went well beyond Lady Worthing's capabilities. Eve mused that after all, these were only ideas, and he was sure his mother still believed deep down that Candide's father was not his father. It must be nothing more than a vague suspicion, aired now with a view to keeping everything as decent and open as possible, due to his and Percy's recent reconciliation.

Anna nodded her false agreement with his theories and excuses and let him lead her to the library to return her books before they were due to meet their friends. She bought him a coffee at the cafe and she worried silently over his almost imperceptible withdrawal from her and everything around them as his mind spun over the revelations.

Candide was already basically a sister, in name or not.

But not Percy.

For Eve and Anna, it had only been a few days since Eve and Percy hated one another passionately. How strong the bond had since become, neither Anna nor Eve knew for sure, but they both knew the inheritance had always been a source of fury for Percy, and Anna knew the thought of losing Percy would take an increasingly large toll on Eve the longer he worried about it.

CHAPTER 24
A SECRET UNVEILED

As a gorgeous pink and purple sunset settled over Endymion College, Anna and Eve slowly made their way back to their building. They were due shortly to go to Candide's apartment where Percy and Joe would be explaining how one gets to Hell, what one does in Hell, and how one kills a demon, and neither of them felt quite prepared for that next step in preparations. Eve suggested they take the long way around by the forest to prolong their evening walk and enjoy what was left of the heartrendingly beautiful daylight. Perhaps he wasn't ready to see Percy yet, and Anna readily acquiesced to lengthening their time alone.

Until they turned the corner.

There stood Percy behind their apartment building, leaning back against the cool stone, staring up at the stars in the sunset above the tree line. He made quite a beautiful picture with the lost, dreaming look on his face—sad, wistful, reflective. He wore his sturdy brown boots under his grey trousers and his navy coat was open to reveal a crisp white shirt underneath, unbuttoned more than necessary, but as though he had carelessly undone the top buttons when he overheated during some adventure or other and then forgot all about it, rather than the more likely possibility that he simply realised how unutterably good looking he was and had decided to do a great and necessary service to all students enrolled at Endymion College that year.

He threw his glorious dark hair most becomingly to the side as he turned his head sharply upon hearing their approach. He pushed himself away from the wall and fixed Eve with an off look—a half-wary, slightly alarmed look. "Eve, I was just thinking about you. And you too, Anna." He began to pace back and forth slowly, looking at the ground, the stone wall, the trees, all around, except very occasionally, questioningly, at Eve.

"Are you all right?" Eve asked. "You seem kind of—"

"Kind of what?" Percy snapped.

"I don't know. Out of sorts."

"What is it, Eve? I don't have time for puzzles."

Eve cast his eye briefly around at the complete lack of anything that could be keeping Percy from puzzling, and failing to find a single thing, gave a vague shrug and proceeded. "I have something to tell you—"

"Well, spit it out then. I haven't got all day."

"It's kind of a big thing."

Percy paused his pacing and sent a side-long glance to Eve. "How big?"

Eve sighed out the entire contents of his lungs in preparation. "For normal people, huge. For us… I don't know. Still big. I think."

Percy recommenced his tread along the grass, smoking, but stayed silent, waiting for Eve, who pushed forward reluctantly, despite Percy's strange reception. "So, my mother, it turns out… uh… How do I put this? She was seeing… not only our father. For a time. Around the time I was born."

Percy shook his head knowingly. "I told you."

"Don't say it."

"I won't. But only because it upsets you."

"Anyway, it has now come to light that my… parentage… uh…"

Anna helpfully jumped in. "Eve's mum doesn't know who his dad is."

"Yes. That." Eve nodded.

Percy halted. "So… So what does this even mean?"

"Well, Percy… I don't know if…" Eve raised his shy eyes to Percy and made himself say it. "I don't know if I'm your brother."

Percy, still facing side-on to Eve, turned his head to take in Eve's lovely, slightly apprehensive face, with a look of shock and rather an unusual aura of agitation.

"Not my brother," Percy murmured, standing dead still in the evening air. He took a final draw on his cigarette, threw the thing to the ground, and he blew out the smoke in a short, sharp puff, then fast as lightning he reached a hand under Evelyn's chin and pulled him in close. Percy placed his beautiful lips on Eve's beautiful lips and kissed him.

Eve stood, frozen, and the kiss lasted much longer than anyone would have anticipated, had it been possible to anticipate at all, and when Percy pulled back, after a few short, breathless moments, he said, "I'm sorry. I had been wanting to do that for a very long time."

Eve, still firmly planted on the spot, looked to Anna for some kind of direction.

Anna felt somewhere deep inside a small, reassuring spark of jealousy. She knew somehow, logically, this wasn't what people did, and there should be some sort of repercussions for Percy's actions. She was vaguely aware of these feelings in the back of her mind, but at the forefront, overwhelmingly, what she knew to be true was that seeing Percy kiss Evelyn was the single most spectacular thing she had ever seen in her entire life.

Eve licked his lips quite innocently and Anna's immediate impulse was to follow suit and kiss those lips that Percy had just kissed, and to kiss Percy, and to watch Evelyn kiss Percy again, but instead she forced herself to stay rooted to the ground, eyes wild with excitement.

He was so beautiful—*they* were so beautiful—and it was one divine moment she may never witness again. Her mind and her heart went into overdrive trying to understand what had just happened, trying to quell her outlandish imaginings and trying to put her thoughts into some sort of useful order. It was a moment she instantly longed to see repeated over and over, and the long and short of this was that she was of no help to Evelyn at all in that moment.

"I said…" Eve murmured, "I said I *think* I'm not your brother. I don't know—"

"Yes, you did say that," Percy replied impatiently. "Yes. What does that even mean?"

"I don't know at all," said Eve. "I'm very confused."

"So, who's the rightful heir?"

"I have no idea…"

"Well, I don't suppose it matters, anyway." And he took up his pacing again.

Eve shared another unsure look with Anna. "It doesn't?"

"No. Not anymore," Percy replied. "We both know the title suits me better, though."

"It does," Eve conceded.

Percy gave a sharp nod, but then asked, "How do we find out?"

"I guess we could get tested?" said an increasingly flustered Eve. "But—we can—but Percy—I don't—or—uh—I didn't, I guess—I didn't want to know. I don't know how important it is to you to know." Eve looked at Percy with a beautiful flush on his pale cheeks and a sad, bashful, loving longing in his eyes that clearly melted Percy on the spot.

Percy walked back over to Eve, threw an arm around him, and placing his forehead gently on Eve's, he said, "I can't say you'll always be my brother, Evelyn, but I will always love you. No matter what happens. I meant everything I said. We won't ever be apart again."

Anna watched the interaction without the least subtlety as their cheeks met, as one of the most beautiful smiles she had ever seen spread across Eve's face, as Percy kissed Eve's cheek, then moved away from him. She felt some small disappointment that was all the physical contact for that time, but she was incredibly happy for the two of them, regardless.

"Was that everything?" Percy said, more softly than before.

"Yes," said Eve. "For now."

"Then leave me. I have a lot of thinking to do." And he took up his place against the wall again as though the whole interaction had never taken place.

Anna slipped her hand into Eve's as they walked away and she smiled up at him.

"Don't," he laughed.

"I didn't."

"You were about to."

"It's just—"

"It's just nothing."

"Would you though?"

"Stop it!"

"I don't mind…"

"I know you don't. But it's nothing. It wasn't anything."

"I mean, if it's good enough for Lord Byron…"

"Why does everything always have to come back to Byron?"

Anna let the subject drop, but noted Eve was a blushing combination of perplexity and thoughtfulness for the rest of their walk, and she stayed steadfastly away from that elephant in the room, letting Eve draw his own conclusions, not wishing to sway him one way or the other.

A Trip To Hell

A PLAY IN FOUR PARTS

Starring :

Anna.........................The Hapless Seductress
Evelyn.....................…The Hapless Seducer
Percy..........................The Sexy Arch-Villain
Joe....................…….The Jaded Would-Be Lover
Candide....................…The Irritated Bystander
Aubrey……….The One Who Brought The Vodka

CHAPTER 25
A TRIP TO HELL – ACT 1

Candide sits in an armchair knitting. Aubrey sits on the lounge. Tea is spread in front of them. Joe paces back and forth behind.

Aubrey: Sit down, Joe. You're making me nervous.

Joe: Sorry. I'm just a little anxious. Candide, have you taken up knitting?

Candide: Something to fill the endless hours of daylight. Also, it's good for anxiety. Tea?

Joe: No, I couldn't drink a thing.

Aubrey: Vodka?

Joe: Yes, perhaps a little. Thank you. You know I don't usually drink very much.

Aubrey and Candide exchange knowing looks.

Enter Percy.

Joe: Percy! Are you well?

Candide: You look like you haven't slept at all.

Percy: I barely have. My house is full of skeletons.

Aubrey: I forgot all about them. Vodka?

Percy: Please. Right to the top. Perhaps I can drink away my misery.

Candide: Not too much. We do have a job to do tonight.

Percy: Jobs, always jobs. To hell with your jobs. Why are we even drinking vodka?

Aubrey: I thought Anna would think it was fun. With her Russian studies.

Percy: She needs calories. You should have brought an ale.

Joe: She is looking quite unwell. Perhaps she would be better off not drinking at all and just eating something.

Percy: She'll be fine. It's done nothing to diminish her beauty. Or to dull the brightness of her very fine eyes.

Joe sighs heavily and averts his own eyes. Candide holds out her glass for more vodka.

Candide: So, she has very fine eyes now.

Percy: She always had very fine eyes.

Candide: She's with Eve.

Percy: Indeed she is.

Candide: And she would never be unfaithful.

Percy: What a waste.

Joe: I doubt Eve sees it that way.

Percy: No. Nor would I in his position, I suppose. But can she really be happy here? What can Endymion College offer her that all the rest of the world can't? Why spend all her life in one place with one man?

Enter Eve and Anna.

Eve: We brought snacks!

Anna: Are we doing vodka?

Aubrey: I thought you might like it… because—

Anna: Because Russian Literature! I love it! Thank you so much, Aubrey.

Eve: Come see what we got. Oh, and Percy: I brought your gun.

Exit stage: Eve, Candide, Aubrey and Joe.

Percy: I bought you Russian cigarettes, Anna.

Anna: You did?

Percy: I thought you might like it.

Anna: What a fun idea! That was so thoughtful, Percy.

Anna takes the cigarette given to her by Percy. He places one between his beautiful lips and leans in close to her to light both cigarettes. Anna walks to the window to smoke. Percy follows her. The silence is thick.

Anna: It's a lovely evening.

Percy. Yes, it's a lovely evening. A lovely evening to hang oneself.

Anna: Someone's been at the Chekhov.

Percy: Have you thought any more about what I said?

Anna: What you said when?

Percy: When I told you I was falling in love with you.

Anna: Not now or ever. It was only an hour ago you kissed Eve.

Percy: And I would do it again.

Anna: I can't understand you at all.

Percy: You understand me, all right.

Anna: Because we're both lonely and unfortunate?

Percy: Because we once were.

Anna: Well, we're not now, so don't look at me like that.

Percy: How can I look at you any other way when—

Anna: Percy, I need to ask you three questions.

Percy: What?

Anna: Have we ever slept together?

Percy: No.

Anna: Have we ever kissed?

Percy:

Anna:

Percy:

Anna:

Percy: No.

Anna: Have you ever slept with a demon?

Percy: That's a funny story, actually—

Anna: Fuck!

Anna exit stage.

CHAPTER 26
A TRIP TO HELL - ACT II

All players are assembled in the kitchen.

Candide: We really need to get to work on this trip to Hell.

Anna: Then we should all go back to the living room.

Candide, Anna, Aubrey and Joe exit. Percy grabs Eve's arm to prevent him leaving.

Percy: I wanted to talk to you.

Eve: I think we should go plan Hell with everyone else.

Percy places two glasses down on the bench and fills them both with vodka.

Percy: I'm sorry about before.

Eve: Don't be.

Percy: Don't be?

Eve: I mean… What I mean is—

Percy: Drink.

Both men drink.

Percy: It doesn't have to mean anything.

Percy refills the glasses.

Eve: Okay.

Percy: Unless you want it to. Drink.

Both men drink.

Eve: I'm not ready to talk about this.

Percy places his hand under Eve's chin. Eve looks at Percy in shock but does not pull back. Percy places his other hand on Eve's cheek. Eve's lips part sexily. Percy runs his thumb slowly over Eve's beautiful lips.

Eve: Anna…

Percy: Do you really think she'd mind?

Percy and Eve stare into one another's eyes. Eve's heart almost beats out of his chest. Percy moves closer.

Percy: You are so beautiful…

Eve: Percy…

Enter Joe. Eve and Percy pull away from one another and look around the room casually.

Exit Percy.

Joe: What did I just walk in on?

Eve: Drink?

Eve turns his back to Joe and refills the glasses with a shaking hand. Both men drink.

Joe: Is that something you want to talk about?

Eve: What? Percy? No. He's my brother and we're very, very close.

Joe: Okay.

Eve: We're just close. That's all. He's my brother.

Joe: All right.

Enter Anna.

Anna: We have to go to Hell. In a couple of days. And you've taken the vodka.

Candide off stage: Eve!

Eve: Anna… I'm sorry. I have to go see Candide.

Exit Eve.

Joe: Drink?

Anna: Yes.

Joe fills both glasses. They both drink.

Joe: What's going on with Eve and Percy?

Anna: What? Nothing. They're just close. They're brothers, you know.

Joe: What's going on with you and Percy?

Anna: Nothing. Not a thing with me and Percy.

Joe: So there's nothing weird with Percy going on at all with anyone?

Anna: No. Not like that. No more than usual. He's Percy.

Joe: I just really want to know because… He's acting strange. And… and I want… I want to…

Anna: If you're into Percy, you should tell him.

Joe: I'm not the one Percy wants.

Anna: I don't think he knows that's an option. Is that an option? You took that vow of celibacy—

Joe: Yes. But I've been thinking about what you said. It is a big thing and I don't know if I want to live like that. You know, maybe not forever?

Anna: You might stop being a priest?

Joe: No, but I might stop being a priest who lives like that.

Anna: And maybe you and Percy could happen…

Joe: Maybe? I don't know. He's so… different. And I've always known that, but I thought he was such a jerk and then suddenly I realised a few days ago… He's not like that, and now I can't stop thinking about him, and—and he just looks straight through me. I thought he liked me before—

Anna: Oh, he definitely did.

Joe: Did? 'Did' as in past tense?

Anna: I don't know. He probably still does. Do you want me to talk to him?

Joe: No, I couldn't ask you to do that.

Anna: No, let me. I need to talk to him about some other things, anyway. Set some things straight. Don't worry, I'll be subtle. I'll just feel it out for you. It's awful not knowing something like that.

Joe: Maybe just an indication. I don't even know where I stand with this. But it would be good to know if I should even think about it.

Anna: I think you should think about it. I would. Percy's something else.

Joe: He's something else entirely… Are you sure you're not—

Anna: Absolutely not!

Candide from off stage: Hell! We have to go to literal Hell. Get out here.

Exit Anna and Joe.

CHAPTER 27
A TRIP TO HELL - ACT III

*A*nna, Eve, Candide, Aubrey, Joe and Percy are all in the living room sitting around the coffee table.

Percy: The hardest part is getting there and back. To do that, Aubrey, you're going to be our most important person.

Aubrey: Most important? How exciting! I'm totally in. I have a nice scythe to take to Hell. What else do I need to do?

Percy: You're not going to Hell.

Aubrey: What? Why not? I don't want Candide to go to Hell without me!

Percy: She can't get back without you.

Aubrey: Okay, well, that is very important, I suppose. What exactly do you want me to do?

Percy: To get to Hell, Anna and Candide are going to need to die. Just a little bit.

Aubrey: Fuck you, Percy.

Percy: Just a little bit.

Aubrey: Fuck you, Percy.

Percy: You would just kill them a bit, then bring them back to life. Doctors do it all the time.

Aubrey: Fuck you, Percy. I'm not killing my girlfriend.

Percy: I must say, Aubrey, you're being very immature about this.

Aubrey: Fuck you, Percy!

Exit Aubrey.

Candide: I'm going to have to go talk to her, but for the record, I'm fine with this.

Exit Candide.

Eve: Candide, no. You're not dying. Candide!

Exit Eve.

Joe: So… I'm going in there.

Exit Joe. Only Percy and Anna remain in the living room.

Percy: Cigarette?

Anna: Yes.

Percy hands Anna a cigarette and pours more vodka.

Percy: Drink.

They both drink. Anna walks to the window to smoke her cigarette.

Anna: Percy, do you remember that time we saw Joe taking a shower?

Percy: I do. In winter. It feels like such a long time ago.

Anna: Do you still think he's more beautiful than Eve?

Percy stands and walks to Anna.

Percy: Why did you bring Joe up?

Anna: I was just wondering if there was something there.

Percy: Are you trying to make me confess my love for you?

Anna: What? No!

Percy: Joe's completely off-limits. Why bring up the one person in this house who's off-limits?

Anna: He's not the only person!

Percy: You're correct. Aubrey's a staunch lesbian.

Anna: Staunch?

Percy: Staunch. And Candide hates me, which leaves only two.

Anna: No, it doesn't.

Percy: Yes, it does. Two people I'm intensely devoted to, neither of whom, I believe, would spurn my advances.

Anna: Neither?

Percy: Neither. Should we test my theory?

Percy steps towards Anna, places an arm around her waist, and pulls her in close. Her heart beats hard against his. She does not pull away. They stare into one another's eyes for a few brief moments. Percy kisses Anna.

Enter Joe.

Joe: Fuck!

Percy lets go his grasp on Anna. Enter Eve, carrying Pushkin's killer's gun. Percy turns to see Eve. Percy runs through the front door. Eve runs after Percy with the gun. A shot rings out in the courtyard.

CHAPTER 28
A TRIP TO HELL – ACT IV

nna, Candide, Aubrey and Joe stand at the bedroom window watching Eve, who stands alone in the courtyard, his gun smoking.

Enter Percy, who falls on the floor.

Percy: Fuck! Fuck! Did you see that? He shot me! That absolute bastard shot me!

Enter Eve.

Eve: I'm sorry! I'm sorry! It just went off! Are you okay? Percy!

Eve falls to the floor by Percy.

Percy: I'm fine, but look at my coat! It's brand new, and it cost a small fortune and there's no fixing something like this!

Eve: I'm so sorry. It's such a nice coat. I'm really sorry.

Percy: What did you try to shoot me for? I never thought you were the type to shoot me over a woman.

Eve: Anna? I don't need to shoot you over Anna.

Percy: Is it about the inheritance, then? Lord Worthing has his revenge!

Eve: I didn't try to shoot you! This gun is one hundred and fifty years old. It goes off so easily. I didn't even know it was loaded.

Aubrey: You see now, Anna? Guns are terrible.

Anna: I don't see what any of this has to do with me!

Candide: What's this about the inheritance?

Eve*:*

Percy*:*

Candide*:* Is this something I should know?

Eve: Yes, but I would prefer when we haven't been drinking vodka all night. Who brought the vodka, anyway?

Aubrey: Me. Sorry. I thought it would be funny.

Eve: No, it was. It was a lovely idea.

Candide: Eve! Spill it.

Eve: Percy might not be my brother.

Joe throws his hands up in defeat and falls on the couch.

Eve: Because my mother isn't sure who my father is. And Candide, that means maybe what we always thought… Well, maybe you are my sister. I hope you are.

Candide sits by Eve.

Candide: I'm sure that's not the case, but I would love it if it were.

Percy: And that means the estate may be mine.

Candide: This is bullshit! I lived there half my life. Just like that, I'm cut out?

Eve: Me too.

Candide: Yeah, but you hate the place.

Eve: Would you live there?

Candide: Of course! I love that place.

Eve: Oh, well, I won't be tested then. As far as the world is concerned, I'm the rightful heir anyway, so you can have the mansion, Candide.

Percy: You absolute bastard, Lord Worthing!

Eve: Stop calling me that! Candide has more of a claim to the place than either of us.

Percy: That's not a bit true.

Eve: Not legally, perhaps. But emotionally.

Percy: Emotions count for nothing. Isn't that right, Anna?

Anna: Why am I always involved in everything? I'm just standing here.

Joe: Yeah, I saw you, 'just standing there'.

Anna: Shut up, Joe!

Candide: Why am I only finding out about this now?

Eve: Anna just told me this evening.

Candide: Anna? Anna, why is Aunt Addie always telling you things?

Anna: I wish I knew!

Percy: You're always in the middle of everything, Anna. You will always carry destruction in your train!

Eve: Percy, no.

Anna: What the hell was that?

Eve and Percy: Chekhov.

Exit Anna.

Percy: I thought she would think it was funny.

Eve: No.

Candide: I still need to talk to you, Anna!

Exit Candide.

Joe: No, I need to talk to Anna!

Exit Joe.

Aubrey: I'm not going to miss this.

Exit Aubrey.

Percy: Eve, I love you.

Eve: I love you too, Percy.

Percy: No, Eve. You're wilfully misunderstanding me.

Eve: Stop it right now! You're drunk and I'm drunk and I'm not going to discuss this with you. Not now. You have to stop all of this right now.

Percy: Fine, but let me declare my intention—

Eve: I will not! Stop talking or I'm leaving.

Percy: All right. Tomorrow.

Eve: Tomorrow?

Percy: I'll come see you tomorrow night. You and Anna. I want to talk to both of you.

Eve: Okay. Until then, we rest.

Percy: We rest.

Close curtain.

CHAPTER 29
A LITERARY DIVERSION

Nine a.m. lectures were Anna's least favourite part of university, unless the lecturer happened to be Evelyn Worthing. Said glorious professor had been up and out of the apartment well before she awoke that day, so she was left alone to drink several coffees and shower. She chose to wear a short-sleeved, white-collared shirt, buttoned right to the top, over a knee-length brown tartan skirt. She slipped on some socks and her oxfords, leaving her legs bare, for it was finally spring after all.

The lecture theatre for Russian Literature was the oldest in the university. Floor to ceiling translucent white windows lit steep rows of smooth, varnished benches sitting gorgeously in a semi-circle beneath richly moulded ceilings, dripping with sparkling chandeliers. One had to keep their notepad on their knees to take notes as there were no desks, but it wasn't something Anna minded. Although she had spent longer than she could afford that morning looking for and failing to find her lovely fountain pen, she eventually settled quite happily on a pencil she found on Eve's coffee table, and took her place in the lecture theatre, fourth row back, next to an aisle. Once the theatre appeared to be full and she wouldn't be in anyone's way, Anna placed her coffee cup down on the floor by her side and stretched her legs out into the aisle.

Evelyn entered the theatre moments later and a warm, happy pink coloured Anna's cheeks. He placed his tea and his books on the lectern and glanced around the theatre. His eyes fell on Anna, and remained there, his face very serious, for entirely too long. He looked down at the lectern and shuffled his books a little. Then he looked back at her and back down again.

"My name is Evelyn Worthing." He turned to the blackboard, paused, then turned back to the audience with a vague look of confusion. "But you already know that." He looked down again and moved some more papers around. Was he looking for notes? Eve never needed notes. Something must be wrong.

He put his head back up, blinked the panic out of his eyes, and said, "Uncle Vanya. My favourite play by one of my favourite writers. What's not to love about Uncle Vanya? A group of people pushed together, each with their own complex histories clouding their judgement and spurring their passions." He paused, looking as though he had realised something new, then went on. "The characters are compelling. We have the wealthy professor and his beautiful young wife." Eve's eyes shifted back over to Anna and she smiled a little at the concept. "And Vanya, whose fortune was lost due to past love, resulting in his bitter resentment of the professor who became the beneficiary." Anna's face became a little more serious, as did Eve's. "Brothers in love with the same woman." They both averted their eyes. "An inheritance that threatens to tear them all apart." Anna swallowed hard. "And at the centre of it all…" Eve locked eyes with Anna again and she turned quite pale. "Chekhov's gun."

The similarities between art and life suddenly became undeniable to Anna. She thought over her history at Endymion College, everything she had studied with Eve—*Frankenstein*, *The Picture of Dorian Gray*, perhaps even *Crime and Punishment*—and she began to see patterns. All the conversations they'd had, in class or in private, had been in parallel with those books and more.

She saw a thousand strange coincidences that... But no, not coincidences. Once maybe, two or three times even, but over and over?

It was clear to her now.

There was something more going on. Something larger even than Michael and Percy and Lady Worthing, and even bigger than Eve and his parentage, and the two of them and their great love. Something bigger than all of them.

The girl who read books. The girl who thrived on books. The girl whose existence was so many times solely dependent on literature... It was almost as though she was now existing inside her own...

No.

It was not possible.

She looked around the room. It was so beautiful. Really, is this where people learn about Russian literature? In rooms as beautiful as palaces? And she looked down at Eve. He was talking about Chekhov and he was so beautiful. So beautiful and so young. And he loved her. How was this possible? It was...

It *must* be.

It was fiction.

The notion struck Anna as clear as day: she had finally gone insane.

But when? And where?

She ran her hand over the smooth seat next to her. It was perfectly solid and real. She closed her eyes and opened them again, and all remained the same. She looked around at the faces of the students—every one of them their own perfectly individual selves. How could she have imagined every one of them? All of this? And how to escape? And where to escape to? But if she had already been forced to escape to the recesses of her mind to come here, wasn't it entirely better to remain here?

She looked back at Eve and he looked up at her, and the same worry clouded his face.

He knew.

He knew they were both involved in something bizarre, and there was no way he could know that unless he too was having his own individual realisations. That was right, wasn't it? Could she imagine his thoughts, too? No. He was his own whole person, with his own thoughts that she couldn't possibly guess at. That was proof enough that he was real. That all of it was real. Wasn't it?

Eve, who had been strangely stumbling over his words and throwing disoriented looks towards Anna this whole time, pulled himself together and delivered a stunning lecture, shot through with passion, melancholy, love, despair, hope and humour—all the things that make Chekhov, Chekhov. He closed the lecture on a high note, and as the newly inspired students slowly shuffled out, he said, never looking up from the books he was packing away, "Ms James, can I please take a moment of your time?"

Anna pushed her belongings into her bag and pulled her legs in close as she waited for the other students to leave. Meanwhile, Evelyn appeared to pay her no attention as he cleaned the blackboard and deferred questions and conversations from a few students. When Eve and Anna were finally alone in the lecture theatre, he walked over to the door and locked it, then he turned back and his eyes fell on her.

She ran down the aisle to him and said, "That was so strange. All those things you said. The way Uncle Vanya parallels everything that's happening in our lives right now. The way all our books do! Eve, are you okay?"

He looked at her in confusion and said, "I guess that is kind of strange. I never thought about that before. Huh." And he looked her over, and he reached for her hands and pulled her close and kissed her.

He kissed her cheek and her neck so as to let her speak while he was kissing her. "But… Wasn't that why you were looking at me like that?"

He paused. "Like what? Was I looking at you?"

"Yes. For the first half of the lecture. You kept staring at me. Weren't you trying to—"

"Oh. Oh, sorry." He blushed lightly. "I didn't mean to. I was so distracted. I need to pull myself together. No, I didn't mean anything, I just…"

"Just what?"

He pushed his lips together as if to stop the words, but they spilled out, anyway. "I never saw you wear a skirt before." Whatever she was about to say was cut short as he kissed her again and his body was pressed so deliciously against hers and he mumbled, "Do you have anywhere you need to be right now?"

She smiled, and she shook a little with delight as she felt his teeth on her neck. "Nowhere to be."

"Thank God for that," he said.

About three seconds later, Anna was pushed up against the blackboard of the most beautiful lecture theatre she had ever seen, having the greatest sex of her life with the most perfect man she could ever have imagined, and any thoughts of anything but Eve disappeared from her mind entirely, except the distant and fleeting acknowledgement that if there were any other reality outside of this one, it wasn't worth waking up for.

CHAPTER 30
A HANDSOME VISITOR

The rest of Monday went on much the same way it always did. Anna went to the library where the huge fire roared endlessly and unnecessarily in its gothic fireplace, and after some time she went home and she read her books. Eventually, Eve also came home, and they cooked dinner and they ate and they sat down to their evening conversation.

Eve began. "Anna, can I ask you something?"

He wouldn't have asked that way if it wasn't going to be hard to answer. "You can."

He came straight out with it. "Do you like Percy?"

She blushed. "Percy?"

He blushed. "Yes. Percy."

She smiled a little. "Of course I like Percy."

He squirmed a little. "I think you know that's not what I mean."

Her eyes sparkled, and she arched an eyebrow. "I could ask you the same thing."

Before Eve could colour any deeper, the door swung wide open to reveal Percy in all his rugged, masculine glory. "I have something very important to tell you both," he said. "Sit down and prepare yourselves. You might find this shocking."

They were already sitting, so they both remained exactly where they were in anticipatory silence, waiting for the tantalising axe to fall.

Anna was, naturally, concerned for Eve's well-being, but she was Anna after all, and therefore she was, for the most part, concerned with her own feelings. She watched Percy as he paced anxiously up and down the room with all his animal magnetism on full display. His shirt hung slightly open in the way it always did, and like he always did, he looked as though he had spent the afternoon swimming in the Mediterranean Sea, then hauled himself up onto the craggy rocks of a rugged Italian coastline to dry in the balmy air with the feverish sun burning down on his hot back, the salt and the sand still clinging to that swathe of dark hair that curled in just such a way around those fiercely sensual, dark eyes. That's what Anna thought, anyway. She noted the agitated movement of his beautiful fingers and she wished very much he would roll his shirt sleeves a little more, the way Evelyn did, such fine wrists as they both had.

Eve looked at her and knew what she was thinking, and she didn't know whether to be ashamed or admit everything. Why not admit everything? He knew! They all knew, so why on Earth not? And if not now, when? Would it be now? Would it be tonight?

Eve, for his part, had more than once noted how very beautiful Percy became in all those years they spent apart, and Percy had made no secret of his adoration of Eve, even before he kissed him. But then he did kiss him, and it was entirely possible they weren't related at all. But they still could be. And what did that even mean, anyway? And Eve looked again at the love of his life and her sweet pink cheeks and her red lips and her irresistibly provocative eyes, and she was wearing another skirt she suddenly found somewhere, and he thought about her with Percy and his stomach flipped and his heart skipped a beat and he was perfectly ashamed of the places his mind went, so he looked away from her and she looked at him and he looked back at her and he looked at Percy who was very, very handsome, and who he was sure couldn't possibly be his brother. After all, other than their appallingly good looks, taste in literature and women and their shared histories, what did they actually have in common? No, no brother to Eve was Percy, and Anna wanted them both and Percy wanted them both and Eve wanted them both and here they all were and would it be tonight?

Percy paused his pacing, swept his hair back dramatically and turned to face them, letting his penetrating blue eyes run cautiously over the two of them before he said: "I slept with Joe."

"What!" Evelyn and Anna cried.

The words came in a fast, anxious, furious wave, spilling out of him as he continued to pace his path back and forth across Eve's carpet. "I slept with Joe! I slept with him and I hate myself for it. In one night, I've smashed all his boundaries, I've ploughed through his vow of celibacy, I've plundered his sense of self-respect, I've completely ravished his career, I've thoroughly fucked—Anna, why are you laughing?"

"I'm not," she said, righting herself and wiping away a tear.

"I thought I could talk to you two."

Eve, warm and pink, made his face as serious as possible. "You can, Percy. Of course you can." He cleared his throat. "How are you feeling about things now?"

"Utterly depraved!"

Anna and Eve lost it completely, mostly with relief the tension had been broken, and Percy walked to the kitchen and poured himself a drink while he waited for them both to calm down.

Anna eventually poked her head up over the back of the couch. "I seriously doubt Joe minds at all."

"Anna's right," Eve said. "Have you actually been to see him?"

"No! I can't face him. Oh, the things I did. The things he did…" Percy lost himself staring into the distance.

"You know, Percy," Anna said, "this isn't the sort of reaction I would have expected from you."

He flung himself down in an armchair. "And why is that, Anna?"

"Nothing… It's just—"

"Honestly, I have to wonder sometimes what I ever did to deserve the reputation you both seem to think I've earned. He's such a sweet boy—"

"He's hardly a boy," Eve put in.

"He's so sweet—"

"I don't think he's that sweet either," said Anna.

"He's—"

"He is sweet," said Eve.

"Evidently, he's never been pissed off with you," said Anna.

"When was he pissed off with you?"

"We're here to support Percy, remember?"

"He's a lovely, sweet boy," Percy said, "and… that wasn't supposed to happen."

Anna kicked his knee playfully. "Why? Joe's liked you forever."

"He's out of the priesthood, Anna!" he practically shouted.

She gasped. "Already?"

"Not yet, but it's just a matter of time."

She shook her head slowly and sadly. "Damn. He looks so good in that outfit."

"I'm sure he gets to keep the outfit," Eve said, helpfully.

"He was wearing it last night, when he came over," Percy sighed.

"Oh. Oh, well, no one would blame you for what happened then," Anna said. "Hot priests…"

Percy nodded his agreement. "I was powerless."

"In an old church and everything…" she exhaled.

"You understand," Percy said. "I knew you would understand."

"I very much do." She thought of Percy's fireplace and of his thick rug, and of his chains, and of the light shining down from the stained-glass windows on both of them, and she thought of how she should definitely talk to Eve about redecorating.

"What I don't understand is how we got here," Percy went on. "All this time I've wasted, heartbroken and pining for you…" He waved an arm towards Anna.

"Me?" Anna cried, still trying to figure out how a brief flirtation in her kitchen somehow became a heartbreak.

"And you with all those things about you…" He waved the same arm towards Eve.

"What did I do?" Eve cried.

Percy narrowed his eyes. "Don't pretend you don't know."

Eve looked over at Anna and shrugged.

Percy continued, "And now I realise I've been in love with Joe the whole time."

"Love!" cried Eve.

"The whole time!" cried Anna.

"You were right, Eve," Percy said. "I should just talk to him. I'll go see him right away."

"Uh, no…" said Eve tentatively. "I mean, you should, but maybe tomorrow? You seem a little bit…"

"I'm very much on edge!" Percy shouted.

"You are. I can tell," Eve said. "Tomorrow."

"Yes. All right. Tomorrow."

"And maybe don't mention the falling in love bit. Just yet."

"That would be weird, wouldn't it?"

"A little bit."

"You're right. He'll be there tomorrow. I'll see him then. And I'll be calm. And I'll be normal." Percy drained his glass, then paused the movement of his arm before he could put the glass on the coffee table. He remained in place for a few moments, thinking, and then in a softer tone, "I want to tell you both, I'm really sorry for the last few days. I wish I could pretend the last few months haven't touched me, but in truth, these have been some of the hardest days of my entire life. And that's saying something."

Eve smiled sadly across at Percy. "It's all right."

"No, it really isn't." Percy gazed back and forth between Eve and Anna, then back down to his empty glass, which he watched as he twisted it around in his lovely fingers. "I look at you two and you have this perfect impenetrable thing. Something that even death can't touch. And I thought I wanted that. A piece of that. So I pushed it, and I tried to test it, and… now I realise what I needed was to know it was impenetrable. I think… I think I needed to know that there can be a safe place like you both have in this world, even if I'm not a part of it. So, I'm sorry I kissed you, Eve."

"That's fine," Eve mumbled with pink cheeks.

Percy turned to Anna. "Anna, I'm sorry I said you would always leave destruction in your train. That's not a bit true. I thought it would be funny, but it wasn't funny at all. The truth is, since the day you came into my life, you changed everything for the better, and I love you, I really do, and I have not, until now, been able to reconcile my feelings about everything you've done for me and for Eve, with the friendship I hope we still have. I see now I've been completely disrespectful. I'm sorry I kissed you too, Anna."

"That's totally all right," she choked. Eve glanced over at her, slightly perplexed but apparently not especially bothered by the revelation, so she did no more than colour at his ready acceptance.

"I honestly don't think I would have coped at all had things gone a different way between us all. Had you two not been so… So strong as you are. Together. It's important to have something to believe in." Percy sat a moment longer in the armchair, reflecting, then said, "When you told me yesterday, Eve, you might not be my brother, the thought of losing you again terrified me, and I lost control completely, and my behaviour last night was appalling. That's all I can say to explain it. And I think, if it's all right with you, and you forgive me, I want you to be my brother. Even if we're not brothers by blood, I would prefer we never mention it again and just go on as we have been. I don't want to get a test, and Candide can have the mansion, and you can be Lord Worthing, and I hope I haven't damaged us too badly."

"Percy, no. We're fine," Eve replied. "I'd like that, too."

"Then come here." Percy stood and Eve walked over to him, and Percy pulled Eve in close and held him tight for some time.

"I have to go now," Percy said. "Thanks for listening to me. And for putting up with me. I think I'm in a much better place now."

They said their goodbyes and Eve and Anna went back to their books and evening conversation, and neither of them ever mentioned out loud how close they had come to spending that night with Percy.

CHAPTER 31
ANOTHER TRY

The next morning, Eve, Anna, Joe, Candide and Aubrey were all assembled in Candide's apartment as required, when the door swung wide to reveal Percy's delicious frame.

"I don't understand how he keeps getting in," Aubrey whispered.

Percy walked into the centre of the room and fixed his eyes on Joe, who had just come out of the kitchen.

"Joe," Percy said, by way of greeting.

Joe stopped. He smiled. "Percy."

In a second, Percy had Joe pushed up against the wall, chest to chest. He slammed his hand down on the wall as a brace to stop him falling completely into that gorgeous man, slipped an arm around Joe's waist and pulled himself in even closer, hips grinding together, and they kissed as though there were no one else in the room, or the world for that matter.

"Joe," Percy said breathlessly, after a time, "I think I'm falling in love with you."

"Then I think I had better come over tonight," Joe replied. And Percy kissed him again.

Everyone else averted their eyes, like people do, except Anna, who needed the soft kick she received from Evelyn to come back to reality.

"Is this a thing now?" Aubrey whispered.

Anna, flushed and excited, nodded her head happily and watched Percy run his hand over Joe's chest and push himself away, and watched Joe grab him by the collar and pull him back in for another kiss. Eve kicked her again.

"So, Hell," Candide said loudly.

"Yes," said Joe, extricating himself and taking a seat on the couch. "About that. I'm not convinced we really need to kill Anna and Candide."

Percy slid into the seat beside Joe. "We don't *need* to kill them. It's just easier that way."

Aubrey laughed. "Easier than what, Percy? I didn't realise you had so much experience murdering people."

Percy stared hard at Aubrey, as though he couldn't make up his mind what to reply. Eve intervened. "She means murder, *then* bring them back. Not just murder."

"Oh." Percy laughed. "Well, you're right there, Aubrey. I don't tend to bring them back. It happens though, doesn't it? And it would be in a very controlled environment. As controlled as it can ever be."

"Do I need to say it again? I'm not killing Candide. Or even Anna."

"I really don't mind," said Candide. "I think Aubrey can do it."

Anna nodded enthusiastically. "She already saved you once. I'm totally down with this."

"That settles it then." Percy clapped his hands together as an end to the conversation and made to stand.

"That settles nothing!" Eve cried, and so Percy sank back into the couch.

Candide tossed her head back in exasperation. "Eve…"

Eve frowned severely at her. "Don't accuse me of being controlling again. I think it's very okay for me to not want you both to die. And also, why are we only talking about Anna and Candide? I'm going to Hell. I'm absolutely going to Hell."

"Eve, no," Anna said softly.

"Anna, yes. You can't imagine I would ever let you go and fight demons without me. Real demons. More than one demon. And I don't even know what else. In Hell!" He ran an anxious hand through his lovely hair, then crossed his arms tight as his foot started to tap. "You know, now I'm thinking about this, maybe it's not that great an idea to go to Hell at all."

"We can't back out now," Candide said.

"What? Why? This seems like the perfect time to back out. We'll summon the demon here and we'll kill it. All six of us together, here on Earth."

Joe screwed his face up apologetically at the suggestion. "It isn't going to walk into a trap. It's a demon. It knows we want to kill it. It must know Anna wants her soul back."

"So it's waiting for Anna?" Eve said. "Then that means Anna and Candide are walking straight into a trap. No." He shook his head resolutely. "I'm not happy with any of this."

Candide rolled her eyes. "This is what happens when we let Eve speak."

"Can you stop being so flippant, please? Why are you being like this? I know you're tough, Candide, but you're acting like this is nothing. It's not nothing for you to risk your life." Candide looked down at the floor, her face hard, so Eve continued, "My best friend in the world wants to take the love of my life to face certain death, without me, and I'm supposed to be okay with this? No. I know how important this is, but no, you're not doing this without me."

"Eve," Candide said, her tone a little gentler now, "I have to go and I can't do it with you there. I'm doing this for you."

Eve's eyes met Candide's sadly across the new coffee table. "This isn't something I want you to do for me."

"Yes, you do. You just don't realise it." Desperate to look anywhere but at Eve, Candide focused on the floor. Eve came to her side and bent close, their faces together, Candide still refusing to meet his gaze as she said, "You love Anna. More than anything or anyone. And you need her back whole and I know—I knew that was always going to happen one day. You two have something and I'm not… Of course we're not like we used to be, that's only normal but—"

Eve shook his head. "Of course we are. That doesn't change."

Candide's voice broke as she took Eve's fingers in her shaking hand. "I can't lose you again. I can't go through that. If I don't go, I know you will. I know you. I know you'll do that, and I would rather die than go through losing you again."

"Candide!" Aubrey cried.

"I'm sorry! He made me say it!"

"Don't ever say that!"

"Look." Candide sat up and wiped the tears from her face, controlling her voice. "It doesn't matter. None of this matters. I'm taking Anna to Hell, and I'm bringing her back, and Eve is not going because I'm a very powerful witch now, and he's not to mess with my skills by making me sad."

Eve paused and stared hard into Candide's eyes. "You're a very powerful witch now?"

"Very." Candide nodded. "See?" She flicked a finger and spilled the tea Percy was taking to his lips.

"Candide!" Percy yelled.

"That was amazing," Anna said. "Do it again."

"Don't you dare," Percy snapped.

Eve watched all, casting his widening eyes back and forth between them. "I'm not okay with this either."

Candide threw her hands up in frustration. "You should be! You said you would support me with whatever choice I made. This is my choice."

"I did! I do, but… What else? How much has changed?"

"Not that much. Not so much that it hurts anything."

"Why didn't you tell me?"

"Because I knew you would react like this!" she yelled. "You should be happy. I can do way more than that."

"Well, I'm not happy," he yelled back. "You said it would be art history!"

"Urgh! Eve, you are going to have to accept that I'm the perfect person to take Anna to Hell, and I will not do it if you go. Got it? I won't do it. I won't do it, and you'll both die, and she'll burn in Hell for all eternity and it will be all your fault for being controlling!"

Eve gasped. "That's a horrible thing to say!"

"Horrible and true." She shrugged. "You want her soul back?"

"Yes!"

"Then sit down and shut up or she burns!"

"Candide!"

"Sit!"

"Fuck!"

Eve threw himself back down next to Anna and scowled at Candide, who winked at Anna, threw her hair back over her shoulder, and carried on. "Joe, you were saying?"

"Yes… I was." He removed his hand from Percy's and sat forward again. "Um. So, I'm not convinced we need to kill you or Anna."

"I like Joe's idea," Aubrey said. "Whatever that is."

"Percy's idea has merit, too," Joe said, glancing at the adonis by his side, who shaped his lips into a kiss at him, sparking a little blush in his cheeks. "Basically, if we do it Percy's way, you don't really die, but you get so close to the point of death you have an out-of-body experience. It's well documented, it happens a lot. We can do that, then when we wake you up, we pull you out of Hell, after a certain period of time. Hopefully long enough to kill the demon. But ultimately, we're in control. Whatever happens down there, we have the power to bring you back any time we want. The other way—that's all on you. If something goes wrong in Hell, well, we can't get you back."

Eve recommenced the anxious tapping of his foot and reached for the cigarettes.

Aubrey furrowed her brow. "Percy… Joe… Anyone… Has anyone here ever actually almost killed someone and brought them back to life?"

"No," Percy said.

Joe shook his head.

Aubrey nodded slowly. "And you want to ask a medical student who has no experience with any of this to what? Do a death experiment on people she loves?"

"I never said it was ideal," Percy replied. "But it might be safer than the other way."

Eve threw his lighter back down on the table and puffed out a sharp plume of smoke. "Explain the other way."

"It's the fire portal we did the other day," Joe said.

Eve gave a nod. "Okay, that's better. Let's do that."

"We can, but it's a one-time thing." Eve commenced a slow, tired massage of his forehead, as Joe explained. "We can't let the fire go out at all. Not once. And they can't come back through unless they can find the other side of the portal. If they get lost in Hell, or if they can't get back before the fire goes out because something happens to them… They're gone.

That's the difference. The first way, their bodies remain here and the spirit goes, so there's a chance to pull the spirit out and get it back in the body in time. The second way, they go. All of them. If they don't come back in time, before the fire goes out, they're dead."

"No," Eve said firmly. "Neither of these things."

"Stop it, Eve!" Candide shouted.

While Eve and Candide fell into a fresh argument, Anna caught Percy's eye and tilted her head towards the kitchen.

She left.

He followed.

CHAPTER 32
A TRAITOR

Anna rounded on Percy as soon as they made it through the kitchen door. "Percy, you have to do this with me."

He leaned in conspiratorially. "Do what? What do you mean?"

"I mean," she lowered her voice further still, "open a portal and let me go by myself. In secret."

A short, sharp laugh. "Absolutely not."

"Yes. I really think…" And she commenced a thoughtful pacing of the kitchen floor while Percy leaned back languidly against the bench, listening and watching her. "I really think Eve will be okay if I don't come back. Eventually. If he has all of you. I can't take Candide with me. She can't risk her life for me, especially after what I did, and Eve can't lose both of us." She came to his side and leaned a shoulder against his, looking up hopefully at his inscrutable face. "Percy, please do this for me. You know it's the best thing to do."

Percy pulled out his cigarette case and lighter, lit two cigarettes, and passed her one. He took a deep drag, then puffed out some smoke, thinking. "I'm sure you realise that's a one-way ticket to death. There's no way you can do it alone."

"It's my fight. I'll… I'll just have to manage it."

He shook his lovely head. "It's really not. It happened mostly to you, and to Eve, but this has affected all of us. You're only one person and one person isn't enough. So we're all going to fix it."

Anna threw her head back and groaned in frustration. "Not you, too, Percy."

He looked down at her sharply. "What do you mean by that?"

"You must see, someone is expendable here. I am. You love Eve. I love Eve. Candide loves him. If I disappear, you can all go on as normal." Anna turned to face Percy, and he did the same, the two of them searching one another's eyes, hers pleading and his increasingly wary. "You're the only one who can see things logically, the way I do. Help me."

Then Percy smiled an odd, sad smile. "Did you really think I would let you do this?"

She shrugged and blushed lightly. "I thought…" She looked away shyly, then back up to him again. "I thought we had an understanding."

He laughed softly. "Our mutual darkness thing?"

She grinned. "Yes, that."

"Jesus Christ, Anna, I'm very tempted to restore your memory right now."

Anna's face dropped at his harsh tone.

"Eve does not want you to die for him. I honestly cannot understand why you need me to tell you this. He won't be okay. Ever. He won't. You're his other half and there is no Eve without you. I know you know that. Or maybe you don't right now, because…" He searched a moment for the words, his face darkening with every second, growing more and more perturbed, then only waved a hand in irritation. "I can't tell you what happened, but you should know, if you go to Hell, Eve will stop at nothing to get you back. If you go, Eve will be damned too."

"Then you keep him here," she said simply, displaying her complete and perfect faith in Percy.

"Do you really believe that's at all possible?"

It probably wasn't, but she'd hardly had time to think it all through. It still seemed like the safest and best option to her, and her mind raced at the possibilities of keeping Eve in some sort of comfortable captivity for a time. Until Percy continued his stern lecture.

"Anna, you may not realise this, but what you two have is actually an incredibly toxic, incredibly co-dependent, very unhealthy if extremely loving relationship, and you should probably look into fixing that in the future—get some hobbies beyond sex and books—but right now, the fact remains, if you die, we all lose him anyway." Anna's face showed she was both offended and appropriately shamed, but Percy went on before she could. "I don't think I should have to tell you this, but I'm not okay with losing you either, so you're going to Hell with the most powerful person I know, and she is going to bring you back to us, and in case you were thinking of talking any more about this—" Percy grabbed Anna's arm and dragged her back into the living room, announcing loudly, "You should all know, Anna's trying to talk me into letting her go to Hell by herself."

"Percy!" Anna yelled. "You traitor!"

He threw himself back down next to Joe. "So we'll all be keeping a close eye on her from now on."

"Anna, how could you?" Eve said, but he knew exactly how, and beyond a heavy sigh and keeping his arms tight around her for some time after she dropped back to the floor beside him, he said nothing else about it, nor did he own that he was about to say the same thing to Percy. Instead, he variously tapped his foot, or twisted the tendrils of his hair around and around, or played with his spoon in his teacup, or any other slightly irritating things he could think to do as he tried his best to keep control of his rising anxiety.

Candide watched Eve as he held Anna close, knotting and unknotting his fingers, and she said to Anna, "Do you seriously think I need to deal with Eve's neuroses if you die?"

"What is with you today, Candide?" Eve snapped.

"All right," Joe said calmly. "We still need to make a decision here."

"The fire," said Aubrey. "I won't be the sole person responsible for whatever happens."

"Fire is fine by me," said Candide.

"Me too," said Anna.

"I'm not okay with any of it," Eve protested.

"I get his vote then," Candide replied as Eve glared at her. "Fire."

"I vote near-death," Percy replied. "Eve, are you sure you won't switch to near-death with me?"

Eve raised a frustrated hand to his temple. "Why are we talking about this like it's just a thing we're all doing? Like what we're going to get for lunch? They're going to Hell and they're probably going to die."

"All due respect, Eve, but you were fine with this until you found out you won't be going," Percy said.

"And now I'm not fine! I'm not fine and I'm not going to be fine and—"

"Eve, you need to stop now," Anna said softly.

"No! I'm going to make no effort whatsoever to adjust to this, and we're going to do some research, and we're—"

"Eve."

Eve stopped talking. Anna didn't lift her head. She pulled his hand in and a tear dropped into his palm.

"Anna…"

Then Eve burst into tears, which caused Anna to burst into tears. Candide lost her resolve entirely and burst into tears, which elicited a great deal of crying from Aubrey, who threw herself onto Candide and they sat in the armchair crying together. It was around this time Percy discovered he had something in his eye and so Joe threw his arm around Percy who leaned on Joe's chest and Joe sat quietly for a few moments watching them all before he sighed and said, "This might be a good time to mention, I've actually been to Hell and it's really not that bad."

CHAPTER 33
YET ANOTHER PLAN

Percy's eyes were hard, cold, and disbelieving. "And when were you going to mention that?"

Joe shrugged. "Now?"

"No, not now! That's very pertinent information!"

"Everyone seemed fine!"

"We always seem fine!" Anna yelled.

"I didn't know!" Joe cried.

"When were you in Hell?" Candide asked.

"It was about five years ago. We had a situation, not hugely different to this—"

"'Not hugely different'," Percy spat. "And you're letting me go on and on about near-death experiences."

"It's a very valid consideration," Joe said.

"So, how did you do it?" Eve asked.

"A portal, of course."

Percy huffed dramatically in response.

"But," Joe continued, ignoring him, "it was different. We had a whole team of priests and monks and all that sort of thing."

"Should we be getting the Church involved?" Aubrey asked.

"No!" shouted Joe, Percy and Anna.

"No," Joe repeated more calmly, casting his eyes involuntarily towards Anna, then immediately down to the table as he attempted a reasonable explanation. "It's not… This isn't something they would help with. What Anna did… They wouldn't see it the way we see it."

"No surprise there," Anna mumbled.

"And," Joe's eyes found Percy's, and he blushed a shade darker, "I don't want them to know I'm involved in any of this."

Percy grinned and shifted a knee against Joe's. "Just how often do you step outside the rules of the Church?"

Joe blushed a little brighter. "Only very occasionally. Only when I think it's necessary."

"It's very necessary." Percy pulled Joe close and kissed him. And then he kissed him some more. And some more.

"Please, can that wait maybe just ten more minutes?" Candide said. "It felt for a second like we were getting somewhere."

"When I went to Hell," Joe continued, shoving Percy off regretfully, "we opened a portal with the fire. We did what we had to do down there, then we came straight back. Hell is a very bad place if you're the condemned soul of someone whose body has really died, but going as a living person, it's not as bad as you would think. There are demons and they will try to kill you. They may also become attached to you and follow you back to this realm, but that's usually nothing a Negative Energy Clearing can't fix."

Eve managed a soft smile. "I never got my refund for that, by the way."

Joe smiled just as fondly. "It's another reason we need you here, Eve. We have to keep the portal open the whole time. And we have to watch it constantly, because things will come through from Hell. We need you on this side to help us stop them."

"Things?" he asked. "Like things Anna and Candide will meet in there?"

"Eve," Joe continued gently, "you don't remember some of the stuff we've seen the last few months. Believe me when I tell you, there isn't a person in this world who could take better care of them both than Candide. If something kills those of us on this side of the portal and the fire goes out, they're stuck there. Forever. You need to understand, your role on this side is just as important as theirs. Just because they have a different fight, it doesn't mean you're not fighting for the same thing."

Eve pulled his arms a little tighter around Anna, though it was barely possible, and sat quietly with his cheek against her hair. Then he said, "When?"

Anna wiped away her tears and looked up at his worried face. "I have a lecture and two tutorials this afternoon."

Eve looked back at her miserably. "So I won't see you?"

"It's okay. I won't be gone long." Before Eve could protest, she addressed Joe. "How long will it take to find the demon in Hell?"

"I honestly don't know," Joe replied. "Candide, can you do your location spell?"

She nodded. "Yes. I'll find him."

"Then it's just a matter of getting to the demon and killing him. And killing whatever else you both meet on the way. If it gets too much, you just come straight back to the portal. We'll keep the fire open until you get back, and we can try another time if this doesn't work. We can try as many times as we have to, so if you think it's getting too dangerous, run straight back."

"Okay." Anna smiled up at Eve. "This is fine. We can do this."

"But there's one more thing," Joe said.

They all looked at each other anxiously.

"Time. It passes a little differently in Hell. It passes slower, which means the fire cannot go out for some time. Maybe even days."

"They'll be in Hell for days?" Aubrey gasped out.

"Not for them. For them it could be maybe an hour, but here, because our time moves faster, that could be a long time. That's why we need you here, Eve. And we also need a big fireplace they can walk through. Somewhere we won't be disturbed, and where we have space to kill anything that comes through."

"I'd like a new door before I try to use my dungeon fireplace again," Percy said. "All of those skeletons that reanimated…"

Joe glanced over at him. "You should probably…"

"No, I know." Percy shrugged. "I've just been busy."

"I mean…" Joe blushed. "I could… If you wanted?"

"Would you?" Percy smiled. "Maybe in a few days or…"

"Yeah. I'll be there."

"I'll get some snacks or something and we can—"

Candide cleared her throat loudly.

"I know where there's a really big fireplace." A slow smile began to stretch Anna's lips. "In a big space, with a stone floor, where the blood will wash off easily."

There came a knock at the door. Candide jumped up to open it. "Aunt Addie!" The women threw their arms around each other, and Percy automatically lit two cigarettes, one of which he held out for Lady Worthing.

"Good morning, everyone. Sorry I'm late, but I had a lot to arrange." She took the cigarette from Percy and walked to the front of the coffee table to address them all. "Candide and Anna will be the only people going to Hell. Evelyn, as far as everyone is concerned, you are leaving for staff training tonight. I'll be taking your classes until they get back. Anna, Candide, I have arranged for you both to make up classes next week. Try not to get too badly damaged in Hell. You're going to have a lot of work to get through. Aubrey, I know you won't be happy with me, but your medical degree really does require a lot more from you than their arts degrees, so you will need to attend classes as usual this week. Nevertheless, should you need a break from study, it will be arranged. We'll still need your help when you're not in class for supply runs, emergency medical aid, and some slaughter of beings from Hell. Percy, Joe, pack some things and cancel all your appointments. You'll be required here at Endymion College, with Evelyn, until they return. We'll be using the library's fireplace as a portal to get Anna and Candide to Hell and back, and the three of you will be defending this side of the fire the whole time they're gone.

The library is closed henceforth to all but us. Is there anything else you need to know?"

Everyone shook their heads in silence.

"Perfect. Ladies, go to your classes, then get some rest. Eat well. You have a lot of killing to do. Gentlemen, get ready for a long and bloody battle. I will see you all this evening. Library, eight p.m. sharp."

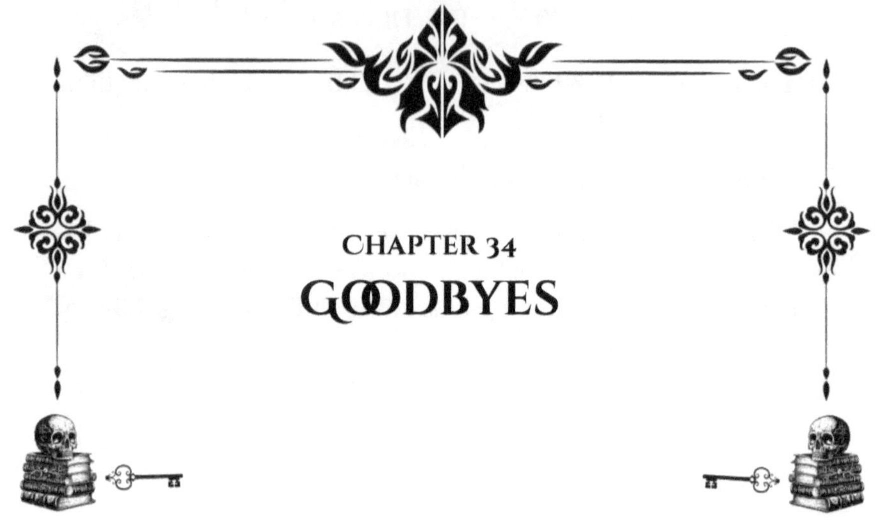

CHAPTER 34
GOODBYES

It was Eve. He was making his way up the stairs to the occult section of the library. Anna heard his footsteps first, then turned and looked over the back of the lounge to see him. She ducked down before their eyes met.

"Are you hiding from me?"

Too late. "No. Not hiding."

Eve took a seat on the couch opposite her. "You are. You're doing that thing where you pretend like the whole world isn't falling in on us."

She eyed him warily. "Have you come to tell me that's unhealthy and we need to talk about it?"

"No." Her eyes went back down to her book. "I was just wondering if I could sit near you and pretend it's not happening, too." Eve tried his best to keep his voice steady as he added, "Since this might be the last time I ever see you."

She kept her eyes down as they began to water. "Do you want to sit on my couch?"

Eve moved across to her and she saw him look at her book as he settled in, but he didn't comment on it, or start any sort of conversation, so she rested her head on his shoulder and they sat in silence and read for a while, until she said, "I love you, Eve."

He rested his head on hers with a long sigh. "I know. You don't have to say anything."

"Thank you."

"That's okay."

She knew Eve was trying hard not to talk again. She saved him the trouble. "I'll be back soon. I just need to kill a demon, and then I'm coming straight back to you. No matter what. I promise."

"I know. I just love you so much." They both blinked back their tears and stilled their shaking hands and sat and tried to read in silence together until the library door slammed shut and they heard Percy swearing loudly about how late they both were.

"Are you ready?" Anna whispered.

"Never," Eve replied. "But let's go."

She smiled at him and their lips met, and they both knew it might be the last time they were ever alone together, so they both pretended it wasn't happening.

They heard a huge crash as they descended the stairs and saw that several loads of firewood and other necessities had been dumped against the far wall. It was easily enough to last at least a few days. Candide, Aubrey, and Lady Worthing sat on the lounges in front of the fire, and the library door was bolted shut.

"Eve!" Candide cried as he made his way down the stairs. In an instant she was in his arms and they looked into each other's eyes and entered into the usual series of declarations, protestations, mutual reassurances, and promises.

Percy didn't look up as he arranged the firewood. "Doing all right, Anna?"

"Yep. You?"

"Fine," he said, throwing down another log.

She settled down next to Aubrey on the lounge. "Are you all right, Aubrey?"

"No." Aubrey smiled. "No, I'm not."

Anna linked her arm through Aubrey's. "I know it probably doesn't mean much, but I promise I'll take care of her."

Aubrey's only response was to nod slowly and sadly. Everything was in motion. It mattered very little whether Aubrey had any faith in Anna or not. She had faith in Candide, and Candide was willing to do this for Anna, so Aubrey had done her best to detach herself from the situation, and Anna wasn't helping. Aubrey gently pulled her arm free and walked to Candide, so Anna turned her eyes to the fire.

She knew she deserved the lack of trust for what she had done to Candide, not that she remembered the incident, so she accepted it regretfully and pushed it down, and waited anxiously for the goodbyes to be over.

"Hey, Anna." Joe was by her side now.

"Hey, Joe."

Anna turned her eyes briefly towards Eve, who was wrapped up in Percy's arms, deep in loving conversation. "Joe, is Hell very scary?"

"Yes. Yes, it is. But like I said, not as bad as you would think. You might see some pretty horrible things in there. But probably not that much worse than things you've already seen here."

"Things I remember?"

"Yes. Things before the last three months. You've seen a lot of gruesome death, so… more of that sort of thing, probably."

She searched Joe's calm, sweet, patient face, his chin resting on the arm of the lounge, his lovely features glowing in the firelight. "It must have been pretty awful, whatever happened that whole time. You know, for it to be worse than everything else we've seen." Joe said nothing, but came around and sat down on the couch next to her with a sigh. He smiled softly and turned his hand up, and in a second she had gripped it tight and whispered, "Joe, am I a terrible person?"

He squeezed her hand in return and shook his head firmly. "No, Anna. No, you're not."

Finally, her tears began to fall. "Do you think I deserve all of this?"

"No, I don't think that. No."

She couldn't stop now she had started, and she spoke in a fast, harsh, desperate whisper, searching Joe's eyes. "Do you think if I wasn't here, none of this would be happening to any of you? Have I ruined all of your lives just by being here? Just by being me?"

If anyone could tell her how horrible she was, surely it would be Joe. No one knew better. And he said, "I don't think that at all. You can't blame yourself if a demon attaches itself to you. It's not your fault. None of this is."

She started sobbing on his shoulder and he put an arm around her while she tried to get her words out. "My life was always, always awful, and I'm beginning to think… I'm beginning to think maybe it was all always meant to be this way, and if I'm near you and if I do anything, everything will just be ruined for you, because maybe I'm just not meant to be happy, and I take that with me wherever I go."

"Anna—"

"I know I did something terrible. Even after I hurt Candide, I know I must have. Only no one will tell me what it was. And it's so bad you won't tell Eve either. What did I do? Did I hurt him?"

"You would never do that."

"Why are we even doing this, Joe? I'm going to end up in Hell anyway, aren't I? That demon, when he possessed you, do you remember what he said? He said I'm rotten to the core. Born broken. He said I'm going to Hell and there's nothing I can do to stop it. He said I was always destined for Hell and—"

"Stop. He was a liar. Are you going to trust what a demon tells—"

"What if I'm going straight to Hell just for being a terrible person, and I'm putting you all through this for nothing and that's exactly where I belong?"

"Anna, no." He turned her teary face up to his own, calm and resolved. "We wouldn't all be here if we didn't believe you're a good person. Your past has nothing to do with any of this, and

I don't care what that demon said, and I don't care what anyone else says—I think you did a terrible thing to do an amazing thing. I wasn't there that night, but from what they tell me, what you did, didn't just save Eve. If you hadn't made the deal you made, Candide would probably have died anyway. Aubrey too. And you. You would all be dead and who knows who else after that. Percy might be dead, or it's possible he could still be possessed even now."

Anna's mouth gaped open at the revelation. "Percy was possessed?"

Joe stared back at her, shock written in every feature. "Anna, Percy killed Eve when he was possessed."

She let out a loud gasp. "It was Percy?"

"You didn't know that? Seriously? Don't these people tell you anything?"

"Apparently not!"

"Oh my god." He ran a hand over his brow and took a deep breath. "Anna, it was Percy. He wasn't warded, and he got possessed by the same demon who possessed me. The same one you're about to kill. He walked into your living room that night and he killed Eve right in front of you and Candide. And he injured you all pretty badly in the process."

"I can't believe they didn't tell me. How could Percy not tell me? He never breathed a word."

Joe cast a worried eye over Percy, still glued to Eve's side. "Don't hold it against him. I think... I don't think you should bring it up to him either. He had to watch himself attack you all, but of course the worst part was Eve. He still isn't coping with that. Or, he's trying, but it's brought out a lot of... We'll say, 'uneasiness' in him. He has… He has some attachment issues. With Eve."

Anna looked again at the two of them, deep in conversation, smiling, staring deep into each other's eyes. "Yeah, that explains a few things, actually."

"He didn't want me to tell you that happened, or anything else that happened, but I thought someone must have told you by now, if not Percy, then Candide. Either way, I think you need to know, so I'm telling you. None of this was your fault. You got the demon out of Percy that night by using the same deal you used to save Eve. That makes five people you saved that night, and I don't know how many more if you hadn't found a way to control the demon. That's what you gave your soul for."

She turned her eyes to the fire, trying to process everything Joe was telling her, but he swiftly reached over and brought her back to face him with a gentle hand under her chin, until she was looking straight into his eyes.

"When you go to Hell, you need to be *that* Anna. You need to be the Anna who makes hard choices, and I hope you'll show no mercy. You fight and you make whatever sacrifices you need to make, because I honestly believe you have the soul of a warrior. Don't ever feel bad about that. And don't ever think any of this is your fault. The demon wants you to believe that because it makes you weak. You're a good person who was forced to do something bad to take care of the people you love. That doesn't make *you* bad. In fact, that makes you one of the best people I know. You're my friend, and I want you to know that I have complete faith in you."

"Joe…"

He wiped a fresh tear from her cheek with the pad of his thumb. "You're not a killer, Anna. You're a survivor. Even if the two things have to intersect sometimes, it's not the same thing. You're a good person. I can promise you that. You belong right here, with us. And we all love you."

Anna could barely speak, overwhelmed at Joe, of all people, having found exactly the words she needed to hear, seemingly out of thin air. Eventually, she whispered, "Why are you such a good priest?"

Joe laughed softly. "I'm just being honest. Go kill that bastard and come straight back to us."

She smiled and dried her eyes. "I will. That's exactly what I'm going to do."

"Eat something first," Lady Worthing said.

How long everyone else had been listening to Joe and Anna's conversation was a mystery, but all eyes were on them. Anna sought Candide first. "Are you sure you want—"

"Yep." Candide smiled and took a piece of bread, so Anna did the same.

Eve stood alone now, some distance away, waiting quietly. She crossed the room, took his hand, and led him a little further. "I'm sorry for being the way I am. It's just because—"

"I know," he said.

"It's so much harder with you. Because I love you so much."

He took her in his arms and she rested her head on his chest. "I'm sorry I'm not stronger when you need me to be."

"I want you to be exactly how you are," she replied. "You're the love of my life and my whole world, and I want to make sure you know that. Before I go. But I can't say goodbye to you."

"Don't," he said. "I don't want you to."

Still they refused to look at one another, or to let go.

"I won't be long," Anna said. "Not for me, anyway. I know it's going to be a bit longer for you."

"I can wait. I'll stay on my side and I'll fight for you. And then we'll be together."

"And no more supernatural stuff."

"No. Not ever."

"With our nice cottage."

"And our cat."

"And our books.

"I love you."

"I love you, too."

"Come back."

"I will."

Before either of them could start crying again, Lady Worthing declared that it was time.

Percy directed Anna and Candide to a table where a silver bowl awaited them. "For anyone who may be thinking of following Candide and Anna into Hell," Percy looked askance at Eve, "if your blood is not in this bowl, the fire is just a fire. You'll get burned very badly. Arms out."

Anna looked doubtfully at Percy's lovely dagger. "This was so much easier after all that scotch."

"I have lots of scotch," Percy said, glancing to a wooden case by the wall. "Would you like some before you go?"

"No," Eve said sternly. "No one's drinking. What's wrong with you, Percy?"

Percy's eyes snapped over to Eve. "No drinking? For *days*?"

"No." Eve shook his head. "None. Absolutely not. This is serious."

"Yes, I'm beginning to see that," Percy muttered. "All right, well, arms out."

Candide and Anna pushed their arms out straight, closed their eyes and turned their heads towards each other to block out the pain.

"Ow."

"Ouch!"

"Just let it drip," Percy instructed.

"Yeah, I know, but, ugh," moaned Candide.

"I have bandages today," Aubrey piped up. "And we can do stitches."

"So civilised," Anna replied, eyeing the carton of scotch.

They let Aubrey do what she needed to do, while Percy added his herbs to the blood. He said the incantation, and just like that, it was time to go.

Eve checked over their weapons, and everyone else's, and his own, and he tried and failed to be stoic, and ultimately he and Anna's goodbye was nothing more than a long kiss, a few tears, and a very strong reluctance to let go of the hand that pulled away from him.

CHAPTER 35
A FEW MINUTES IN HELL

As they emerged from the fire, Candide's disappointment was as palpable as Anna's relief. "It's just… It just looks like a cave."

Anna cast her eyes over the rough, dark stone walls, which curved around and formed an oppressive ceiling not very far above them. All was grey, except some greenish-blackish, unsavoury-looking mould scattered here and there. Underfoot was dirt and rocks, such as one might find in any regular cave on Earth. "Is this really Hell? You don't think we've come to the wrong place?"

The tunnel ran long and black in two different directions, further than their eyes could see, and there was no indication which direction would take them where they needed to be.

"It's cold, too," Anna said. "I thought it would be hot. Isn't Hell supposed to be hot?"

She looked back at the portal with a touch of longing. It was no more than a fire burning in the side of the cave wall, though very faintly, she could see the reassuring outline of shapes moving in the library.

"Let's explore. Joe did say it isn't that scary— Wait…" Candide tilted her head to the side. "Did you hear that?"

Anna listened. "Screams?" She listened some more. "Yeah. That seems exactly like the sort of thing you'd hear in Hell."

"Let's go that way then."

"Towards the screams?" Anna swallowed hard. "Sounds like a good idea."

"Oh, hang on." Candide halted her with a hand on her arm. "Let me do my magic thing."

"Yeah, okay. Do that." Anna stood back and watched as Candide shut her eyes. Her fists closed tight, and a few seconds later her eyes opened with their eerie green glow back in full force.

Candide focused on Anna, very serious, worried, curious, alarmed.

Anna's lips parted in fear. "What is it? What's wrong?"

"My magic…" Candide looked down at her hands as though she couldn't quite believe they belonged to her.

"What is it? Is it working?"

"It's working." Candide's surprise was quickly replaced by a disconcertingly confident smile. "It's working really well. It's… Anna, this is so odd, but… I feel more powerful down here."

The knowledge of Candide's magic working especially well in Hell did little to alleviate Anna's fear at that time. "M-more powerful?" she stammered.

Candide nodded slowly, then closed her eyes again, breathing deep of the stagnant cave air as though it was a fresh spring morning, a beauteous glow spreading all over her, a sensation which she seemed to savour. "I have the strangest feeling that… something's right, like…" She opened her glowing eyes again and looked at Anna with an unguarded happiness that Anna hadn't seen in Candide for a long time. "Did you ever go somewhere for the first time, but it felt like coming home?"

Oh fuck, Anna thought to herself, but she nodded and smiled and said, "That's really good, Candide. Keep your sword ready. Shall we go that way?"

Candide nodded her agreement. "I can't quite place the demon, but I think that's a good decision, anyway." And so they walked on through the long tunnel towards the sounds of lost souls being tortured for all eternity.

CHAPTER 36
SIX HOURS IN THE LIBRARY

Eve wiped the blood and sweat from his face, breathing hard as he pulled his knife free from the dead hellhound. "These things are so hard to kill. And what are we supposed to do with the carcasses?"

"Aubrey will be by in the morning with a cart for them all," Joe replied, sucking fresh air deep into his lungs. "Start another heap by the door. They can burn them over at the medical centre."

"Can you imagine the smell?" Percy cut the final piece of sinew free and pulled a leg off the beast. "All that hair burning. How's she going to explain that?"

"I'll clean the floor again," Eve muttered. "It's getting too slippery to fight."

"Yeah, no, watch out," Joe called. "Some kind of tentacles are coming through."

"Again?" Eve sighed, picked up a hatchet, and went to work on the thing.

CHAPTER 37
TEN MINUTES IN HELL

"This tunnel just never ends," Anna whined. "Do you think that's the actual Hell? Like, we're condemned to walk through this tunnel forever, and we think we're getting somewhere, but we never will?"

"You watch too much television," Candide replied.

"I think I would actually like something to jump out and attack us at this point. I'll probably die of boredom otherwise."

Candide clacked her tongue and pulled Anna back to their former conversation. "Okay, so, Freddy Krueger, Jason Voorhees and Michael Myers."

"Seriously?"

"Deadly serious."

Anna breathed out long over her lips, thinking hard about the difficult choices. "Kiss Jason, kill Michael, marry Freddy."

Candide sent across a fierce side-eye. "You would marry Freddy Krueger?"

Anna shrugged. "I think he'd be a better conversationalist."

"What's wrong with you, Anna?"

"I don't want to have to kiss him, though. Do you have to kiss the one you marry?"

CHAPTER 38

TWELVE HOURS IN THE LIBRARY

"Coffee!"

"Oh Aubrey, thank God for that," Percy said.

"You look so rough." Aubrey passed the cups over, wrinkling her nose. "And the smell in here…"

A loud crash sounded in the corner as Joe began to throw huge chunks of monster and demon into a large black plastic box. "We have about twelve carcasses waiting for you. Maybe more. And some other bits and pieces. They're kind of chopped up, so we lost count. But yeah, they smell."

"Thanks," Aubrey murmured, "but, um, did you remember deodorant?"

"What? Really?" Eve sniffed himself disgustedly. "Ugh, it's this fire. It's so hot in here. And all the killing things."

"I've got an hour." She crossed the room to him, holding out her hand for his weapon. "I'll stay and watch things while you freshen up a bit."

Eve wafted the collar of his shirt about, trying to cool off a little. "No, it's all right. I'm sure it won't be that much longer."

"No." Aubrey, too close to enjoy his scent half as much as Anna would have, said, "Seriously. Go."

Eve relented with a heartfelt "Thank you," and handed Aubrey the bloody hatchet, stumbling to the bathroom with his coffee.

Percy joined Joe, throwing carcasses into the box. "You too. Then lie down and take a rest. You'll need some sleep."

Joe laughed softly. "Thank you, but I can't sleep in the middle of all this."

"It's fine." Percy pulled the head from Joe's arms. "It will slow down now it's daytime, anyway."

Joe took the head back. "That doesn't sound right to me."

"I'm absolutely sure of it." Percy snatched the head again and threw it into the box decisively, before turning Joe with a firm hand. "I've spent a lot of time studying this, you know. And you need to recharge for tonight."

Joe leaned into the hand Percy held against his back. "You're sure?"

"Yes. Freshen up and rest." Percy slid the hand over his shoulder, around his neck, and planted a light kiss on his lips.

Mollified, Joe sighed out, "All right," and wandered off to the bathroom, too exhausted to put up more of a fight.

"That's a relief," Aubrey said, watching him go.

With some effort, Percy turned his attention to her instead of Joe's handsome form. "What?"

"That they stop coming as much in the daytime. Your pile of corpses is pretty terrifying, to be honest."

"Oh, that." Percy threw another leg in and snapped the box shut as he waited for the door to close behind Joe. Then he said, "Actually, I lied to him. If anything, it will be even worse now. Cancel your classes and ready your blade."

CHAPTER 39
FIFTEEN MINUTES IN HELL

"I don't want to have to kill Kafka!" Candide cried. "He was depressed enough as it is."

"Well, I'm sorry, you should have thought about that before you kissed Jane Austen."

"Wait!" Candide grabbed Anna's arm. "Look, there's a path. It's this way. I'm sure of it!"

"We're leaving this tunnel? I'm comfortable in the tunnel now." She looked around at the all-too-familiar landscape. "I feel like we should leave some breadcrumbs or something if we're going in a new direction."

"Lipstick?" Candide smiled.

"Labyrinth! Love that movie. But no. I have nothing. I'll just…" Anna took one of her knives and attempted, unsuccessfully, to mark the wall with it. "This is bullshit. Will your magic work to get us back?"

Candide shrugged and tugged at her arm. "Let's worry about that later."

With a small rumble in her throat akin to a whine, Anna let Candide lead her down the new pathway.

CHAPTER 40
EIGHTEEN HOURS IN THE LIBRARY

"Just ditch the shirt, Eve," Percy snapped, wiping his bloody dagger clean.

"No!" came the stern reply. "I'm keeping it on. I feel like I'm always losing shirts whenever we do anything. They always get ripped or I leave them behind or we need them for some reason. Something always happens to them. And they're expensive."

Joe shook his head sadly, looking Eve over. "It's ruined, anyway. I don't want to have to tell you, but that blood isn't going to come out."

"Nothing gets demon blood out," Percy agreed.

"It's way worse than human blood," Joe added.

"Is that why priests always wear black?" Eve asked.

"I can't let you in on church secrets." Joe smiled. "But the collars, I have to soak them all the time. Unless it's demons. Then I have to get a whole new one."

"Ugh, it's so hot in here." Eve threw another log onto the roaring fire. "All right. Fine. I'm just going to do it."

"That's more like it," Percy said as Eve pulled the soaking-wet shirt from his oppressively hot body. "Go rinse it now. You might still save it."

"I'll be two minutes," Eve called over his shoulder.

"We've got it," Percy replied. "Save your shirt. We'll kill things."

As Eve disappeared into the restroom, Joe and Percy both paused what they were doing. Their eyes locked, and in an instant, the scorching gothic library faded into nothingness between the two of them.

"I don't think you need your shirt either," Joe said.

"The feeling's mutual," Percy replied.

Within seconds, they had had ripped the shirts from each other's heaving chests and were locked in a passionate embrace, Percy's hands deep in Joe's dark curls, running over the scars on his back, Joe's hands sliding eagerly over Percy's hot, wet, hard, rippling muscles. Joe shoved Percy down onto the lounge and was on top of him, their lips pressed hard, his hand tugging at Percy's belt, even though they both knew they couldn't possibly go as far as they wanted to that night.

A millisecond later, they were shocked out of their romantic diversion by the death cries of some odious creature or other.

"I'm not sure that was even two minutes," Eve muttered, throwing the carcass into a box.

"Sorry," Percy muttered.

"I wish Anna would come back," Eve sighed.

CHAPTER 41
TWENTY MINUTES IN HELL

"How many are there?" whispered Anna, looking out from their hidden alcove in the rock.

Before them were the first creatures they had seen since they entered Hell. The hideous beings occupied a large, craggy opening deep within the cave, the walls dripping with slime and stinking abominably. It had grown increasingly hot as they left the main tunnel, and Anna and Candide were sweating heavily. The smell of sulphur permeated the air, making every breath harsh and sickening, and finally they could see the fire and lava that Hell is so famous for, bubbling in deep pools and running in small rivers here, there and everywhere.

"At least five." Candide ducked back down. "Five that I can see. Do you think we can take them?"

"I don't think we have much choice."

Suddenly, they heard a noise behind them.

A demon.

Anna supposed it was a demon.

She had never before seen a demon in its corporeal form, other than those in the cave.

"It's you!" the demon cried.

Before they could take the time to exchange worried glances, Anna turned her axe over and belted the thing in the stomach with the blunt end. Candide approached the fallen creature and shoved her sword under its chin. Then they exchanged worried glances.

"What did it say?" Candide asked.

"It's you!" the demon repeated, only louder, and with a flush of hot adrenaline they realised the other nearby demons had heard and were moving quickly towards them.

"Fuck!" Anna whispered.

"Time to fight." Candide pushed her blade straight forward, slitting the demon's throat, while Anna gripped her axe tight in readiness.

CHAPTER 42

TWENTY-FOUR HOURS IN THE LIBRARY

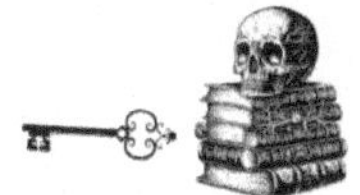

Percy's voice was thick, his cheek smooshed against the couch. "No, I'm getting up."

"Just take another hour," Eve insisted. "We're fine."

"Yep." Aubrey yawned. "We can take them."

Percy sat up anyway, rubbing his bleary eyes. "When is your mother going to get here with the hard drugs?"

Eve looked over at him with a withering scowl. "I'm not taking drugs this week."

Percy rolled his tired eyes. "Don't be stupid. Not even love can defeat sleep."

"Just… have some of my Adderall," Eve said. "It's in my bag. Top pocket."

"You don't need it?" Joe asked.

"There's a whole box."

"Perfect." Percy walked over and began rummaging through Eve's satchel.

"I think you're being ridiculous though," Eve said, watching him. "It's only been a day."

Percy threw himself back down on the lounge next to Eve and began cracking pills out of the packet. "And a night. And the days prior to that. I've barely slept all week. We had to kill all those skeletons. And there was the vodka. And then Joe kept me up all night."

Joe's frantic eyes ran to Eve and back to Percy. "You're going to tell him just like that?"

"It's all right, Joe," Eve replied. "He already told me everything."

Joe's cheeks, already pink from the heat, turned a worrying shade of red. "Oh. Thanks for that, Percy."

Percy crushed the pills with the back of his dagger. "It was pertinent information at the time."

"Yeah," Eve said, fighting off a blush of his own. "It's weird to say, but it really was."

Percy cut off Joe's response. "Joe, did you want some Adderall?"

Percy's perfectly innocent-looking face got about two seconds of Joe's ire before he relented through sheer fatigue. "Yes. Please. Aubrey, do you want some?"

"No," she said, eyeing the dubious white powder. "Though, I hope no one minds me saying, I thought Lady Worthing might offer a little more help with all this than hard drugs."

"Welcome to my childhood," Eve yawned.

Percy climbed to his feet. "All right, you both lay down and rest. I'm wide awake now."

Eve collapsed onto the couch immediately and was asleep within seconds. Aubrey took the other couch and nodded off very shortly after.

CHAPTER 43
TWENTY-FIVE MINUTES IN HELL

Anna and Candide sprinted forward into the opening, ready to battle. There were more demons behind them. Others poured in from holes and alcoves and crevices all around. Within seconds, they were surrounded by perhaps one hundred demons—perhaps more. They turned, pressing themselves together, back to back, ready to fight to the death.

Anna held her axe high, her knuckles white with fear as she looked over the hideous mob, a sea of scarlet skin and terrifyingly sharp teeth, scales and horns and black and yellow eyes, their inscrutable faces watching, waiting, as they silently planned whatever it was they were about to do.

"I'm so sorry," Anna whispered.

"Stop saying sorry," Candide whispered back.

Anna would have said it again, but at that exact second, the demons all fell to the floor, began to cower, to cry:

"The chosen one!"

"She has arrived!"

"The chosen one!"

Candide turned and looked at Anna with a mixture of shock, apprehension, and even a small modicum of respect. Anna was thankful to see it there; it buoyed her spirits considerably. She cast her eyes around at the demons, the ghastly creatures crawling in the filth, climbing the slimy walls, slithering all around. It was a terrifying sight, to be sure, but she was here now and…

She was the chosen one.

She understood, very suddenly, that she must have known it to be true all along. Somehow. Somewhere deep inside, she briefly reflected, her survival instinct had been leading her to this extraordinary fate the whole time. She realised now that she had always known she was destined for some form of great-ness. All the suffering, all the pain, everything must have been for this reason. Finally, it all made sense. Her moment had arrived and she would right all the wrongs of her life and walk boldly, with her soul and with her friends, into a better future.

Anna stepped forward with her axe, while Candide hung back, carefully brandishing her sword, ready to battle whichever of the hideous creatures should try to challenge Anna's newly discovered supremacy.

Anna looked around proudly at her dominion of rocks and slime and oozing orange liquids. Was she to rule all of this?

"It is I, Anna——"

"What is it you want?" snapped a small, ugly, stinking creature with too many eyes to count.

"Uh, I have come to——"

"You dare speak for the chosen one?" a demon cried.

"You dare interrupt?" another demon yelled.

"Guards! Seize her!" a third screamed.

Two of the more hideous looking beings started forward. A look of panic was exchanged between the two women, and Candide stepped forward in Anna's place, holding her sword defensively. "Touch her and I'll kill you all!"

A sea of gasps filled the room. Anna turned to behold Candide with fierce embarrassment, and more than a touch of horror.

"This is Anna," Candide yelled. "She's my... servant. My favourite servant! And you're not to go anywhere near her!"

"Guards! Stand down!" a demon yelled.

"We mean you no disrespect, my lord," another said.

The title drew a smile from Candide, who was abruptly enjoying herself in Hell far more than she had thought possible. She ran her eyes, her glowing green eyes, around the room. She lifted her sword high into the air. "Bow down!" she yelled.

At once, all fell to the floor, averting their eyes, cowering before her. Candide's face showed nothing but excitement and delight as she looked over at Anna.

"Me too?" Anna whispered.

"No. You're good there."

"Okay." Anna blushed. "Thanks. My lord."

Candide didn't bother to hide her smirk. "You there!" She pointed her sword randomly at a group of perhaps twenty creatures of Hell. "Bring me the demon who dared to inhabit the body of Evelyn Worthing."

More gasps. More averted eyes. Shaking hands and tentacles. Whispers.

"What are you whispering about?" She pointed to a creature that appeared to be some sort of leader. "Tell me now or die."

"My lord, I beg of you, take pity," the thing sobbed. "We need… We need only the name of the demon and we shall bring them forth immediately."

"Of course." Candide nodded grandly. "Anna! Tell us his name."

"I don't…" Anna mumbled. Anna paused. Anna ran a lock of hair behind her ear with nervous fingers. "Sorry, I never got his name."

"Goddamn it, Anna," Candide snapped. "That's like rule number one for dealing with demons."

"No one tells me these things!"

Candide sighed heavily before addressing the demons again. "Bring me every demon who has been to Earth in the last month."

More gasping and wringing of hand-like appendages.

"What? What now?" Candide spat.

"My lord, that's…" The demon shuddered with fear. "That's all of us."

"Seriously?"

"Of course. You—you are the chosen one. You would know this." And the thing made a little more eye contact than Candide was comfortable with.

"I do. I do know that." She threw her hair back and stood extra tall, pointing her sword at the one who had looked at her the wrong way. "You. Come here."

"Me?"

"Yes." She kept her sword levelled at the creature. "You."

The demon looked around anxiously, then slumped off its rock, half-crawling, half-lumbering towards her.

"Closer," Candide said as she looked down her nose at it.

The creature, staring at the floor, hobbled closer.

"Closer," she said.

It moved slowly, unwillingly, ever closer, until it was just beneath the point of her sword. A triumphant smile lit her beautiful face and Candide brought the sword down hard and fast, decapitating the creature in one slice.

The room filled with screams, fights, creatures clawing at one another to escape.

"Silence!" she shouted.

All was still.

"You!" She pointed two fingers at another of the demons as her eyes lit a shade brighter. Then with a twist of her hand, she drew two of its five eyes slowly forth from its head, the revolting sinew stretching and twisting as the creature screamed in agony, until she flicked her wrist back and its head exploded entirely.

"Fuuuuuuuck," Anna breathed involuntarily.

Candide wasn't the least bit distracted. "You have five Earth-minutes to bring me the one who inhabited Evelyn Worthing or you all die!"

The creatures ran about in a panic, trying to flee the room, all terrified and with only the instinct of survival to push them on.

"Horribly!" Candide added.

Somehow they moved faster still.

"And you there!" Candide swished her hand back and one of the creatures was frozen in its tracks. When only they and that creature were left in the room, Candide lowered her voice substantially. "You will bring me Charlotte and Marcel Lenoir."

Anna's stomach sank to her knees. Now Candide's very strong desire to be the only person to accompany Anna to Hell made a lot more sense.

"You have two Earth minutes," Candide called after the demon.

Anna stood very still and very quiet next to the chosen one, who felt like visiting Hell was a homecoming, whose powers were appallingly powerful in this space, and who had never breathed a word of her true intentions to any of her friends.

They waited together in perfect silence as they watched the creature slither away.

Then more silence, until Anna gathered the courage to ask softly, "You came for your parents?"

Candide's smile was reassuringly embarrassed, and gorgeously familiar. She was still, absolutely, hopefully, to Anna's eye at least, the same Candide. "No. No and yes. I may as well take them too, right? Since we're here, anyway."

Anna had never been good at not saying what she was thinking. "Candide, I don't want to be awful, but… They don't have bodies to go back to. What happens—"

"It can't be worse than Hell." Candide refused to look at Anna from that time, so they remained exactly as they were in the cavernous space, only the drip-dripping of some kind of sludge from the walls and the occasional bubbling of lava to break the awkward tranquility. That and the intermittent screams of damned souls.

After a time, Anna threw out, "I can't believe you're a chosen one."

Candide turned to Anna excitedly. "It's pretty brilliant, isn't it?"

"Actually, no." Anna laughed. "I can believe it. It suits you perfectly."

"How great is this?" said Candide.

"So great," said Anna. And she tried very hard to believe it.

CHAPTER 44
THIRTY HOURS IN THE LIBRARY

"Speed makes me tetchy," Eve snapped.

"You can just take a Valium to balance it out," Joe replied gently. "I have plenty."

Eve shook his head resolutely, eyeing the fireplace with hopeful anxiety. "No. I'm not taking anything until they get back. I'm just going to carry on like this."

"Coffee," Aubrey called.

"Thank God," Eve replied.

"It's all just drugs," Percy mumbled, rearranging his neat line of white powder.

Joe pointed towards the fireplace. "Look, Aubrey, you wanted to see a basilisk?"

She looked over delightedly at the creature just coming through. "So that's what they look like. I was beginning to think I'd never get to see—"

Percy finished his line and threw his dagger across the room, killing the creature in one blow. "Get that for me, would you, Eve?"

Eve groaned deeply, then ripped the dagger free. "Sorry, Aubrey." He dragged the corpse across the room and hacked into the thing, covering himself in blood-spatter, before adding several more pieces to her box of monster detritus.

CHAPTER 45
THIRTY MINUTES IN HELL

"Charlotte and Marcel Lenoir are not here."

Candide tried and failed to hide the mix of emotions that hit her with the demon's message. After all, how could she be disappointed that her own parents didn't number among those condemned to an eternity of torture? Her weak voice asked, "Are you sure?"

"Very sure. They have never been here."

Anna spoke up to fill the stretching silence. "Then where are they?"

"Forgive me, I do not know. They are not residents of Hell, nor have they ever been."

Candide let the creature scamper away with its life. Anna waited for her to say something about it, but she refused, so Anna squeezed her forearm and Candide tilted her head against Anna's. Anna, by way of changing the conversation, said, "I wonder when we can kill this guy. It feels like it's taking forever."

She regretted her words immediately.

They heard it before they saw it. Two huge feet slamming down on the earth, then a dragging sound—the harsh, heavy breaths of a gigantic demon.

Candide and Anna made as much noise as a potato as they took in the enormity of the hideous thing they would have to fight. It was all muscle. It looked as though it had no skin and was thick red and yellow sinewy meat all over, with the ripple of its spine, pectorals, thighs and buttocks all exposed. The surface was pock-marked and blistered and leaked pus from pustules in such a way it seemed as though it must have been painful for the thing to walk or stand or exist at all. It was humanoid, somewhat, with two big, bulging, round eyes, and two long, pointed ears reaching far back behind its sloping head, and when it spoke, its horrifyingly long, forked tongue sucked and slurred all about its words and its sharp, foul teeth. Its voice was so deep they both felt the vibration in the pit of their stomachs when it spoke. "Challenger… It is time to meet your fate."

Up went all kinds of slapping and screeching that seemed to serve as some sort of enthusiastic applause in that damned place.

"Is that still you?" Anna whispered. "Or is the chosen one different from the challenger?"

Candide shook her head, shrugged her shoulders, and kept her eyes and sword on the demon.

"Okay… I'll just…" Anna stepped forward with her axe held high. "It is I, Anna James—"

"You dare to speak for the challenger?" cried one demon.

"Silence, servant! Or your tongue will be removed from your head!" screamed another.

Candide's eyes widened in fury, then she did her hand thing and pulled the offending creature's tongue completely out of its head, at which point Anna, appropriately mollified, said to Candide, "I think you're the challenger too."

Candide stepped forward in Anna's place. "Who do I have to kill?"

"Me." The giant demon lumbered forward into the middle of the opening. It was perhaps twenty times Candide's size.

Sword still trained on her rival, Candide walked closer. "Are you the one who killed Evelyn Worthing?"

"I am the one who killed him. I am the one who resurrected him. I am the one who owns her soul." He pointed a long, black, curling claw straight at Anna, and she shuddered, beholding the hideous beast. This was the thing she gave her soul to. The thing she almost pledged her mortal life to. The thing she kissed and almost made love to.

No, she reminded herself.

It was handsome, virginal, Catholic Joe she had done those latter things to.

Then she shuddered again.

"Anna," it drooled, "it is good to see you. Though you are here a little earlier than expected." Its meaty arm did a circle of the cave. "Welcome to your forever home."

"No," Candide said. "Anna's home is with me. I'm taking her and her soul back to Earth, but first, I'm going to kill you. And I'm going to enjoy it."

Then Candide did her hand thing. She pointed all five fingers out long at the demon's face, scrunched her hand into a fist, twisted it over and pulled.

And nothing happened.

Anna started, "Was that—"

"I don't know!" Candide pointed her hand at one of the smaller creatures, and with a flick, pulled an arm off. Ignoring the screams, she tried focusing her power on the demon in front of her again.

Nothing.

She pressed her lips hard together. "Fine. Demons, kill him now!"

The smaller demons stayed perfectly still.

"Do it, or I'll kill you all!" Candide yelled.

Still nothing, except now the low rumbling of the huge demon's mocking laughter.

"Fuck this," she muttered. She used her powers to throw a group of the smaller demons at the enormous beast. But with a wave of his finger, the lot were dispatched into a river of lava where their death-screams were more than enough to disconcert Anna and Candide.

Even if the demon's face was that of a monster and not a human, the expression of ridicule was readily discernible. "You are not yet strong enough to fight a creature like me. And now, thanks to Anna James, you never will be."

"Me?" Anna looked from the creature to Candide and back again. "What did I do wrong this time?"

CHAPTER 46
THIRTY-SIX HOURS IN THE LIBRARY

"It's not that I especially want to get married or anything," Eve reflected, leaning his beautiful, sweaty self against the mantelpiece of the fireplace, "but I want to do something special for her, you know? And that seems to be the thing people do, giving each other rings."

Aubrey flicked her sweaty hair back, sending a shower of blood, not her own, over Eve. "There's no faster way to piss off a woman who doesn't want to get married than to propose to her."

Eve wiped the blood from his cheek. "No, I know. I would never want to put her in a position like that. I just want her to know how much I love her."

Joe threw himself down on the lounge and lit a cigarette. "You've been killing Hell spawn for days to help her get her soul back from a demon. I think she knows."

"Yeah, but…" Eve turned his lovely head upwards and stared off into the dark recesses of the library, thinking. "I mean… something *special*."

Percy also lit a cigarette and leaned against the other side of the fireplace. "Evelyn, you are fast becoming one of the dullest men of my acquaintance."

Eve scowled at him. "Well, what do you want to talk about? Demons again? I'm sick of talking about demons."

"Ugh, here's another one," Aubrey said, advancing confidently with her scythe.

CHAPTER 47

THIRTY-FIVE MINUTES IN HELL

"Candide, The Black. The Challenger. The Chosen One. And you: stupid, useless, Anna James," the demon laughed. "The weakest link in the chain. So easy to lead, so easy to manipulate, and the only person incompetent enough to bring Candide Lenoir straight to Hell, right where I wanted her." Then he laughed some more while Anna turned a nauseated shade of white.

"Oh. Oh shit…" she whispered. "What did I do?"

"You did everything you were supposed to do," the demon cackled.

Anna stared back at him, aghast. "I was supposed to lead her to Hell? To *you*?"

"No." Candide shook her head confidently, but that confidence somehow seemed a little false under Anna's distraught eye. "He's lying. I chose to come. This was my decision and you know that."

"But only because I lost my soul!" Anna cried. "Which I traded for Eve. Because he killed Eve. And because… because…" Before Anna could lose herself entirely retracing each and every step that had led to them both being in Hell on that glorious spring day, the demon cut through her thoughts.

"Because you're a very bad person, Anna. When I offered Candide a deal, she wouldn't take it. Then I tried to take the Necronomicon, which would have stopped her from coming into her full power, yet somehow you thwarted my plans. But I learned something that day. What I discovered is that you, Anna, all along, were the sickness that would lead to her destruction."

"A sickness?" Anna whispered.

"A plague on your friends!" he shouted gleefully.

"So everything that happened…" Anna crossed her guilty arms over her churning stomach. "That whole time you were just using me to get to Candide?"

"The important thing was always, simply, to stop her. While I toyed with you, she gained just enough power to think she had a chance down here. To believe she could protect you. To believe she could protect Evelyn Worthing." The creature let out another hideous laugh. "Evelyn Worthing… He *will* be devastated when neither of you return. Mostly because he knows you'll both suffer the worst possible fate any human soul can suffer down here. With me. But don't worry. He'll soon be dead, too. But not before I do a deal with him to obtain his soul."

Candide scoffed at the odious beast. "He would never do that."

The demon's golden eyes burned into Anna. "He would do it for her."

CHAPTER 48

FORTY-TWO HOURS IN THE LIBRARY

"They're both dead. They're both dead, I just know it."

"Eve, darling, stop crying," Percy said, wrapping a hand around Eve's bulging biceps. "I promise, they're going to be fine."

Eve shoved him off. "You don't know that! How could you possibly know that?"

"Eve, if you don't get up off the floor, one of these slugs is going to kill you," Joe offered.

"Good! I'd rather die by venomous slug than live without them."

"Get up off the floor right now, Evelyn!" Percy yelled.

Eve stood up begrudgingly and wiped his face, then he set about stabbing slugs again.

"You need to man up," Percy continued, kicking a particularly large slug across the room. "You have no idea what they're dealing with, and I guarantee you neither of them are sitting on the floor in a pitiful heap crying about you."

CHAPTER 49

FORTY MINUTES IN HELL

"No, not Eve!" Anna cried. "Anyone but Eve! You can't have him!"

"Anna, stand up." Candide's irritated voice pulled her, somewhat, back to her senses. "If you're done listening to this, let's just kill him and go home."

"Yes. Yes, I think that's a very good idea." Anna jumped to her feet and ran towards the demon with her axe. The thing swung its tail around and hit her full in the face, not only knocking her off her feet, but giving her a mouthful of foul liquid from the pustules that burst against her lips.

"Oh!" she spat. "God!" she convulsed. "That's absolutely disgusting," she retched. "Bastard!" She ran forward with her axe a second time, and she very nearly made contact, until he swung one of his long arms down and floored her with a strong blow to the ribs. The axe was thrown across the room into a wall, where it broke into three pieces.

All this time, Candide was doing her best to use her powers. The other creatures she could still destroy easily, but any she attempted to throw at the demon wouldn't move at all now. Rocks in the cave reacted the same way. She gave up in frustration and ran into battle, the sharp tip of her sword aimed at the beast's belly.

He didn't even need to sidestep. His arms and his tail were so long that before her sword could make contact, he brought a huge claw down from above and knocked her to the ground.

"Now, Anna," he slurped, "watch as I crush her skull."

Candide let out a scream as the giant thumb pushed her face hard against the jagged rocks.

"No!" Anna cried. "Please, no!"

A deep laugh burst from the creature as he held Candide so she couldn't move, and so Anna dare not move. He leaned his foul face above Candide, who struggled beneath his painful grip. "Now you learn, I am your master. You will submit, or you will suffer."

"Never," Candide seethed through gritted teeth, sharp rocks cutting deep into her cheek. "I'll never do anything for you."

A low, satisfied rumble escaped from deep within the demon. "Anna James, leave us."

The shock of the request made Anna sick to her stomach. "No. I won't. Candide, I won't leave you. Not ever."

The demon turned hateful eyes on Anna. "Leave her now, or I take Evelyn Worthing's soul."

"He would never let you do that," Anna said, knowing even as she said the words it was a complete lie. There wasn't a thing he wouldn't do for her or Candide.

The demon's hideous mouth turned up into a curious smile. "It seems you need a reminder of just how bad I can make things for you."

The beast waved a hand and Anna's brain felt like it was on fire. A thousand knives seemed to stab at her skull in every direction and she fell to the ground with a scream. But the pain of that was nothing compared to what she suddenly remembered. Everything the demon had done, everything she had done, everything that had happened to Eve. All her horrifying memories came crashing down on her in one eviscerating cataclysm.

The demon watched on, mesmerised by her pain, the same smile on its face, and Candide was forced to watch too, as Anna sat there in a stupefied flood of tears, gasping for air, sobbing.

"He's whole again," the demon prodded. "Just like you asked for him to be. If you go back now, you know they can make you whole, too. They can make you forget Candide ever existed. They can make *him* forget she ever existed, and then you both get your happy ending. It's a very small sacrifice after all, isn't it?"

"No," Anna whispered pleadingly, between sobs.

"I will keep your soul, but if you want to save the soul of Evelyn Worthing, if you want to live a long and happy life with him, if you don't want him to end up like he did, then go to him now. This is your last chance of happiness, before eternal damnation. Choose wisely. Choose now."

Anna looked up helplessly at Candide, still struggling against the demon's grip, tears running down her face. "Candide…"

Anna gasped as a loud sound echoed around the chamber. The sound of the demon clicking its fingers, once. "The portal is now closing. Run fast, or lose your life, and lose Evelyn Worthing's soul."

She searched Candide's face. "Candide…"

For the first time during the whole ordeal, tears slipped from Candide's eyes. "Anna, please… no…"

"I love you, Candide."

Anna sprinted with every ounce of strength and fear and desperation she had in her, never pausing to look back at the expression on Candide's face that would have stopped her in her tracks had she seen the moment she broke her best friend's heart.

CHAPTER 50

FORTY-EIGHT HOURS IN THE LIBRARY

Eve dropped the note and threw his head back against the couch. "Why didn't I just take the drugs hours ago? This is instantly so much better."

"Of course it is," Percy said. "Go freshen up. And don't wake Joe and Aubrey."

"I can't leave you here by yourself."

"I'll call if anything comes through. You smell again. Go."

"All right, I'll go." He paused to smile his handsome smile at Percy. "I want to smell nice when Anna comes back."

Percy passed a patient hand over his brow. "So you've said. Several times. Go."

The instant the door clicked closed behind Eve was, coincidentally, the instant Anna burst through the fireplace and fell over in a puddle of blood.

Percy pulled her to her feet. "Anna! Thank God." He turned expectantly to the fireplace. He turned back to Anna, a touch of panic in his eye. "Where's Candide?"

Percy was perfectly unaware that he was still holding her hands tight as he waited for her answer, but the alarmed manner with which she held his gaze, before withdrawing her own hands, elicited his quick, curious attention.

She averted her eyes as he studied her, then removed herself swiftly from the close interaction, running for the table in the centre of the room. "Candide's trapped in Hell and I'm going back for her. Don't let the fire go out."

At her words, Percy's gaze fell on the fireplace. His voice came hoarse and horrified. "Why is the portal closing?"

"It's the demon. He's closing it." Anna grabbed at whatever she could find on the table. "Is it these herbs? Do I need this bowl? I'll take the bowl. Will any knife do or do I need your special one?"

He was at her side, still thrown by her refusal to look at him. "Use anything. You just need blood from everyone who's going through."

"Good. I'll take it all back to Hell, I'll murder that fucker, we'll open a new portal and I'll bring Candide back." She finished throwing everything she could find into the bowl and ran to the fireplace, only to be repulsed by the heat of the flames. "Fuck! Fuck! Fuck! Fuck!"

Percy stood frozen to the spot, his skin taking on an unsavoury pallor. "Without these things, she can't get back through."

Anna stared hard into the fire for a moment, firming up her resolve, then she pulled herself together and started for the door. "I have to get these things to her. I'll make sure she can open it from the other side, but I don't know how long it will take and I need you to keep this side open, no matter what."

Percy arrested her movement with a swift arm around her waist before she could take another step. "Anna, what are you doing? Where are you going?"

She grasped his hands, freeing herself, but gripping him tight this time. There wasn't long. Every second was precious, but she had to tell him, so she did what she had been avoiding and looked straight into his eyes. "Percy, I'm going to see Aka Manto."

His words were swift and firm. "No, Anna. You're not."

She only nodded her head and tried not to let her fear get the better of her. "Please, don't tell Eve what I've done. And please…" She took a deep breath before pushing forward. "I need you to promise me you won't let him come into the bathroom in our building until… um… I'm sorry to have to ask you this, but will you check it first? For my… For my body? Or send Aubrey or Joe, but please, I don't want Eve to find me. Not like that. You understand, don't you?"

He refused to understand. "Anna, no. Not Aka Manto. He will flay you and hang you with your own skin—"

"He might not."

"He will!"

"It's all I can do." Her voice broke, so she pulled her hand away from him and made a tight fist, digging her fingernails deep into her palm in the hope the physical pain would wrench her away from her overwhelming emotions. "If he kills me, you can't let Eve see it. Promise me."

"No. We'll do the near-death thing. I'll go get Aubrey now. She's asleep up there somewhere——"

"We don't have time. Candide needs me right now. She's with the demon and he wanted her all along and I don't know what he's going to do to her. I'm taking this and we'll make a portal from the other side if I find her. *When.* I mean *when* I find her. Or if I don't make it… then I guess… that's all from us. So…" Her harsh whisper softened, and she held his hand tight again and looked up at him. "Goodbye Percy. It was so lovely to know you." She kissed his cheek, ready to fall apart with the safety and the scent of him, then said, "And one more thing. If Aka Manto does that, or if I get trapped in Hell, please don't let Eve remember me. Please. Make it like I was never here."

Percy shook his head, holding her hand to his heart. "Absolutely not. I'll come with you. We'll do it however you want, but don't ask me that. I could never do that to him."

She shook her head sadly. "You won't have a choice. The demon said it will offer him a deal to get me back and you know Eve would take it. You do because…" She hadn't wanted to tell him. She knew it would only hurt him if he knew, yet she had blurted out the words before she could stop herself, whispering, "Because you're the only other person who knows how bad things were."

At the sharp spark of pain in his eyes, she knew what she had done, and she turned to leave as though, had she been faster, he might not have caught it.

But she was stayed by the tone of his voice. She could never pinpoint exactly where it lay between surprise and sadness and heartbreak, but whatever it was, he only said, "You remember."

Anna turned back to him, ashamed of herself. Ashamed all at once that she had tried to keep something so important from him, betrayed him in that sense, but also ashamed of the impossibility of the situation. Her eyes filled with tears as she looked into his. "I remember… And I'm so sorry."

The thick silence sat heavy between them for several long, harrowing seconds until Percy whispered, "I miss you so much."

Anna held herself still a little longer, then took two steps forward and collapsed into his ready arms. Collapsed there because she believed it was the last time she would ever do it. Even if she survived Aka Manto, even if she came back unscathed with her soul and all her memories, it could never happen again. Not like that.

Percy's arms were tight around her, his lips against her hair, but he didn't kiss her. They had all made choices and there was, in practice, no going back, but in reality, just for those very few seconds, they had gone back, and she was in his home, safe and protected, and gathering all the strength she could before he, resolutely, could no longer be what he had become for her. They accepted the fact with no discussion or challenge, yet there was something deeply, permanently unsettled in both of them that insisted maybe, from that very first day, had things been a little different, he might always have been that for her. "I miss you, too," she whispered. Then she swiftly forced out the words, "Eve can't ever know."

Just as swiftly, he replied, "I would never tell him."

She held him a little tighter still. "I love him so much, Percy."

He wiped her tears away and firmed his own voice. "So do I. I'll take care of him."

"I know you will."

He lifted her chin with the side of his index finger, just as he had before. "Anna—"

She shook her head, because she knew what he was about to say, and in the stifling intimacy that held them together, even in the fervour of chaos, it was one fatal step too far. "I feel the same way about you." She squeezed his hand one last time, then slipped away, gone before he could say another word.

Percy made a very small figure standing in the centre of that great room, the huge fireplace burning incessantly behind him, staring into nothingness, all the strength gone out of him. He walked slowly over and bolted the door behind her, then turned back to see Eve.

Eve took in his tear-stained face and asked gently, "What is it? Did something happen?"

"No," Percy replied. He searched his brother's sweet, caring, lovely face. "Can you come here?"

Eve walked over to him. "Are you okay?"

Percy threw his arms around Eve and Eve held him tight. "It's nothing," Percy said, fighting to control himself. "Nothing at all."

CHAPTER 51
DRAG ME TO HELL

Anna ran through the door of her apartment and flung Candide's sheets from her bed. There it was: the *Necronomicon*. She grasped it and she was running back down the hall whispering over and over, "Please don't kill me, please don't kill me, please don't kill me…"

She halted at the bathroom door and took a deep breath. She let it go. She took another. She placed her hand on the door and pushed. It groaned deeply as it slowly swung wide to reveal four empty toilet stalls.

"Aka Manto? Aka Manto, are you in here?"

She went straight to the fourth toilet stall and inspected it. No sign of a ghost.

Hesitatingly, one by one, she pulled back the curtains from each of the shower stalls. All were empty. She closed and opened all the toilet doors. Still, he did not appear.

"Aka Manto? Please, can you come out? I'm sorry I never talk to you and I always ignore you. I just don't want to die, but… Oh. Sorry. Um."

High school. It wasn't that long ago. They had offered neither Latin nor French, so she had chosen the next best thing.

"Konnichiwa, Aka Manto. Watashinonamaeha Annadesu. Uh. That's maybe the limit of my Japanese there. Uh. Onegai, Jigoku? I think, I hope that means, please take me to Hell. Please?"

She looked around the room in despair before an idea popped into her mind. "Oh! Oh, got it."

She dashed into the cubicle and closed the door behind her, locking it automatically. She sat down on the toilet, holding the *Necronomicon* tight. "Okay, I'm here. I'm in the toilet stall, which is exactly where I need to be for someone to offer me toilet paper."

Still nothing.

"Aka Manto? Paper? Ah, no, you're not going to make me…"

Anna sighed and swallowed down her pride. She wondered vaguely what else she would do for these irreplaceable friends she had made less than a year ago and she stood again. She pulled her belt open and her hand was on her top button when she heard him. That familiar shuffle. She sat back down. She waited. She heard him approach. This was it.

Then silence.

Not quite silence. Her breath, harsh in her throat, in and out, in and out, her blood pulsing in her ears, her heart beating hard.

She saw a flash of his red robe under the door.

His voice was clear as day: "Akaikamiga hoshii desuka? Aoikamiga hoshii desuka?"

Red or blue toilet paper. Not yellow. Never yellow.

"None!" she replied. "Uh, nashi. Jigoku. Hell. I want you to take me to Jigoku."

Blades. She heard the sharp clash of at least two blades.

"Oh. Oh no. Uh. Please don't kill me!"

She looked up. The lock on the door was sliding open. "No!" She reached for it, but all her strength was no match for whatever supernatural force this was, and the latch slid open anyway.

"Oh fuck. Fuck!" She pushed herself as far back in the cubicle as she could. "Book! Take my book! I know you want it. Oh, what's the word for 'book'!" The door came open excruciatingly slowly. She watched, and she shook and she hyperventilated, then she screamed, "Necronomicon!"

The door paused.

"Aha! Everyone understands that word! Necronomicon! Totta? Take it!"

Now the door completed its procession, crashing open in one fast movement, and Aka Manto stood before her. His red robe reached from a hood over the top of his head, all the way down to the floor, covering his toes. He was nothing but red except where his face should have been. Instead of the face, there was a white porcelain mask, black holes for the eyes to look out, a black space for the speech, but too much darkness for her to see anything beyond. In his red, gloved hands he held two short and obviously exquisitely sharp blades and she shrank to look at them—to wonder what he was about to do to her. He let the knives fall to the floor with a clang. "Necro-nomicon?"

"Here, see?" She held it up. "I will give it to you. Take it. Totta. Get me to Hell. Necronomicon, totta, Jigoku, okay? Deal?"

Anna watched, transfixed, as he reached his hand up to his mask. He put two fingers in the eye-holes, a third in the mouth, and pulled it free.

Everything Percy had said was true.

He was knee-quiveringly handsome. His lips were full and his lashes were long around his dark brown eyes. A strong chin and high cheekbones, unutterably beautiful skin and straight dark brows, his glorious, thick black hair now breaking free of its confines as he threw his hood off.

This entire description, of course, is as nothing compared to what Anna saw that day. It defies the written word.

She gasped only once, then cast her eyes to the floor because she knew he didn't want her to look at him that way.

"Why do you want to go to Hell?"

"Oh! English!" Anna cried, happily. "Um. Okay, so my best friend in the world is trapped in Hell by a demon and I have to go save her."

"That's a very good reason."

"Thanks. I really love her and I have to get to her. I have to kill a demon and free her. This is her book, but, well, I hope she won't be too mad with me if we survive." She searched his too-beautiful eyes. "If I give it to you, will you help me?"

He offered a slow nod. "I will."

"All right." She squeezed the book tight one last time, then handed it over to Aka Manto.

Then she watched in horror as he reached into the folds of his cloak and drew forth a new and terrifying sword.

"No…"

His voice remained calm and steady. "The demon who was here, in this place. Is this the demon you mean to kill?"

"Ye-yes," she stammered, eyes glued to the impossibly long, shiny and keen edge of the weapon.

"Then take this." He held out the hilt of the sword for her. "I hate him too. I hate what he did to Evelyn."

"You…" She stared back in amazement. "You know Eve?"

"Evelyn is very kind. He came to talk to me. For a while. He left books for me. Then the demon took him away. This sword will help you kill it."

She accepted the sword with a shaking hand. "Oh. I didn't know that. I will kill it. Thank you." She tried a small, scared smile, and he smiled back with a kind nod. Then she asked, "So, what happens now?"

In an instant, the whole room began to shake. Anna pushed her arms against the walls of the cubicle to steady herself, then her breath caught in her throat as she slipped downward. The floor below her cracked open, the tiles parted, and all that was beneath was an increasingly huge and dark hole.

Seconds later, Anna was gasping for air as the fall onto the stone floor of the cave where her journey in Hell had commenced had knocked the air out of her completely. She clambered slowly and painfully to her feet, grasped her sword, and ran.

CHAPTER 52
EVEN LONGER IN THE LIBRARY

"God, this is boring," Eve said. "This book is so boring! Why is it, as soon as I take the drugs, nothing happens? It feels like hours of nothing. And I could have been sleeping this whole time."

"Do you want that Valium now, Eve?" Joe suggested.

"Why do you keep asking me that?" Eve snapped. "I'm fine. It's just this book is so goddamn boring."

Percy scowled at Eve, tap-tapping his foot on the stone floor all the while. "Evelyn, you have a whole library at your disposal and you choose to read James Joyce. You have no one to blame but yourself."

"It's a very important book," Eve mumbled.

"That doesn't mean it isn't boring."

"You're not supposed to say that."

"You just said it!" Percy spat. "It's a boring book! Just accept that it's a boring book!"

"I didn't! I—" Eve stared down at the copy of *Ulysses* in his hands. "I did, didn't I? Joe, maybe I will have that Valium."

"I think that's a good idea." Joe began rummaging through his belongings.

Eve stood. "I'll put some more wood on the fire."

Percy stood. "No, no, I'll get it."

Eve took a step. "No, I can do it."

Percy stepped in front of him. "No, let me."

Eve stopped. "Percy… I've noticed you don't seem to want me to put wood on the fire. And… And nothing has come through there in a really long time and…"

Eve's suspicious eyes locked with Percy's alarmed eyes. Eve made a dash for the fireplace. Percy held him back. Eve shoved him and ran and Percy caught him and they both fell over in front of the fire, at which point they engaged in a very messy if exceedingly attractive shirtless wrestle for fireplace supremacy until Eve kneed Percy in the stomach and pushed him off.

Eve's eyes grew wide with horror. "It's closed. Percy, why is it closed? You knew it was closed!" He turned back to Joe. "Did you know it was closed?"

"Detain him!" Percy cried, gasping for air.

"No," Joe said. "I'm not getting into a fight with Eve. You detain him yourself."

"What is going on?" Eve yelled.

Percy staggered to his feet. "Evelyn, I really need to go to the bathroom. Right now. It's an emergency."

CHAPTER 53
EVEN LONGER IN HELL

"Candide!"

"Anna!" Candide, until that time sitting bored on a rock, jumped to her feet. "I thought you left me!"

"Never!" Anna yelled back victoriously. "I would never leave you!"

She held Aka Manto's sword high in the air and Candide clapped her hands in delight before she turned to the demon. "I told you she would never do anything so stupid." She yelled across the room, "Anna, you're amazing!"

"Aw, thanks, Candide." Then Anna stretched her arm out long, pointing her sword at the demon. "Prepare to die."

All eyes turned towards Anna. A sea of gasps moved around the rocky chamber.

"The chosen one!" they yelled.

"The second challenger has arrived!"

"That's more like it," Anna said proudly, and it was with some confusion that she noticed Candide's face fall.

"You dare speak for the chosen one?" a demon screamed.

Anna turned green and her voice came in a weak croak. "What?"

"You dare to interrupt the challenger?"

She beheld the growing anger with increasing fear, unsure what to do next, until she heard the familiar voice from behind.

"Hey, gorgeous. What did I miss?"

And there he stood on a rocky outcrop, just as glorious and confident as ever, shirtless, muscles glistening in the red glow of hellfire, impossibly fresh and beautiful, no doubt smelling very nice, his handsome gun pointed unnoticeably slightly to the right of the space in the middle of the demon's eyes.

It was a very serious swoon. Not quite the swoon of secreted Keats on a spring morning, but very close. It wasn't just because he was exquisitely statuesque and heroic-looking in that moment, the glow of the lava lighting up his ethereal beauty in contrast against the black slime dripping from the walls of literal Hell, but more than that, Anna had the sudden and almost overwhelming realisation that although she now remembered every single horrible thing that had happened between them, she felt no fear of him. In a flood, she remembered the poem and the daffodil, running from skeletons with him. She remembered the yellow room and the lecture theatre. She remembered his complete, unerring faith in her, his complete adoration of her, his promises of a cottage and a cat, and every single time he had kissed her and placed his arms around her and told her how much he adored her. Above all, she remembered how safe and loved she had always felt with him since the first day they met. With Eve. Eve, who she had resurrected from the dead. Eve, who that demon had tried to take from her.

"Eve," Anna sighed.

"Anna!" Candide yelled, furiously.

"Candi!" Eve yelled back happily.

"Eve!" Candide snapped. "You're not supposed to be here! Anna, how could you be so stupid?"

"I didn't bring him!" Anna cried. "I left him with Percy. How did you get away from Percy?"

"I kicked him in the stomach!" Eve yelled back.

Anna gasped. "You didn't!"

"Just a bit. Then Joe made Percy tell me everything and Aka Manto brought me down."

"Aka Manto?" Candide and Anna cried in unison.

"Yes! He's so nice. When he's not killing people. But listen, should I go ahead and kill this demon, or do you two want to do it?"

The demon let go a deep, guttural laugh. "Thank you, Anna. Now I have them both."

"No," Anna protested breathlessly as a new terror crept over her. "No, I was—I didn't do this! I was trying to do the right thing—"

"When will you learn that you can never do the right thing?" the repellant voice threw at her. "You are rotten to the very core, Anna. Everything you touch will always turn to ashes because you are irretrievably impure. And now," he glowered, a hideously evil grin pulling across his foul face, "take one last look at your friends, and remember, this was all your fau—"

The demon's side burst open in a spray of pus and bile as a shot rang out across the cavern.

Anna's eyes snapped adoringly over to Eve, who jumped down from the ledge and walked to her as he packed more gunpowder into his gun. "Why are we listening to this thing? Let's kill it already."

"It's not that simple," Candide said.

Eve fired again, this time blowing a chunk off the demon's leg. "Why not?" he yelled over the screams of the beast as he packed in more powder and another shot.

"Because—" Candide started.

The demon roared furiously and stood tall. Eve and Anna stared with some alarm as the wounds began to close and heal in front of their eyes.

"Probably should have seen that coming," Eve said.

"Demon stuff," Anna whispered.

Eve stepped closer and kissed her cheek. "I missed you."

She smiled up at him. "I missed you, too."

"Eve, pay attention!" Candide called. "Apparently we're chosen ones and challengers, and we have to fight him in open combat. He says that's the only way we can defeat him, and I've been tricked into coming down here before I was at full power—"

"Full power?" Eve called back.

"Yeah." She used her magic to paint the wall with the innards of a small demon.

Eve scrunched his handsome face up. "What? That's not full power?"

"I know. I'm sorry I didn't tell you—" she began. She paused. She looked over his annoyingly unperturbed face. "Eve, have you taken something?"

He bit his lip and coloured a little. "Maybe…"

"Unbelievable!" she yelled. "Anna and I are trying to fight demons in Hell and you're all having a party up there!"

"No, it's not like that!"

"Has it even been an hour?"

"No, no! It's been three nights and two days on Earth and I've barely slept in maybe sixty hours and I have killed so many things and I was really worried about you both—and—and I know it's not relevant but Percy never stops talking and I can't tell you how irritating he is and I'm quite worried I'm going to start hallucinating soon—but I might be already hallucinating—to some extent—aural ones at least—but it doesn't matter anyway, I just really want to sleep soon, so please can we wrap this up and do a battle or whatever it is and go home already?"

Candide narrowed her eyes. "You seem tetchy."

"I'm not tetchy," he snapped. "I had a Valium."

"Okay. That's just great. All right." Candide hid her eyes in her hands for a few moments before she looked over at the demon and sighed out the words, "Let's just get this over with."

CHAPTER 54
FIGHT TO THE DEATH

"Candide Lenoir," the demon growled.

"Yeah," she muttered.

"Evelyn Worthing," it snarled.

"What?" he snapped.

"Do you both accept the challenge? Defeat me and you retain your souls and gain back the soul of Anna James. Lose, and you all die." He raised two thick arms. "And this, Hell, shall be mine."

"Yeah, sure, but we still don't know your name," Candide said.

The demon laughed menacingly. "My name is…" Anna waited on tenterhooks as the demon glowered back at them. "Mammon!"

"Are you kidding me?" Candide moaned, throwing her head back in anguish.

"The indignity!" Eve spat, turning his face away in disgust.

"What is it?" Anna asked quietly.

Eve curled his top lip in a move angry and sexy enough to give Percy a run for his money. "He's not even a proper demon."

Candide rolled her eyes. "He's a lesser demon."

"How dare you!" the demon roared.

"I'm just…" Eve searched for the best way to express himself. "I think 'ashamed' is the right word for this. All this bullshit, coming down to Hell, and it's just this guy. Demon of wealth or misplaced trust or something."

Candide nodded her disappointed agreement. "I thought we were going to be fighting Beelzebub or a proper demon like that."

"Right?" Eve replied. "Or Belial or someone exciting."

"Aren't they the same thing?" Candide asked.

"I don't know, but this is just… ugh." He aimed his gun and shot another round into the creature's giant belly, just for the sake of it. After the gargling howl and the expected ejection of blood and pus, the creature staggered to its feet and loomed over them as the wound began to heal again. Eve went on, "I don't see how this is a fair fight if he can keep doing that."

"No one said it would be fair," Mammon hissed. With that, he threw his arm back, tossing Eve into Anna, knocking them both to the floor, where Eve surprised Anna (not for the first time) with his agility, bracing her descent with his strong arms.

Candide dashed forward with her sword aimed at the creature's leg and managed to slice a deep wound into the thigh. The demon screeched and brought its tail around, knocking Candide off balance. It reached down, grabbing her by the neck with its claw, then pulled her to standing and slammed her against the wall. It leaned in close, peering into her face. "Your power is mine."

Instantly, Candide's eyes rolled back in her head. Her entire body shook, just as the demon's arm did, holding her tight. Eve ran forward with his newly loaded pistol and shot Mammon in the same arm. It let go at once, and Eve dashed to Candide's side, catching her before she could hit the floor, choking and gasping for air.

The creature turned its eyes on Eve and smiled. Even in its non-human state, Anna recognised the demon's evil grin. It was the same one he always gave her when he was about to do something especially horrible. Malignant pleasure. And Anna knew exactly what he was going to do.

The thing raised a finger before she could take a step and Eve froze in place, right there against the wall, with Candide in his arms. He stared into space, into complete nothingness, as one staring deep into an infernal abyss. His hands began to shake, his arms, his body.

His eyes met Anna's, nothing like the way he'd looked at her seconds earlier.

And she knew.

The demon had restored his memory.

She ran towards him.

"Seize her!" the demon yelled. Anna was immediately set upon by a dozen of the foul, smaller creatures. Aka Manto's sword was long, but it was light. She'd never touched a sword in her life, but her instincts moved her hand down on a sharp diagonal. The blade passed from the shoulder of one of the beings, slicing clear through his guts, which spilled out in a steaming heap on the group. She completed the movement, arcing up, and in doing so easily took both legs of the nearest creature.

A thing jumped on her back and she let out a scream as it bit hard into her shoulder. Frantically, she swished the sword back, and she managed to take the head of another demon, which rolled across the floor only to melt by the side of the lava river, but it was all her inexperienced hands could manage.

A nasty looking little red creature with more boils pulsating on its malodorous skin than could have been comfortable grasped her sword arm, bringing it down with its full body weight. Working together, another pulled her legs out from under her, and yet another shoved her over, where she landed hard on her stomach. In a last-ditch attempt to do any damage at all, Anna wrenched her arm free and threw the sword at the demon, glancing its side in a wide cut, drawing out a satisfying howl from the beast, before the sword clattered to the floor, far out of her reach. The demons overwhelmed her, holding her down on the sharp rocks, clawing at her body, pulling at her hair. She saw Candide, still gasping for air, flick her wrist towards them. But then she saw the bereft flicker of desperation on Candide's face, and Anna realised her powers were gone.

But then, something inside Candide rallied. Determination, perhaps, to hide her fear from Eve. She lay eyes of fury on the demon, then reached for her sword. The demon's huge hand closed on her and Eve at the movement, and he threw them, sending them crashing into a pile of rocks. Candide let out a scream as her back smashed hard against a boulder. Eve, another scream of pain as his side was ripped open on the sharp stone. He fought his way across to Candide, pulling her in close to him, the only thing he knew to do as he struggled to maintain control over himself and the situation. He held her, just as he had before, just as protectively as he ever did, but both Candide and Anna could see he was no longer the Eve that walked into the room. He was an Eve that had seen things no one should ever see. And he was an Eve with none of the fight left in him.

The demon lumbered towards them, his insidious eyes burning into Eve. "Do you understand now? Her soul is not one worth saving." Eve lifted his exhausted, despairing eyes to the hideous beast as it spoke. "You remember now all the things she made you do." Tears formed, and began a slow roll down Eve's cheeks, though he never looked away, and he never said a word, even as they came faster while the demon continued. "You see their faces still, don't you? All those people you killed. Do you enjoy the memory of their screams as much as I do?"

"Eve, don't listen to him!" Anna yelled. "You never did a thing wrong."

The demon turned on her. "Did you truly believe I wouldn't know the difference?" He laughed. "This is where you learn: never cross a demon." It gazed back down at Eve, who still watched him, but with an ever-growing hatred in his expression. "For every person you failed to kill to bring me fresh meat, I harvested those organs myself. With his hands."

"No," was all Anna could manage. All those people. How many people? How many people that she had lost count of with her clever workarounds, saving herself the horror of murder, only to pass it on to the person she was supposed to be protecting.

Eve, breathing hard, managed to force out the words, "He's lying."

But Anna knew from the look of miserable disgust on Eve's face, it was all true.

It was never just the things his hands had done to Anna, which was more than enough to drive a man like Eve to despair. There was so much more he had never breathed a word of. He was always, always protecting her. Even the day she walked out on him.

All Anna's hatred and self-reproach that she had worked so hard for so many months to overcome wrapped around her like a noxious fog.

Eve hadn't been able to tell her because she wasn't strong enough to hear him. He hadn't been able to tell her because he wanted so much to protect her, when she should have been protecting him. But she had never protected him. She let a demon use his body to do unimaginably evil things because she was too selfish and obsessive to let him go. She knew it, and when he finally raised his eyes to her, she knew he was thinking the same thing. That the person he trusted most in the world, the first person he ever let in, had betrayed his trust and condemned him to a wretched existence, just like she always knew she would.

The understanding that she had ruined Eve ruined Anna too.

They stared at one another across the room, broken, both knowing in their own way that it was over and completely unsalvageable. Their two hearts were breaking all over again, and neither cared at all about their own impending death anymore.

And that was the exact moment Candide noticed the gash Anna had made in the side of the demon's body.

The wound that was still bleeding.

"Eve." She placed a hand under his chin and turned his face towards her, looking deep into his eyes. "I need you now."

Whatever feelings Eve had for Anna, whatever doubts and loss and desolation he felt, all were at once subdued as he looked back at Candide, who still believed in him so unreservedly. His best friend. His sister, perhaps. The one person he had always managed to protect, and no matter what he had done in the past, or what he may have yet to do, there wasn't a thing he wouldn't do for her.

Eve climbed to his feet, turned, and landed a hard punch on the demon's chest, which did not a thing but distract it long enough to allow Candide to run to Anna's sword. She brought it down swiftly on the beast's tail and chopped the end clean off.

"That's more like it." She jumped back out of reach as the creature swung a claw around for her. "Anna, where did you get your sword?"

"A ghost gave it to me," Anna sniffled.

"Then it's supernatural. Eve!"

Eve understood the one and only shot they had, and dashed for Joan of Arc's sword. But the demon grabbed him with its gigantic claw and threw him back to the floor, where the weapon was thrown out of his grasp, landing in front of Anna. The beast stomped a gigantic foot down hard on his chest. Candide brought her sword down again, this time into the demon's leg, slicing a nice chunk off. It screeched and turned and lunged for her, enabling Eve to roll free.

At the same time, Anna rammed her elbow back as hard as possible, breaking the grip of one of the distracted creatures that were holding her, and sending it falling into another. The skin scraped off her arms as she wrenched her body forward along the jagged rocks towards the sword. Eve made another break for it, but was thrown to the ground again as Mammon caught him. Anna kicked at the things still holding her legs, then fell, crashing painfully over a rocky ledge as she escaped their grasp. She stumbled to her feet, took the sword in hand and bolted forward to Candide's side.

Finally, they stood together, swords at the ready, as the creature rounded on them.

"I'm sorry about all this," Candide said. "I didn't know I was a chosen one. Or that Eve was."

"There's no one I would rather die beside," Anna replied. "Whatever happens, I'm glad it was with you."

"Me too, Anna," Candide smiled. "But let's try not to die."

"Let's try."

Candide did a very impressive roll as the creature reached for them both, but unfortunately, Anna, who had none of Candide's agility, was caught off guard and her sword fell again to the floor as she was swept off her feet, crashing painfully to the ground. A shadow fell over her. She looked up to see the sharp, broken claws of the demon's gigantic foot coming down fast and heavy upon her.

Then she was standing.

And she was pressed hard up against Eve, who had pulled her to safety.

The creature let out a ghastly scream and clutched at its belly where its innards poured forth from the huge slice Candide made right across the thing, though Eve and Anna barely noticed.

Anna took in a soft gasp at Eve's sudden, unexpected closeness. She felt the heat of him against her skin, his breath on her cheek, and his lips trembled slightly as he looked down at her, the two of them together again with all their memories. Anna felt his grip loosen, and in a move as desperate as if their lives depended on it, she grasped the forearms that were gentle at her hips, wrenched them tight, and brought her two hands to his cheeks. "I love you so much. I'm sorry for everything that happened. I know I'm horrible and I do awful things, Eve, but I love you and I don't ever want you to go again."

"Even now?" he whispered above the pained screams of the mortally wounded brute leaking all over the floor. "After everything?"

"Forever. Just the same. And nothing will ever change that."

His face broke into a beautiful smile, all relief and hope and love, and as his sparkling violet-grey eyes stared into hers, he lifted his arm and fired into the creature's approaching face, covering them both with mucus and a smattering of brains and tongue. "I thought it was all over."

"It will never be over." She raised a hand to wipe away some demon pus from his temple. "If you'll have me."

"Forever. Anna, I love you more than life itself." A severed claw landed on them, and before it had time to hit the floor, they kissed.

"Let's kill it," she breathed.

"Swap," Candide called. She held out the hilt of Aka Manto's sword, which Anna took with more satisfaction than anyone had ever taken a sword.

She turned, and she sliced straight through the ankle of the beast, taking its foot off in one blow. The demon crashed to the floor with a howl. Eve smiled at her lovingly and reloaded his pistol. Candide swept in and took an arm off with Joan of Arc's sword, and though it made little difference now, Eve shot the beast again. Anna applied as much pressure as she could to a writhing leg, but when it wouldn't give, she threw a hopeful smile over to Eve.

He melted, even more than he already had, just to be near her again. He wrapped an arm around her waist and she leaned back against him, and he placed his hand on the hilt of her sword and pushed firmly. Together, they felt the whole thing give way, and as the demon cried out in agony, Eve kissed her neck and she turned and kissed his lips and Candide said, "You're both being really weird. Could you please stop what you're doing and help me kill it?"

Eve stepped back and loaded his gun again. Anna pushed her blade deep into the side of the creature and continued the cut Candide had already made from the base of the belly, all the way up to the neck. Candide smiled an acknowledgement and took the other side with her own sword. Then Anna reached over and traced her blade straight down the middle, and all the guts were set free. She dug the steel into the gaping cavity and then, quite forgetting herself, went about slicing off and ripping out every organ she could find. There were many to choose from, and given her substantial experience harvesting organs from humans, she found the process of comparison surprisingly fascinating. The creature was, in fact, quite still, by the time she realised how completely she and her sword were covered in blood. She looked over proudly at the pile of innards she had amassed, then she looked back and she saw Eve and Candide waiting patiently, indulgently.

"Do you think we should decapitate it?" Eve asked. "For good measure?"

"You can't be too careful with demons," Candide suggested.

"Let's," said Anna.

Approaching from opposite sides, Anna and Candide applied their blades and sliced back and forth, back and forth. Huge squirts of blood sprayed them as they severed the major arteries, but undeterred, they carried on until the lump that was the head rolled across the floor and hit Evelyn's boot. He steadied his gun and unloaded a round straight into the demon's face, blowing it to pieces.

This time, it did not heal.

A round of applause went up from the audience of creatures who had been entirely forgotten by Anna, Candide, and Eve.

"Mammon has been defeated!" they shouted. "All hail, the new rulers of Hell!"

CHAPTER 55
THE GREAT ESCAPE

Anna, Eve and Candide exchanged worried glances until the demon continued its speech. "That is, if they can defeat the next seven challengers, and thus, the prophecy will be fulfilled!"

Anna bit her lip, then asked, "Um… Do I have my soul back?"

"Your soul is returned. Make haste and depart, servant! The new challenger approaches…"

They heard the heavy steps in the passage.

Thud!

"Uh." Anna turned to Eve and Candide. "Did you two want to… rule Hell?"

Thud!

Eve shook his head sternly.

Thud!

"No," Candide said. "I really don't."

Thud!

"Then… fuck this prophecy?" Anna suggested.

Thud!

"Mmm," Eve agreed.

Thud!

"Fuck this prophecy," Candide announced.

And they all ran out of the cave and through the tunnel as swiftly as their many injuries would allow.

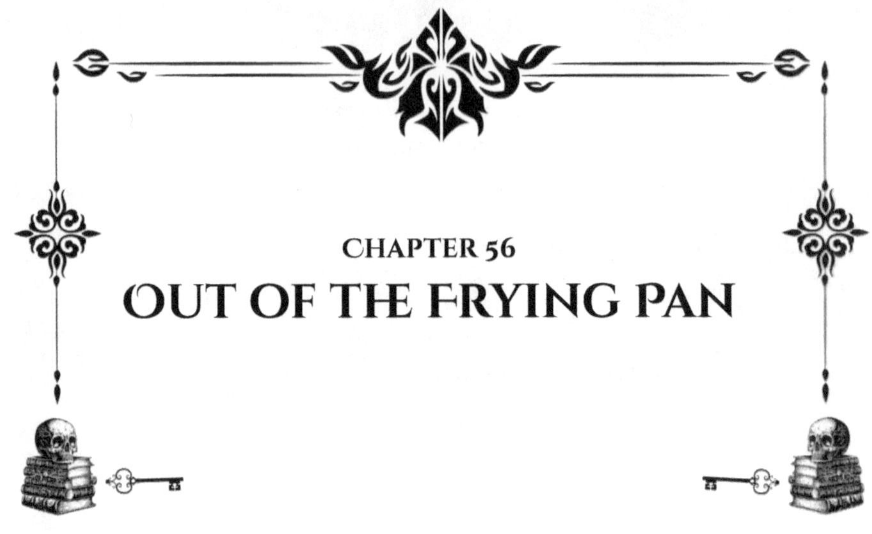

CHAPTER 56
OUT OF THE FRYING PAN

After they had been running for some time, Candide panted, "Do we have a plan for getting out of here?"

"Look!" Anna yelled. Straight ahead lay Percy's silver bowl and herbs.

"You never stop amazing me," Eve said proudly, as they pulled up at the bowl, bracing themselves against the grimy walls and each other to catch their breath.

"And how nice is my sword?" Anna wheezed.

"It's gorgeous," Eve replied breathlessly. "Like you."

Anna blushed very happily, cut and filthy and bloody as she was.

"Okay," Candide said, gathering herself, "Where's the spell?"

Anna shot her a bewildered, vaguely guilty look as she heaved in the stagnant cave air. "Huh?"

"The spell," Candide repeated. "You know, the words that will get us out of here and save all our lives. Where is it?"

"Uh. Um…" She winced. "I don't have it…"

"Anna!" Candide snapped.

"I thought—but," Anna blustered. "You know Latin, don't you?"

"Yes, but—"

"And Eve has a very good memory, don't you, Eve?"

"Uh, yes. Yes, Anna. That's all very good thinking…" He watched down the tunnel apprehensively and began stuffing his gun again.

"I can't," Candide wailed in exhaustion. "I can't battle another seven challengers. That one sounded even bigger. Oh fuck! Fuck!"

"It's fine." Eve turned the package of herbs over in his hand. "We'll just try the incantation. What's the worst that could happen? We're in Hell already, so… Let's just wing it."

"Eve!" Candide clapped her hands in front of his shocked face. "No! I want Evelyn Worthing. The guy who never wings things. The guy who turns himself inside out with anxiety and never fucks thing up! I need Evelyn Worthing, who fixes all my mistakes for me and takes care of everything all the time!"

He looked very hard at her for a moment, then said confidently, "Give me the bowl." She passed him the bowl. "Arms." They held out their arms. He put the blade to Anna's skin, then back to Candide's, then back to Anna's. "Can you do each other or something?"

"Yep." Anna nodded, suppressing a smile.

Eve smiled back, thankfully. "Sorry." He slit his arm open and let the blood drip into the bowl.

Anna took the blade and sliced into Candide's arm. "Ouch!"

"Sorry." She put the blade back to her own skin. "Uh, oh, I… I can totally do this."

Candide grabbed the blade out of her hand and cut her arm.

"Ouch!"

"You're welcome."

"Okay," Eve said. "Just let it drip and I'll put these herbs in and… Fuck. We need a fire. We need a fire! Where are we going to get a fire?"

"Your shirt!" Anna cried, before looking over his delicious naked chest again. "Oh. Oh, I forgot. Um, all right then." Anna ripped off her own shirt, then pulled her pants off. "You too, Candide."

"Fuck." Candide pulled her clothes off.

Eve removed his own pants, and they threw them all in a heap. "Is this going to be enough?"

"It has to be." Anna fetched her cigarette lighter out of the pile. "We need to light something first."

Candide ripped the collar from her shirt.

Eve looked at Candide. "What?" he said.

She shook her head doubtfully. "I didn't say anything…"

"Oh." His confused eyes focused hazily back on the task.

Candide and Anna exchanged a worried glance, then began to work faster still. Anna lit the collar on fire. She put her lighter down on the clothes and smashed it with the heel of her boot, releasing the lighter fluid.

"So clever," Eve sighed.

Anna smiled at him, then her face dropped as a look of panic hit Eve. "Wait! Gunpowder!" He desperately rifled through his pants pockets, tearing out all remaining packages of gunpowder and bullets.

Candide reprimanded him firmly with a hard scowl, then dropped the burning rag into the clothes, which burst easily into a roaring fire.

"All right," Eve said. "It was something about the river Acheron."

"And gods being merciful," Candide added.

"Yes! Then we renounce Christianity, I think. Then the bit about Beelzebub."

"Was Mephistopheles in there?"

"No, that's Faustus. It was… uh… Demogorgon!"

"Yes! Then offer the blood and we're good."

"Okay. I'm going to do this."

"Do it!"

"Okay." Eve stood tall and took a deep breath, the bowl held high over his head, the blood from his cut arm running over his biceps, down his shoulder and chest.

"Sit dies Acheronis nice! Abrenuntiemus Christianitatem nostram! Beelzebub gehennae rector. Ardet infernus. Demogorgon, gratias ago tibi quod me in tenebras tuae transitus reducens. Accipe hoc sanguinis donum et ad bibliothecam eamus. Quaeso."

"Eve," Candide started, paused, then went on, "did you just thank Demogorgon for accepting you into his dark passage?"

Eve frowned.

"It sounded very good to me," Anna whispered.

"Just chuck the blood, Eve," Candide sighed. "We'll see what happens."

Eve stood there holding the blood a moment longer, then said, "Actually, no."

"I'm about to hit you," Candide hissed.

"These are all the herbs we have. If I got that wrong, we don't have a backup at all."

"Chuck the goddamn blood, Eve!" she shouted.

"No!"

"Yes!"

"No!

"Yes!"

"You told me! You told me, be the Eve who doesn't do stupid things. That seems like a stupid thing to do!"

"Eve!"

"The fire's getting smaller," Anna said.

"If it goes out, we're stuck here anyway," Candide yelled. "Just throw it while we still have a fire."

"I—I don't know what to do," Eve stammered. "Why am I even doing the Latin? You're the Latin-speaking one!"

"There is no other way out! Put it on the fire now!"

"I think maybe…" Anna looked up at Eve and Candide. "I'm so sorry I didn't get the words. Oh god… I think maybe… I think this is it for us…"

Candide and Eve stopped yelling, and all three looked at one another in hopelessness as the devastating realisation began to take hold.

Then they heard an exceptionally loud crash and a cough and a gasp directly behind them as Percy fell to the floor.

"Percy!" they all cried delightedly.

He rolled over, regarding the three of them unsteadily, as they crouched around their burning clothes in their underwear.

Anna jumped to her feet and pulled him up, barely giving him time to get his balance before she said, "Thank God you're here, Percy! I want you to take your pants off immediately."

His face cracked into a handsome smile. "And they told me this would be Hell."

CHAPTER 57
INTO THE FIRE

Eve's heavy eyes assessed Percy. "You look wired."

"What?" Percy replied.

"Wired."

"What?"

"I said, wired."

"What?"

"Take your pants off!" Candide snapped.

"Oh. Okay." Percy automatically wrenched the end of his leather belt free from its clasp. "Why is that again?"

"We need to burn them to make a portal to get back," Anna explained.

"Oh good. We're on the way back." He asked in a tired voice, "You got your soul?"

"Yes. And you arrived just in time. We don't know the incantation to get back at all."

He handed his trousers over to Anna with a smile. "I'm glad I came then."

"Me too." Anna smiled back at him.

"Eve, wake up." Candide slapped his face gently.

With a start, Eve pushed himself off the wall. "Sorry."

"Wait," Percy said, taking his pants back from Anna. "I need the drugs and the dagger."

She watched him extracting the precious items. "You brought drugs to Hell?"

"I wasn't sure how much longer I would need to stay awake. I thought you were probably all dead, but just in case."

At that, Anna properly studied Percy's glassy, bloodshot eyes. "How long have you been awake?"

He regarded her absently as he searched for the answer, eventually coming up with, "I have no idea. Time has become… meaningless."

"It was around fifty-five hours when I left," Eve murmured. "How long have I been gone?"

They all noticed for the first time that Percy's speech was a little slurred as he replied, "Another whole night and another whole day. It was evening again when I left."

Anna, who was already crouching down to set Percy's clothes on fire, had a sharp intake of breath. "Percy, no…"

Candide was far less concerned about Percy's state of sleep deprivation than Anna. "Percy, can you do the spell now?"

Percy stared off into the distance as though watching something.

"Percy?" Candide repeated.

Eve followed his eyes. "Shadow people?"

Percy shook his head a little as he stared. "So many now."

Eve nodded. "I'm seeing them too."

"Percy, the spell!" Candide insisted.

Percy continued his distracted watch. "I'm maybe thirty-six hours ahead of you, Evelyn. Maybe more. It's not good here."

"Percy!" Candide yelled.

He turned back to her. "I'm sorry. What were we doing?"

Candide raised a hand of frustration to her temple. "Okay, what did you bring? Speed? Is it speed?"

"Yes."

"Okay, take some now, very quickly, and wake up. We need you to do this spell right away or we're all going to die."

"Candide…" Anna said.

Candide snatched the small parcel of drugs from him. "Give me your hand."

"Candide…" Anna repeated.

"Here." Candide poured out a large line onto the side of his palm. "Quickly."

"Candide!"

Percy inhaled the powder.

"What is it, Anna!" Candide yelled.

"Candide, my dad died of a drug overdose and…" She shook her head. "And this…" Her words cut off with the clenching of her throat.

Candide's face fell. "Oh, Anna. I didn't know. Anna, I'm sorry."

Eve brought an arm around Anna, and she continued softly, "I'm getting scared now. What is that? Eighty—ninety hours awake? More? He can't be far from psychosis. I don't want him to have any more. Either of them. It's been too long. This isn't okay anymore."

"I'm sorry," Candide whispered frantically. "I'm sorry. I'm scared too. I'm really sorry. I would never have done that unless we were about to die. I'm sorry."

The combination of the immediacy of insufflated amphetamines, combined with Percy's already powerful attachment to Anna, brought about a fast and profound change in him. He took Anna's hand and pulled her to her feet. "It's only speed and I promise you I've been awake a lot longer than this before. You never need to worry about me. Eve's fine too, and I'm taking us all home right now."

Percy sliced into his own arm without another moment's hesitation and poured his blood into the bowl. He lifted it above his head, said the correct words, then he threw it on the fire. Candide disappeared into the flames first. Eve took Anna's hand and led her through, and Percy followed behind.

Seconds later, they tripped over a very nice, late eighteenth-century fireplace grill, falling on top of one another and into Lady Worthing's spectacular drawing room.

As soon as they realised where they were, there were cries of jubilation, of relief, of exhaustion, from all but Percy, who was busy stomping out the fire so nothing could follow them through. But even as they celebrated, they gradually became aware of the smell of cigarette smoke from the doorway. Then the familiar voice. "Welcome to your own personal Hell, Evelyn."

Eve let out an embarrassed but fond laugh. "Mum, I said I'm sorry for saying that. Can we please forget it already?"

"No, Evelyn," the cold voice replied. "I'll never let you forget."

Eve turned ghost-white with the words, reeling back against Anna, who instinctively wrapped her arms around him. Other than his panic, no one else understood that anything was amiss until the edges of Lady Worthing's face began to bleed. Only a little at first, then in drips and drops down her neck, down her white nightgown, until it was pouring in thin, repellant streams all down her body, pooling on the floor around her feet.

She gazed mercilessly into Eve's terrified eyes as she lifted the cigarette to her lips and took a deep drag on it. As she pulled it away, her entire face disintegrated into chunks of odious dead flesh, pieces dropping one by one to the floor, crawling with maggots, leaving only the front of her skull, pale and bloody, cigarette smoke escaping between the teeth, out through the nose holes, drifting up from the empty eye sockets.

"Candide," Eve whispered. "Can you see it?"

Candide darted forward and slammed the door shut. "Yes, Eve. Yes. It's her. She's really there."

Eve slumped over against the wall, turning his face away from the group. "Why tonight? Why is she back tonight?"

Anna kept her arms tight around him, looking silently to Candide for an explanation.

"She usually just haunts the attic," Candide said apologetically.

"The attic?" Anna said. "As in, where Eve slept alone when he was little?"

"Yeah," said Candide. "She's always haunted him. She's like… Eve's worst ghost."

"My god," Percy cried. "That's hideous. Why did Adeline let him sleep alone with that thing on the loose?"

"Uh…" Candide's head tilted to the side, much like one trying to explain the unexplainable. "She says ghosts are nothing to be afraid of. And that we should get used to them."

"She's absolutely terrifying," Percy muttered. "And so is the ghost."

"It's very rare she comes down here," Candide offered, then she walked over to Eve's side. "But that means we're home, Eve. We got out of Hell and we're home." She looked up from him to address Anna and Percy again. "We just have to survive tonight in the house and we'll be okay."

Eve's eyes shot over to the far corner of the room and he stared for a short while, then looked back at Percy, who nodded some sort of understanding.

Perfectly terrified, Anna did her best to appear functional. "All right. Then we just keep that door shut tight, and stay here together, and—"

"No!" Candide and Eve cried.

"No," Candide continued, "this room is a very bad room and we need to go. Pretty much right now before we all die."

"Go where?" said Anna, accepting the statement for what it was, as she had seen enough for one day to feel no need to second guess Candide where the supernatural was concerned.

"Shall we make a break for the front door?" Percy suggested.

"Um, no," Candide replied. "The house is bad, but outside…" She shook her head.

"Should we call for help, then?" he asked.

"We can't. The crying woman is on the phone at night."

Anna felt the need to ask for a little clarification after all. "The what now?"

"She's on the line all night," Candide said. "As soon as it gets dark. She just cries and cries and she never answers if you ask her what's wrong."

"Except that one time," Eve muttered.

"We don't talk about that," Candide replied sharply.

Anna took a deep breath to cope with the chill that ran down her spine. "Okay. Then where did you go when you were little?"

"The tv room," Candide said. "But… It's some way off. If we all go together and stick together, we should be fine. It's perfectly warded for everything and perfectly safe."

"How far is it?" asked Percy.

"It's in the East Wing."

"Ugh, why do you have to live in a house with wings?" Anna moaned.

"I am never coming back here," Eve mumbled. "Never again."

"Yes, good plan," Candide agreed. "Now, everyone up. We, of all people, know you never separate in a haunted house."

"That's right," Anna said. "We'll stick together, and if I see that ghost again, she's going to eat my steel."

"We call her Lady Worsing," Candide put in.

Anna worked very hard to control herself, but she chanced a look at Percy who had already cracked a hugely inappropriate grin, and then she and he both coughed uncontrollably in a pathetic attempt to hide their laughter, which had the pleasant effect of releasing Eve from his miserable reverie. He smiled and put his arm around Anna and pulled her in to kiss her cheek, then they all stood.

"I'm going first," Candide announced. "Then Percy, then Eve. Anna's going to watch behind us." Anna nodded her agreement. "You two," Candide pointed between Percy and Eve, "I'm pretty sure you're both hallucinating by now?"

"A little bit," said Eve.

"Very much," said Percy.

"So before you try to fight anything, please just check with me or Anna to make sure it's real. Okay?" They nodded. "Okay. I'm opening the door now. Stay in a line. Stay together."

Candide moved to the door, and they all shuddered a little as she pulled it slowly open. But Lady Worsing had disappeared. Candide looked around, her sword at the ready, and took her first tentative steps out into the hall. Percy followed close behind, and Eve was next.

"Are you okay?" Anna whispered.

"Yeah. Fine," he whispered back. "Are you okay?"

"Yes. But I need my hand back. To hold my sword."

"Oh, sorry." Eve smiled. He let go of her hand with a squeeze. "Stay close."

"I will."

Eve stepped out into the hallway and Anna stayed right next to him. But despite that, there was nothing she could do, nothing to stop the arm that reached around her waist and wrenched her back into the drawing room. The door slammed shut with her friends on the other side, leaving her quite alone in the haunted house with something she was perfectly sure meant to harm her.

CHAPTER 58
WORTHING HOUSE HORROR

Anna pressed her bare back up against the cold wooden door and held her sword at the ready. She couldn't see anything in the room, but it was a very bad room to be in—that much she knew.

"Anna!" She could hear Eve calling from the hall, trying the door handle, which had become utterly useless. "Anna, stand back. We're going to break it down."

"Okay." She refrained from rolling her eyes, but she was at least reminded that her side of the door was the one with the hinges. She cautiously moved over and tried the exquisitely thin blade of her sword against them. It slid in like a dream, and she started manoeuvring it up and down, up and down, concentrating hard and smiling at her own ingenuity as she watched her plan work, and the bolt that held the thing together started to slip free.

"Anna." The voice was so close, right beside her, and in her horror she jumped and fell back, hitting the wall and sliding to the floor.

Staring up, she beheld the glorious features. "Bad Eve!"

She righted herself and cautiously pushed her way to standing against the wall.

He looked exactly the same as Eve. The same injuries Eve had sustained that very day, the same patches of dirt and bruising, everything down to the smallest detail.

"Can I show you something?" He started forward, and she put her sword out defensively. He paused, a look of confusion on his beautiful face. "Anna, why would you do that?"

"You're not Eve," she said. "I know you're not Eve. What do you want?"

Bad Eve's eyes turned cold, and he smiled at her.

Then the lights went out.

"Eve!" she screamed. "Eve, I need you!"

The door crashed open, and he was there, by her side again. She felt him, his arm on hers and his beloved presence, but unable to see a thing in the dark, she still asked, "Eve?"

"I'm here," he said. "It's me. Anna, are you okay?"

"I'm fine, it's fine. It was Bad Eve but—" The lights flickered on and to her horror Anna beheld two Eves awaiting her response.

"What the hell is…" they spoke in unison. Their two heads turned to look at Candide, who, for the first time in her life, reached for Percy. They looked at each other again, then they both said, "He's Bad Eve!"

"No! He's Bad Eve!" they said again, and every movement was a mirror.

"How can he know…" they said. They both turned to Anna.

"Candide…" Anna squeaked, but all she could see of Candide were her eyes peeking over Percy's shoulder.

"The tv room," Percy said. "Let's go."

"Yes." Both Eves stood back from Anna, watching each other, ready for a fight.

Anna walked between them tentatively to the open door, pressing her back against it. "Eves first." Neither of them said anything as they made their way, side by side, out into the hall, where they waited, still regarding one another anxiously. Candide came next, and as Percy passed by, he put an arm around Anna and pulled her close, making sure she stayed with them this time. They all jumped as the door slammed shut behind them of its own volition.

"Fuck this house!" Anna yelled with the latest fright.

"Agreed," said Percy.

"This way," Candide whispered.

"I'll go first," said the Eves. Candide pushed herself back against the wall to let them pass, drawing a sorry, sympathetic look from each of them. From there, they took a right down the hall, then a left, descending the wide staircase. The wood creaked and popped beneath their shoes, echoing throughout the cavernous space around them.

The Eves paused. "Did you hear that?"

Everyone listened.

Not a sound.

"It's… It might be the sleep deprivation," Anna suggested softly.

"No, not the voices…" Both Eves looked at the staircase above them, but apparently unable to detect anything else, they turned and walked. A few steps later, "That! Did you hear it?"

They all stopped again, listening carefully. Then a huge crash sounded on the stairs above and they heard loud footsteps chasing fast after them.

"Run!" Candide yelled.

They fled in a panic, down the grand staircase and through the entrance hall, around a bend and into another larger, seemingly endless hall. They ran through the doorway and each Eve grabbed one side of the huge double doors and they slammed it closed together, the other three throwing their backs against the doors to keep them shut.

Something slammed its weight against the doors from the other side and it almost gave way entirely.

"It's the beast," Candide whispered, as though her low tone was going to hide their location somehow.

"The beast?" Anna whispered back, trying the same desperate game.

"The beast that walks," came Candide's horrified and unhelpful clarification.

Percy looked over at her with a raised eyebrow. "As opposed to?"

"It used to kind of crawl everywhere," she revealed on hitching breaths. "Then one day it stood up… and walked."

The thing rammed into the door again.

"Hold the door and it might go away," she said.

"Might?" Anna yelled.

"Might!"

The thing rammed the door again, then one of the Eves looked at the other and whispered, "What are you?"

The other looked back at him fearfully. "I'm Eve."

"You can't be," the first one whispered. "You don't exist outside this house."

"Is that what you think?"

They eyed one another, then the thing rammed the door again.

"Spiders!" Percy yelled. "It's spiders again! And we have no weapons to kill spiders!"

"Not again!" Anna cried. "Where?"

"There. There on the wall! Or… Over there!"

Anna and Candide searched the hallway frantically.

The thing rammed the door, and they all screamed.

"No!" Candide yelled. "No spiders!"

"No spiders?" Percy cried.

"None. You are properly hallucinating now."

His eyes ran down the walls with a mixture of fear and disgust. "Okay. Just my… temporary insanity."

"Only temporary," Anna tried to reassure him, then she was almost knocked off her feet as the thing rammed the door once again.

"And her? Over there?" Percy asked.

"Who?"

"The nanny. There."

They all followed Percy's line of sight, but only Anna had an inkling of what he must be seeing—a hideous memory from his childhood that was, even now, fresh and living in front of him. Anna shifted a little closer to him. "No. She's not real."

She felt Percy shudder as he looked away.

"Why won't you talk to me?" one of the Eves said.

The other replied, "Because you're not… You're—"

"Do you remember the red room?"

A sad shock of remembrance came over the other Eve. "I do… I thought… I thought it was a dream…"

"Do you dream?"

Eve stared hard at Eve. "What are you?"

The thing rammed the door again and this time Anna was knocked off her feet, and caught and pulled back by one of the Eves. She wrenched her arm away in fright, and they both looked horrified. "Sorry!" they said.

"I have had enough of this!" Anna yelled. "Candide, where's the tv room?"

"Right at the end of the hall. Way down there. Second door from the end on the right."

Anna looked off into the dark. "And how fast can the beast that walks run?"

"I've never tested it."

"Then today's the day. Next time it attacks, we run."

"It might just go away on its own if we just—"

"It might not."

"Okay. You're right. Good plan. Lets…" The lights began to flicker on and off. Each door started to rattle, to open and slam shut. They heard scraping and scratching as huge slashes appeared in the wallpaper, and the walls themselves began to drip with blood. They looked down as they each felt moisture on their feet and saw their shoes were soaked through with the blood from the walls that ran fast into the thick carpet.

"How much of this am I hallucinating?" Percy asked.

"Not a thing," Anna replied. "Is everyone ready?"

They all agreed. The ensuing thirty or so seconds they spent waiting for the beast that walks felt like the longest of their lives. None of them said a thing as they held the door fast, each wondering how well their hurt and exhausted limbs would move, wondering how much harder it would be to run in wet, bloody carpet, wondering what might appear from any of the doorways and try to pull them in.

The thing rammed the door.

They sprinted, all five of them, as fast as they still could. Anna felt something reach out for her and trip her up, but she was swiftly pulled to her feet by Candide, who was wrenched towards one of the doorways and wrenched back again by an Eve, who she slapped in the face for having touched her at all, but even with these many obstacles they made swift progress to their destination, halting only when the hideous figure of Lady Worsing appeared at the end of the hall, walking stiffly towards them, her skin, now regrown on her evil face, a sickly greenish hue and her eyes bloodshot, her expression furious and vengeful. The Eves were the first to slow their progress, then Candide paused, watching them, then Percy halted too.

"Into the room now," Anna commanded. "I can take her."

"Anna, no!" both Eve's yelled. Percy pulled them both towards the tv room but they wrenched themselves free before they could cross the threshold.

As Anna approached Lady Worsing, she swung her sword as impressively as someone who had handled a sword for the first time more than two hours, Hell-time, prior could. Lady Worsing's black mouth grew wider, wider, until it became a huge gaping hole in her face, nothing but swollen red eyes and the mouth and rotting teeth and bad air and a frenzied, ear-piercing screech.

Anna didn't flinch.

"You mean!" She sliced an arm off the thing.

"Nasty!" Off came the other arm.

"Abusive!" Off came both legs, and the body fell to the floor.

"Classist!" She sliced the body in half and the entrails spilled to the floor as Percy and Candide raised an eyebrow at one another.

"Self-satisfied!" Off came the head, which rolled along the floor.

"Fucking bitch!" And Anna stabbed the thing's head clear through from one ear to the other.

"Leave my boyfriend alone!" She lifted the sword, spilling blood and brain all over herself, then brought it back down fast, flinging the head across the hall and into a wall, where it broke in two and slid down, making a satisfying squelch when it hit the blood-soaked carpet.

Anna nodded approvingly and turned back to both Eves, who were looking at her like there had never walked a more wonderful or magical creature on the planet.

The door at the end of the hall burst open and both Eves reached for Anna and they, Percy and Candide, all tumbled back into the tv room. Percy kicked the door shut and when they finally looked around, one of the Eves was gone.

"Anna!" The remaining Eve reached for her and kissed her and she threw her arms around him and knocked him backwards to the floor in her enthusiasm, the two of them landing in a very happy, very bloody, very exhausted heap together.

"And we're safe in here?" Percy asked.

"Completely," Candide sighed.

Anna lay her head on Eve's chest and let herself and everything else disappear into the rise and fall of his warm body.

CHAPTER 59
SAFE AT LAST

The tv room was small, cosy and modern. White walls, white couch—about to be permanently stained from the bloody doings of the night—a small fridge and cupboards stocked with all the necessary supplies for enjoying movie marathons. Percy and Anna threw themselves down on the lounge while Candide and Eve gathered blankets and snacks.

"We'll stay here until the sun comes up," Candide said, "then we'll go back to Endymion."

Anna looked Percy and Eve over. "Can you sleep?"

Eve dropped down next to Anna. "I think so, but if you're worried, I'll stay up with you."

"Please, no," Anna said. "I want you to eat and sleep. Right now. Okay?"

"Okay." He looked doubtfully over the chips on the coffee table, the only food in the tv room. "I'm not very hungry."

Anna ripped a packet open. "You'll eat."

Eve pushed down his nausea and did as he was told, then she shoved the packet at Percy and he did the same.

"I'll put something on to watch." Candide raised her chin towards Anna. "What do we feel like?"

"Nothing with ghosts," Eve muttered.

"I wasn't going to," Candide protested.

"Yes, you were."

Candide grinned at him, then relented. "We'll just flick channels then." She threw herself down next to Percy and they all ate chips and drank juice and flicked channels, until Candide said, "I miss our movie nights, Anna."

Anna's exhausted heart beat hopefully. "Should we do one? Next week?"

Candide said nothing for a few seconds, thinking, then when her silence drew Anna's attention, "Will you move back in with me?"

"Yes!" Anna couldn't and didn't even try to hide her excitement. "Yes, I would love to!"

"Good. Then it's settled. Poltergeist on Saturday night?"

"Yes. Poltergeist."

Eve's head fell back with a groan. "I will never understand you two. And can I stop eating now?"

Anna assessed his almost-empty packet of chips. "Yes. Lie down here." Eve lay his head down on Anna's lap as directed.

Stroking his hair softly, knowing he was safe and loved and within her reach, filled Anna with more happiness than she had ever thought possible, then still more when he turned his beautiful face up and said, "Do you see why I was worried about asking you out?" She laughed and leaned down and kissed him, then he closed his eyes and snuggled into her. "I'm glad you didn't listen to me."

"Me too, Eve. I love you so much."

He muttered an 'I love you' back, but even as he said it, he fell asleep. Candide was next, drifting off on Percy's shoulder only minutes later.

Anna glanced up at Percy. "How are you feeling?"

He offered her a tired smile. "I'm all right. You don't need to worry about me."

"It's all fun and games until fifty hours, right?"

Percy laughed. "Quite right. Now go to sleep. You must be exhausted."

They sat together for a while, then she asked, "Do you still see her?"

Percy continued to look straight forward. "Yes. Just out of the corner of my eye. If I look at the television it helps."

Anna took his hand in hers. "Thank you. For everything."

He squeezed her hand. "You needn't mention it. Off to sleep."

She shook her head. "Pass me a Coke. I want to stay up with you."

Percy looked down at her sad, hopeful face and realised it was more than the desire for company that made her want that. It was something she needed, deep inside, so for the next few hours, though barely capable of conversation or logical thought, Percy let her fuss over him and insist he eat chips and drink juice, and she pulled his blanket up repeatedly, and he listened to her comments and musings and jokes very happily, and he let her feel like she was taking very good care of him. Which she was.

It was during these quiet hours their relationship became something else entirely. Neither of them could have put it into words, but there had been something missing inside of both of them for so much of their lives—Percy since he was five and Anna since she was nine—and from that time, that night, Percy unwittingly but permanently slotted into that empty space in her heart, and she into his.

Anna felt a deep, primal satisfaction when Percy's eyes finally closed and his head rolled over against Candide's. She checked over each of her friends, made sure her arm was wrapped tight around Eve, took hold of Candide's hand, laid her head on Percy's shoulder, and finally, she let herself fall asleep.

CHAPTER 60
REINFORCEMENTS

Neither Eve nor Percy were roused from their deep slumber by the small commotion caused when Joe and Aubrey burst into the room a little later.

"Aubrey!" Candide jumped up from the couch and threw her arms around her.

"I was so worried about you!" Aubrey said between kisses. "Where are your clothes? Whose blood is this?"

"Not mine." Candide smiled, brushing Aubrey's sweaty, blood-clotted hair back. "Are you all right?"

"Totally fine. All better now."

Candide led Aubrey to the other lounge, where they curled up under a blanket.

Joe, meanwhile, paused in the doorway, taking in naked Percy, shoulder to shoulder with naked Anna, who had a naked Eve asleep on her thighs. She motioned for Joe to take his place beside Percy, which he did, a little gingerly.

"Have you been awake this whole time, too?" she asked.

"No. Adeline watched the fire for a while, since the portal was closed, so we slept in the library, waiting for you to open the other side again. Then she said you opened it but she rerouted your exit point here. She said you'd rest better in the mansion, with all the bedrooms here, and we came as soon as we heard." Percy shifted in his sleep, and as though sensing him there, rolled his head onto Joe's chest. Joe took an arm around him and grasped his sleeping hand with an adoring blush. "Are they okay?"

Anna continued to stroke Eve's hair. "They're fine. Just tired."

The door cracked open behind them.

"All accounted for?" Lady Worthing cast her eyes over the group. "Very well. Goodnight, children."

Anna scowled as hard as she could as the ghostly figure disappeared into the dark hall.

"Goodnight, Addie!" Aubrey called after her.

"What time is it?" Candide asked.

"About four a.m.," Aubrey said.

"Didn't you meet any ghosts in the hall?"

"We did, but Adeline just used her powers. Pretty amazing stuff to watch. I can see why you and she can operate in this house so well."

At those words, Candide's eyes dimmed. She kept the smile on her face, but held Aubrey's hand a little tighter.

Aubrey didn't miss the shift. "What is it?"

"Um…" Candide looked down, toying distractedly with Aubrey's fingers. "I lost my powers. In Hell."

Joe and Aubrey gasped audibly.

"You got past all that stuff without any magic?" Joe said.

"Yeah. We did it together. And we had a very special sword, too."

Aubrey, raising Candide's chin, said gently, "You must be devastated."

Candide stopped trying to put on a brave face and wiped away a tear. "I am. You know how much that meant to me. But it's okay." She forced a smile. "I've still got the book, and that's the important thing. I'll study and I'll work hard and I'll get it all back."

Anna looked at the tv. At the ceiling. At the floor. At her blanket.

Candide looked at her. Hard. "Anna, why are you doing that?"

"What?"

"That."

"What?"

"Anna, is there something you should tell me?"

"Uh…"

"Anna?"

"Oh…"

"Anna!"

"Um…" Anna swallowed. "I did something. I did something for a very good reason but… You're going to be pissed."

CHAPTER 61

LATER THAT DAY

It was evening when they all arrived back at Endymion College. Candide and Aubrey said goodnight in the courtyard and went to Aubrey's apartment for the night. Joe and Percy accompanied Eve and Anna home to say goodbye.

"Goodbye?" Anna choked, an unprecedented panic rising inside her.

"Yes," Percy said. "I know it's not the best time to bring it up, but we've been busy, so… I need to tell you I'm going to Poland."

"Poland!" Anna tried very hard but unsuccessfully to hide the tears that were fast forming. Eve and Joe exchanged uncertain looks and stood around awkwardly as Percy took her hands in his and they stared dramatically into one another's eyes. "It's just very sudden. And unexpected. That's all."

Percy cupped her cheek with his soft hand. "I can see I've made a mess of this. Anna, it's a short trip. For work. And then we're coming straight back."

Anna brightened a little. "We? Is Joe going?"

"Yes. Joe's coming with me." Percy looked across proudly at his quietly irritated boyfriend.

"Oh." Anna's eyes flicked between the two, not noticing much other than that Percy was leaving. She said casually, "Is this because you have friends who need you to watch their paintings again?"

"Something like that." He chuckled, then explained, "It's a… a very important work has resurfaced, and it needs to be… relocated. Appropriately. It may keep us busy for some time. I had meant to tell you sooner, but I hadn't expected all of this to take an entire week. But honestly, it's only a short trip. A few weeks perhaps. A month at most. And then we'll go out for lunch or something. All of us."

"Okay." Anna smiled, quite embarrassed by the even stronger feelings she had only just realised she'd developed for Percy.

"I just mention it now because we're leaving in the next few days and…" He addressed Eve. "Did you two talk?"

Anna walked over and slid under Eve's waiting arm. "We did," he said. "And for now, I think we're okay. Is that right?"

"Yes. We'll be all right." Anna gave him a confident nod.

Eve returned it, then said to Percy, "There are so many awful things to remember. But so many good things too. So we're going to try to keep going."

"I'm happy to hear it." In fact, Percy was more relieved than he could ever say that he and Anna would be able to stay exactly where they were with one another, so all he said was, "If it gets too much, and you do want to forget, leave a message at my Paris office, and wherever I am, I'll be in touch."

"Thanks, Percy." Eve hugged his brother. Then they all hugged and said their goodbyes, and Eve and Anna went, more or less, straight to sleep.

CHAPTER 62
SPRING MORNING

Sunday morning, Anna woke fresh and happy, with one thought on her mind: Eve.

She sat upright in her own bed, in her own apartment, and stretched her arms high over her head. She flinched at the pain all throughout her body, but this sensation was nothing new to her. The sun was soft and yellow as it streamed through her gigantic gothic window and bathed her in its gentle warmth. The huge ash tree outside was still covered in a blanket of beautiful white flowers, but just as she was about to push the window open, she froze.

A presence.

She turned back to see, for the first time in a long time, Candide in her own bed, awake. "Hey, Anna."

"Hey, Candide." Anna lay back down on her side and looked across at her best friend, who returned her smile. "Thanks for the sleepover. I had a really nice time."

"Me too. We should do it every week."

"Let's."

"Breakfast?"

"Yes."

Anna and Candide wandered around their gorgeous, sun-soaked apartment together, cooked together, ate together, sat on the couch and read together, until eventually Candide said, "You know, you're going to have to see him sooner or later."

"I know." Anna coloured, sighed, grimaced. "And I want to. I'm… I'm only dreading this a little bit. Or maybe a lot."

"He won't be happy, but…" Candide studied Anna carefully as she fiddled with the pages of her Tolstoy. "Are you sure this is what you want?"

Anna didn't look up, but she nodded. "It is."

"You don't have to tell him everything."

"I can't lie to him."

"Maybe not lie, but you could certainly massage facts… a little… Soften the blow."

Anna stared doubtfully at the floor, her intestines wrapping themselves in a guilty knot.

Candide moved over onto the couch next to her and took her hand. "I love you, Anna. You're the best friend I could ever ask for."

"Don't." Anna hid her face on Candide's shoulder. "Don't make me cry in the morning. I love you, too."

"I know that." Candide put her arms around Anna and hugged her tight. "I'm sorry I ever doubted you."

Anna pulled back and looked her in the eyes. "I'm sorry I gave you a reason to. But it's all over now." Then she took a deep breath and threw her book down. "And it looks like we're onto the next thing."

"Are you going then?"

"I am. Wish me luck."

"Good luck."

Anna stood to leave.

"Anna?"

"Mmhmm?"

Candide raised her sympathetic eyebrows. "Just bullshit him a little bit, okay?"

Anna laughed softly and started down the dark hall to Eve's apartment.

CHAPTER 63
THE PROPOSAL

Anna turned her key in the lock and there was Eve, sitting on his couch in a soft, pale grey sweater, reading and making notes studiously, with a now cold and untouched cup of tea by his side.

"Anna!" He threw the book down, jumped up, and kissed her. "I'm so glad you're here. Did you have fun?"

It was the first night they had deliberately spent apart in a long, long time. How odd it was to meet in the morning, rather than wake up together. Anna felt a small knot tightening in her stomach as she gazed at his happy, trusting face, his warm arms around her. "We did."

"Was Poltergeist as good as you remembered?"

"Even better."

"Maybe I will watch it sometime." He kissed her again, soft lips that she loved so much, and though she was concentrating on feeling more than a little guilty about what she was about to say to him, she sensed an odd nervousness in him, too—a sort of worried excitement.

"Did you have a nice night?" she asked.

"I did. I got a lot done. But I missed you. And…" He became a little more serious. Disconcertingly so. He blinked long lashes over grey eyes that flitted away from her and back again. "I wanted to talk to you about something."

"Oh, good." She paused and took a deep breath. "Because I have something to talk to you about, too."

He took in her apologetic, nervous face, and she saw his enthusiasm die out. "It sounds important."

That familiar sensation of bile in the chest. "It is."

"Do you want some tea?"

"Okay."

Eve squeezed her hand and moved towards the kitchen. He went about making tea, paying an inordinate amount of attention to deciding on the most appropriate cups, opening and closing tea canisters noisily, distractedly.

She watched him, wondering how she best begin. Unconsciously, she put it off, saying, "Eve, you look anxious."

With nearly a glance back, but not quite, "Shouldn't I be?"

"Maybe—"

"Is it to do with Percy?" He concentrated hard on filling the kettle to just the right level and he didn't look up as he dropped the stark words.

Anna's heart leapt into her throat as she made her way swiftly to his side. "Eve, No. No, why would you think that?"

He flashed her a half smile, embarrassed. "No reason…"

"I thought I explained."

"You did. I know." He set the kettle to boil. "Complex feelings."

"Complex non-romantic feelings," she corrected, taking his busy hands in hers.

"Yeah, I know. Sorry. Maybe I'll just sit down and listen. Sorry." He did as much, leading her to the couch and taking his place beside her, his body turned attentively towards hers. His eyes and expression were patient, but there remained a note of alarm about his deliberately calmed features, so for his sake, she pushed down her concerns and came straight out with it.

"Eve, I'm going to take a trip."

His lips parted a little in surprise, then he said, "You're going away?"

"Yes."

"For how long?"

"Not long, but I don't know exactly." He was very quiet, trying not to say what he was thinking, but Anna could guess what he was thinking, because Percy had left on a trip that very morning. He needed to know, and she had to tell him, so she pressed forward mercilessly. "I'm going with Candide."

At that, an understanding came into his eyes, and a curious spark there too, as his left eyebrow raised just a little. "And where are you and Candide going?"

"Japan."

He forced back the smile that tugged at the edges of his lips. "You and Candide are going on a trip to Japan?"

"We are."

"You know you both have a lot of work to catch up on, right?"

"Yes." She let out a little laugh, half nerves, half adoration. "And it wouldn't be until the break."

"Okay." He gave a sharp nod. "And is this a 'you and Candide spending time together because you're best friends' type of thing, or is this a 'don't tell Eve we're going to do something incredibly dangerous with supernatural elements' type of thing?"

She bit her lip. "It's… maybe… the second of those things."

Eve looked at her very seriously for a moment, then his own beautiful lips turned up into a loving, if somewhat exhausted smile. "You can't help yourself, can you?"

"She just wants her book back," Anna explained. "And I gave it away, so it's kind of my fault."

"You saved her life."

"No… I think that was the other way around, really."

He replied gently, "When are you going to accept how wonderful you are?"

Love and guilt battled in her heart. There he was, so, so sweet, and here she was, destroying all his hopes and plans for the future in one blow. She felt her tears welling up, so she looked down and let her hair fall in her face to hide it.

Eve knew, of course, so he changed tack. "You want to fight ghosts, too, don't you?"

"A little bit," she admitted. "But only this one last time."

"So you're going to travel to Japan with Candide to see Aka Manto? The bathroom ghost who kills people horribly."

"He was very nice to us," she murmured. "Mostly."

"I understand." Eve offered a hurt but encouraging smile, walked back to the kitchen, poured out the hot water, and began thoroughly assessing an array of teaspoons.

"Eve?"

"Mmhmm?"

"I won't go if you don't want me to. If it's something that…" He said nothing, the fridge door open and between them, obscuring her view. "I know all of this was supposed to be over for us. Paranormal things. But Candide is going to go no matter what I do. And I want to be there for her."

"Yeah. I understand," he called back, selecting more than he needed and taking it all to the bench to push around aimlessly. "I just wasn't expecting this. Not quite so soon, anyway. But it's something you want, so you should go. And—"

By his side again, she stilled his tense, fast-moving hands, then caught his lovely eyes with her own. "What is it?"

He looked at her sadly, and said, "I just got you back. And I'll miss you."

Her stomach and jaw dropped as she realised. "Eve, you know this is an invitation, don't you?"

His face became the aghast mirror of hers. "What? It is?"

"Yes!" she practically yelled. "It very much is!"

His face lit, and he pulled her in against his chest, letting out a relieved laugh. "Anna, that's easily the worst invitation to anything I've ever had."

"Sorry," she laughed out, her face muffled against his chest. She worked herself out of his grip, but only slightly. "What I meant to say is, Candide and I would love it if you would come to Japan with us. Except…"

"Except?"

"Except you're not allowed to tell us to stop and think things through, and to not do the stupid things."

"Can I say those things if I don't come to Japan?"

"You can, but we probably won't listen to you either way, so you may as well come along." She kissed his cheek, then made her way back over to the living room with her tea. "But you don't have to give me an answer now. I know it's a lot to ask, or to tell you, or whatever it is. We talked about wanting to move on with our lives, and maybe this is a huge step backwards for us. I don't know. Just know that I love you. I don't ever want to make you sad."

"You could never make me sad, Anna, but…" He picked up his tea, took two steps towards her, and said, "About that. About our future. Together. That's what I wanted to talk to you about."

He had become serious again. He placed his tea down on the coffee table, took hers from her hands, and placed it down beside his. She watched, and she waited. He remained quiet for entirely too long, until he frowned, looked back at her, and though he had clearly made his mind up by that time about what he was going to do, he was even more nervous somehow.

He commenced, "I don't want you to take this the wrong way, because you've been very clear that you don't want to get married and settle down, and if I'm honest, I don't think you're ever likely to want to settle down. And I love that about you. But..." Anna's heart beat a little harder in her chest. "I wanted to do something, to let you know how much—how much I love you and how much I want to be with you, so if I've overstepped some boundaries just let me know and we'll just— we'll chuck it, okay? And we'll pretend it never happened. No pressure." Her lips parted slightly, and she drew a short, sharp breath. "It's that..." Eve faltered. He pushed on. "I got you something, as a kind of... a symbol, I guess, of our lives together. Whatever direction they take. And now I've done it, and I'm about to give it to you, I'm worried you might find it... A bit weird or a bit too intense, maybe, but I just wanted you to know, I always want to be with you. No matter what. So I hope it's not too much."

From the time he began to speak in such a way, Anna had felt a small flutter of unease rising in her belly, which, by the time he finally finished speaking, had spread all throughout her body, and now her hands shook a little, and there was a light sweat breaking about her brow. "Eve—"

"I'm rambling again. Sorry." His own slightly shaking hands, quick movements and adorable flush to his cheeks, his anxiety that she should love whatever this gift was, endeared him to her even more, if it were at all possible, but still, she worried what might come next, as he murmured, "I'll just... I'll just get it."

He reached into his bag and pulled free a black velvet box. He turned and handed it to her.

She knew at once what it must be.

She looked into his eyes and he into hers and he smiled hopefully and she took a deep breath.

Ever so slowly, Anna opened the beautiful box to reveal the loveliest, most elegant, shiniest, sparkling, golden, deathly sharp fountain pen that anyone ever beheld.

"Oh, Eve! I love it so much!"

"Do you really?"

"Yes! Really! So much!"

"And see now," he smiled delightedly, his whole being aglow with happiness, "it's like the whole thing never happened."

"Yes, Eve! Yes!" She beamed back at him. "Like it never happened."

"I love you so much," Eve said.

"I love you so much!" Anna replied.

And she kissed him and he kissed her and the relief and contentment they both felt was palpable. She wrenched her new pen free from the box and turned it over to reveal the inscription.

Anna and Eve. Forever.

"I believe that with all my heart," he said. "I just wanted you to know… I've always felt that, since the day we met, and for me, that won't ever change."

"I believe that too, Eve." And she threw her arms around him and they kissed again. Then she admired her beautiful pen some more. "You didn't have to do this. But I love it. Thank you so much."

"I'm just happy it was the right thing."

"It really is," Anna said. Then she looked up shyly at Eve, his beautiful grey eyes sparkling down at her. "So what do you say?"

His smile widened. "Anna, of course I'll go to Japan and fight monsters with you."

"Really? Do you mean it?"

"Yes! With all my heart."

"Oh, Eve!" she cried. "You've made me the happiest woman in the world!"

The End

A Letter to Aubrey

earest Aubriest,

How to begin? I know I haven't written for a long time, so I'll start with my apology. Please know I received every one of your letters and please don't stop writing simply because I'm a terrible correspondent. In truth, Joe and I have been far busier than either of us thought possible, but that's no excuse.

Speaking of Joe, things are going remarkably well. I read him all the parts of your letters fit for public consumption (which, don't worry, isn't much) and he misses you terribly too, though not as much as I do. He's annoyingly insistent we come and see you all again soon, however, as you will soon see, this letter will be stamped from Lerwick in the Shetland Isles, which makes it rather difficult to get to Endymion College. In fact, even Lerwick is located a considerable distance from where we're actually staying, but the journey to town is a pleasant one and worth it to bring you your salvation.

Here we come to the point of this letter. I have, as you will no doubt have seen by now, enclosed the document you requested. I told you already, never to do this in spring or summer, only winter or late autumn at a push, but as you sounded desperate, and as I hear it is unseasonably cold there, I will allow it just this once.

I provide one final warning and I hope you will take my words seriously: if you do this on a warm day, you will regret it. Not only will you never forgive yourself, no one else will forgive you. People have longer memories than you think for this sort of thing. Don't fuck it up.

Now, we've discussed stock at length, and I know you're on the same page here. (I'm sure you appreciate the joke as I am writing at the time.) (That probably didn't need pointing out, but I'm not getting a fresh sheet of paper now.) Your stock is going to be beef stock, and of course you will be making it yourself. Don't skimp on this step (I know you won't).

I will pause briefly here to add one more word on the stock. I notice you didn't mention who your guests are, and whether this is due to delicacy (and you should know you need not be delicate with me—we'll have it all out when I get back) or because you know I'm unlikely to care who your friends are, but if you are inviting Evelyn, you may, this time only, use a good vegetarian beef stock. You know, I say 'good' and I know what you're thinking, but it's Eve and we must make allowances for his sensitive nature, and these things have come on in leaps and bounds over the years.

I know. Believe me, I know.

You're only going to use brown onions. DO NOT think you can add an expression of artistic intrigue here. Brown onions or nothing. If you use red onions, shallots (god forbid), any mixture of onions, you are going to sink the thing before you even start. Brown onions only. Yes, I know, you call them yellow onions. I'm not going to fight with you about this again.

You will fry your brown onions in butter and olive oil, and I swear, Aubrey, if a pinch of sugar so much as approaches that pot, I will know, and I will never give you my risi e bisi recipe. It goes without saying that I got it from the best and wisest of all Venetian nonnas (yet here I am saying it) and I will not betray her trust to a person who puts sugar in her onions.

Your sweetness, of course, will come from an appropriate cooking time. Slowly, slowly, in butter, oil and salt, you will fry your onions for at least six hours. Eight is better. Don't you dare tell me you have more important things to do. This is not a soup you can rush and if you turn it off one minute too soon, I will know. The veil is very thin here in Scotland (which is probably why we're here, coincidentally), so don't think I won't smell it.

Watch your onions religiously, adjust the heat appropriately, scrape the pot over and over. This makes your soup rich in flavour and colour. This is the key. If you fail to give your soup the appropriate care during this time, it will be an embarrassing failure no one will ever forget. No one worth mentioning, anyway.

When AT LEAST five hours have elapsed (and I know you're watching the heat carefully), you're going to add some garlic. Here is a small flourish of your choice. I like to slice them lengthways, paper thin, but you do as you see fit.

Yes, I know, but fuck the purists. Those bastards would have the leeches on you trying to suck the impurity from your soul. It clearly didn't work on me, because here I am telling you to put garlic in the soup. Everyone will say, what is it that sets your soup apart, Aubrey? Flavour, Aubrey.

When you add your garlic, you will also add a few sprigs of thyme. I know you want to put a bay leaf in, but this isn't fucking cottage pie. Constrain yourself.

You will cook it for AT LEAST another hour. Then (and here is the most important thing) add your Armagnac. No, not wine, not even beer, not anything else. Believe me, I have tested every possible ingredient myself, and this is the final word. DO NOT cut corners here. Make sure you get a good Armagnac. If you wouldn't serve it to me, then don't put it in your soup. And don't use a thimble-full either; you're entertaining. Use a good glug and completely clean the pan with it. Make sure every speck of brown that was coating your pan is incorporated seamlessly into your onions.

By now it should be looking rich, glistening, sticky—all the things a good onion soup should be. Now you may add your hot stock, stir, and walk away while it simmers, knowing you have done a good thing.

When you return an hour later, longer if you like, you can finish the soup. Take it off the heat and add another glug of Armagnac. Just do it. A big one.

I know you bought that baguette the day before and it's a little stale. You're still going to toast it. Make your slices thick and slice them on a bias. After you toast them, add butter and yes, rub more garlic over the top. It's fine.

Grate the cheese. Comté or go home. Buy three times as much as you think you will need and then grate it all. Don't think about it, don't look back. No one is going to tell you there's too much cheese, and if they do, ~~you have my permission to stab them in the eye~~ you won't be inviting them back.

Then everything can sit and wait until you're almost ready to serve. This is a good time to shower. No one wants you to smell of onions.

Reheat the soup. Cover the top with your toasted baguette slices, then cover those in Comté. I don't want to see even a hint of bread or soup through the cheese. Just pile it on there. Then the whole thing goes in the oven. Keep the lid off, and I know you will know when it's ready. Golden! Completely melted! Bubbling. You must get it to the table exactly like this, with the brown liquid forcing its way up through the few tiny holes you didn't realise you left in the molten cheese. You can thank me later.

It's been impossible to sleep here as the inn is quite haunted and the screaming skull… Well, it's exactly as one would imagine, so I am sleep deprived and if I've forgotten anything, I apologise in advance. Give the recipe and the method a good study and see what you think, but I've done this a thousand times and I'm quite sure that's everything.

~~Say hello to Candide for me, and~~

I'm going to ask you to keep this letter to yourself just for now. If that would be all right with you. It's rare I would let you claim the glory for a soup such as this, but consider that my gift to you. You may not be able to keep the truth of my having made contact from Candide, but I trust her to let that lie. The fact is, other than a postcard here and there, I haven't written to Eve or Anna at all, as I promised I would, and you know things are ~~a little complicated~~ ~~difficult right now~~ ~~somewhat touchy~~ not in need of any explanation. Let's just make this our little secret, seeing as you owe me for saving your dinner party.

We might have a lot of killing to do this evening, so I best be getting on. If nothing horrifying pops up between tonight and next week, Joe and I are planning a small break, at which time I will sit down and write you a real letter. There is so much to tell from the last few weeks I could make a novel of it. Or a series of short stories, at the very least.

As I said above, please do not stop writing. Your letters sometimes take a while to reach me, but I will make sure this gets to you in time.

I miss you. I honestly don't know when I'll be back. I do want to see you all again soon.

Enjoy your dinner party. I know you'll be amazing because you always are.

Percy.

THANK YOU FOR READING!

If you enjoyed *An Education in Evil*, please leave a review. This is a great way to support authors and to help the series thrive.

Sign up for the newsletter at www.whlockwood.com for special content, new release news, ARC opportunities, and to keep up to date.

ALSO BY W.H. LOCKWOOD

Find the first Endymion College trilogy here:

Endymion College 1: A Lesson in Love and Death

Endymion College 2: A Study in Survival

Endymion College 3: An Education in Evil

But wait… What's that I hear? Someone typing out a brand new Endymion College novel? A whole new Endymion College adventure kicks off with *Endymion College 4: A Vicious Vacation* in 2024.

Meanwhile…

There's something a little unsettling happening in Manchester… In the year 1844. A brand new historical gothic romance with lashings of monster horror is also coming your way in 2024.

Visit www.whlockwood.com for more information.

AND YES! PERCY AND JOE HAVE THEIR OWN SERIES NOW!

Degenerate Art

The Reliquary of Saint Martin

Kidnap the Girl

A Sicilian Romance

The Beast of Barmiston Hall

The Horrendous Haunted Heist of Horror

Coming Soon:

Low Down in London

ACKNOWLEDGMENTS

A huge thank you to everyone who supported me, offered advice and helped me shape this novel into what it is today.

Specifically, a huge thank you to Letizia Lorini for the monumental amount of work you put into this, and for forgiving me when I made you cry. You have forgiven me, right? If not, I have a bottle of wine with your name on it. Kisses.

No one out there can comprehend exactly what this woman does for the world of literature, but there are hundreds authors whose books might never see the light of day without this gorgeous woman in their corner. I cannot say enough about her and I am honoured to have her as my friend. She's too talented, too clever, just too kind to even describe. Please go read her wonderful books.

Lety, I love you!!

Ally Blythe, you have been a rock. Thank you for the many hours of hilarious discussions and for sharing your writing with me. Thanks for being on call for every one of my author breakdowns about how many orgasms Anna may or may not have, etc, and for all your help with all my books. I love you.

Shelby, thank you so much for helping me whip this into shape. You are an absolute delight and I'm so happy we met. Thank you.

TJ Rose, same goes for you. Thank you for the hours you spent on this, but also for writing one of my favourite books.

Krystel, Joe (the other one) and Daphanie. Thanks so much for all the back and forth and listening to me. You three know how much I love you.

Emma, Mycroft and Hannah for being the best book club in town who put up with me talking about my own books for months, and especially to Emma for all the time you put into my books, even if you are the fastest reader I ever met. Thank you!!

Thank you to Atalienart (Anna and Eve, front and back) and Jenn Dove (interior portraits) for the beautiful artwork. Go check them out. Their work is amazing.

Tiffany, Alyssa, Natalie, Annie, Katie, Kim and Bethany. Thank you for the time you spent on these books. I will always appreciate all your help and advice.

Last but not least, Matthew. This could never have happened without you. To the most romantic romantic lead in all romances: thank you. To you, to Alex, Ada and Mary, too, I love you all so much!

ABOUT THE AUTHOR

Author of the Endymion College series, W. H. Lockwood writes gothic romance, MM action-romance, historical fiction, dark academia and cosy horror.

Raised on a diet of teen horror books and Pepsi, only willing to leave her den to attend chess club at public school, W.H. Lockwood started writing at a young age and has kept this passion throughout her life.

Always a voracious reader, she obtained an undergraduate degree in literary studies from a gorgeous sandstone university, following that with a masters in publishing and editing, then a masters in astronomy, thus uniting her two great loves of the arts and science, leaving her utterly unqualified to cope with the real world.

These days, W.H. Lockwood can often be found aimlessly wandering the coffee shops and bookstores of the beautiful city she calls home.

She's known to be a scatty writer, but updates Instagram most frequently, so follow her there for news and random pictures of skulls, coffees, and books.

Thank you so much for taking the time to read the series.

 instagram.com/w.h.lockwood.books

SALT